Salamander

by

David Friedman

To the late Patri Pugliese

My consultant on cleverness and much else.

Chapter 1

He relaxed, closed his eyes, let his mind wander out. Behind him the dying embers of his fireplace, beyond it the fires in neighboring houses. At his right, just the other side of the wall, the little furnace, at its heart a single, impossibly brilliant, point of light. He pulled shadow over it until it vanished.

Farther out, the near edge of the vast sphere of woven fire that held the College, half its height above ground, half below. He melted into it, fitting himself to the dancing flames, through.

A classroom, at its head a magister, young for his robes.

...

Magister Coelus scanned faces as he always did at the start, searching for gold. Not for power so much as perception, control. Intelligence. The stragglers took their seats. A boy at the back caught his attention, his glow an odd pattern of woven flame. It seemed brighter, more intense than the others. Power certainly. And a lot of it. The boy looked up at the magister; the light vanished. Not a boy but a girl, with a shy face neither pretty nor ugly.

He wondered if she had blocked him out of training or talent. No girl student yet in the four years since he and Maridon had persuaded the College of modern scholarship's relevance to their admission policy had shown more than average ability. If the girl turned out to be not merely a fire mage but a prodigy as well, it would shake up the greybeards—and a good thing too.

Seated now, the students watched him intently; time to begin.

"Let us start by listing that which everyone knows about magery.

"Mages have magic; common folk do not.

"What makes a truly great mage is power, the ability to set a forest on fire or freeze a lake.

"Mages train, as apprentices with one master or students with many, in order to learn to increase their power.

"The power of mages comes from the elementals—

salamanders for fire, sylphs for air, and the rest. Elementals know mages by their names. Hence, giving a child the name of a past mage gives him easier access to that mage's elemental.

"Every one of the facts I have just listed is false. The first step to wisdom is not learning but unlearning."

Coelus looked up from his notes into silence, held it for a long moment, continued.

"First, and most important, magic is not limited to mages. Human beings without magic, if they exist, are far rarer than humans beings with magic. Modern research suggests that magic is not even limited to human beings. Many, perhaps all, living creatures have some portion of magic used in some way.

"All of you know people who are not mages but use magic. The cook at the inn whose food tastes better than anyone else's. The lucky hunter. The farmer with a green thumb. It once was thought that the success of ordinary people in ordinary tasks depended only on mundane skills. But this is not so, as scholars have now proved beyond dispute. Nearly everyone has magic and very nearly everyone uses it, mostly as an additional aid in their ordinary business."

If possible, the room became more silent still. Coelus looked up at faces blank, some obviously shocked. Spoke into the silence:

"This has been suspected for a long time and was proved by experiment more than a decade ago. It is not a secret of mages. Mages have little need to keep secrets, considering how unwilling people are to believe the truth when it is told to them.

"Some of you are now wondering why you are here. If your parents' laundry maid—the one who always gets the clothes to come out brighter than anyone else—would do as well, why not send her? Why are you more suited to be mages than she is?"

Again he stopped, to let them think and tension build.

"The answer is not that you have magic and she does not but that you have more than she—enough to be used for more than washing shirts. That is half the difference between mages and other folk, the half that got you sent here. The other half, how to use that power, is what you are here to learn.

"You will start learning it very soon but you have more to unlearn first. I have just told you that one part of what makes a mage is having more power. How, then, is the power of great mages false?

"Even the greatest mages have very little power. You have all heard stories of how a fire mage waved his hand and set a forest ablaze. Some may be excellent stories—but none of them are true. If a fire mage wants to set a forest ablaze, he must do it the same way anyone else does—with a lot of kindling. Durilil, one of our founders, one of the most powerful fire mages that ever lived, is reliably reported to have been able to set a hearth fire of plain logs ablaze. A forest holds many more logs than a hearth.

"What makes a great mage is not his power but the skill with which he uses it. Consider a healer—yes, within these walls, healers are mages. No mage has enough power to go through the whole body of a patient and set everything aright, at least not if the patient is anything bigger than a mouse. What a skilled healer does is to find the one crucial fault and heal that, then let the rest fall into place by its own nature. The more skill a mage has, the less power he uses—needs—to accomplish his task. That is what you are here to learn.

"We cannot teach you to increase your power. You are here to increase your skill. We can increase your power no more than we can teach you to increase your height. It is possible, although difficult and dangerous, to obtain the use of more power by pooling with another mage. There are also potions to let you draw down your power today at a cost tomorrow, although I do not advise you to use them. The pool itself we cannot increase."

Coelus fell silent and looked out over his audience. To start backwards, with all they knew that wasn't true, always worked. Everyone in the class was now wide awake and watching him. Now it was their turn. "Questions?"

A long silence before a hand went up. "How can people use the elements for magic in daily life? Cooking has something to do with fire and farming with earth, but hunting? What is the element for a tailor?"

Coelus waited a moment to be sure the student had finished before responding.

"There is no element for a tailor or a hunter. There is no element for cooking, as far as I know, and I have my doubts that a good farmer is simply an untrained earth mage. Nor is there an element for healing. Yet I have told you that a healer is a sort of mage. There is no element for weaving. Yet the sphere of woven fire that holds this College safe from the world, and the world safe from the College, was the work of two mages, and only one was a fire mage.

"The belief that all magic is tied to one of the four elements is both true and false. All magic is indeed earth, air, fire and water, in many combinations. But all magic can equally well be seen as hot, cold, wet and dry, or woven, shaped, refined and tempered. Hot magic may be combined of air and fire, but equally fire magic is combined of hot and dry."

The students looked puzzled at the paradox, the central paradox of magical theory—except for the girl in back, who watched only with careful attentiveness. Coelus wondered if she had failed to follow, which would be a pity, or if she already knew. Some students came to the College already apprenticed and at least a few witches were technically competent in magery. If most were not, that was in part the fault of the College. If the girl had not come with an adequate understanding, at least she could leave with one.

"Explaining how this can be and the simpler implications will take me most of two months, starting here first period tomorrow. For now, the best I can offer is metaphor."

He turned to the broad slate that occupied most of the front wall of the lecture hall, chalk in hand. "Imagine this slate is a map. A is where you are starting. B is where you want to go to."

He drew an arrow pointing up, over it an N for north, below a rough distance scale in miles, turned back to the class. "How do you get there?"

The same student who had asked the question raised his hand; Coelus nodded to him to speak.

"Go about six miles east, then two north."

"Yes. Can someone give me another answer?"

No one spoke. Coelus looked at the girl in back; in a moment she raised her hand, a bit reluctantly. "A little less than six miles North-east, almost three miles south-east."

"Yes."

He turned back to the board, drew in her answer as two arrows, turned back to the class. "Which is true? Is point B east and north from point A?"

He held their eyes for a moment, turned back to the board, waved his hand—what they would expect of a mage. The grid, white on the black slate, appeared suddenly. "Or is it north-east and south-east from point A?"

He stepped to the slate, caught the grid at its bottom edge and swung it up—it pivoted on the lower left corner until its lines lay along what had been the diagonal. "Class dismissed."

* * *

"How does the new class look?"

Maridon glanced up from the papers. "Forty-nine new students, six of them women. Mostly children of minor nobles, tradesmen, small landowners, but there are two farmers' sons Dag searched out and sent here. Three are the children of mages, so probably half-trained or half mistrained already. Also the daughter of Duke Morgen, who may be a problem. Less power than most, but it might be prudent not to say so."

Coelus shook his head. "And then when she can't do things … I suppose there's the usual nonsense with names?"

Maridon nodded. "At least there is only one each of Durilil, Georgias, and Helmin. Remember year before last? Three Durilils and two Gilbers. Good thing most people do not plan on their children being mages or we would be down to four or five names for the whole class. Far as I can see there's no truth to it—damn superstition."

"No truth at all. I went through the school records for the past twenty years and just finished up last week. A kid named Durilil is no more likely to end up a fire mage, or Gilber earth, than anyone else. And it's getting worse. Mage names are much more common than they were twenty years ago. Why won't people believe us when we tell them it doesn't work?"

Maridon contemplated, not for the first time, the limits of his colleague's formidable intelligence. He might be the best theorist in the college, but understanding people was another matter. "They don't believe us because they think we are trying to keep down the competition. Too many talented mages and what would …?"

Coelus cut in sharply. "There can't be too many. Just think of all we could do if there were five or ten times as many mages. We could put out forest fires before they spread, maybe halt plagues.

5

That's why …"

"That's why you talked Dag into spending his free year seeking out talent in unexpected places. We may know that, but who else does? People believe what they want to believe.

"Oh well. Perhaps in fifty years half the newborn boys in the kingdom will be named Coelus!"

Coelus shook his head. "Not even one in a thousand. If I am very lucky, fifty years from now a handful in the College will remember my work. Nobody else. Theory doesn't impress ordinary people. They want results, nice showy results. If Durilil had come back with the Salamander on a chain instead of never coming back at all, half the class would be named after him, not just one or two. And we've never had a student named after Olver.

"Let me have a look at the admission papers."

The two fell silent for a few minutes while Coelus leafed through the stack. At last he looked back up. "That's very interesting."

"What? I didn't see anything special about any of them."

"That's what's interesting. According to Hal we have three or four moderately strong students—one of them named Helmin, and one a find of Dag's—plus a bunch with enough power to be worth training but not much more and a few I'm not sure we should have taken. That's what he saw. But I was watching the class before my first lecture and it isn't what I saw."

The other mage looked at him curiously, waited.

"I'll leave you to see for yourself. Let me know when you've spotted him. Or not."

Maridon noticed the suppressed smile—Coelus was not nearly as subtle as he thought he was—made his own deduction, said nothing.

Chapter 2

The lecturer droned to a halt, put the chalk down and turned to the class. "I hope that is clear. If not, make sure it is by tomorrow; some of this will be used in what we do then. If your own notes are not sufficient, the library has a list of written texts that cover the same material."

He looked them over a moment and then, satisfied, turned and left the room.

Mari looked down at her tablets, pale yellow wax in ebony, the outside panels inlaid with a pattern in gold wire. Other students were jotting final notes in theirs, so she used her stylus to add, in her untidy script, two more notes on wedding garb for a (hypothetical) future wedding.

Her notes were not likely to make the lecture any more understandable, nor, she suspected, would the texts in the library. The only one she had tried to read so far might have been written in archaic Dorayan for all the sense she could make of it. What she needed was a helpful human being to explain things for her.

One or two of the younger magisters might be possibilities, but probably not this year; that could wait until her first individual tutorial. With ten men to every woman, not to mention her natural advantages, getting one of the male students to help her would be easy enough. But on the whole she preferred to keep her alternatives open. Might as well keep them all hoping.

The answer was obvious and sitting two chairs away. The girl had no clothes sense and no particular looks, but she seemed pleasant enough if a little shy and she obviously understood the lecture better than anyone else in the room. She had been transparently puzzled when the other students — including, once, Mari — were unable to answer the magister's questions. She answered those put to her immediately, clearly, and apparently correctly. By the second half of the class the lecturer had fallen into a pattern of putting a question to some other student and then, lacking a satisfactory response, asking Ellen.

There was a clatter and rumble of scraping as the students got up from their chairs. Mari decided to approach the girl directly.

She made her way to the back of the room against the exiting flow of pupils where Ellen was still putting away her things. "You seemed to understand all of that much better than I did; would you be willing to join me at lunch and try to explain it?"

Ellen looked up at Mari, smiled. "Of course. At the noon bell?"

Mari decided not to suggest the cookshop to meet. The other girl was wearing no jewelry and her clothes gave no sign of rank or wealth. If she was too poor to want to buy lunch when it was free in the college refectory the suggestion would embarrass her; offering to buy it for her might make matters worse. In the setting of the College the girl was her equal—at least her equal—and it was up to Mari to remember that. "At the noon bell then," Mari said.

* * *

Mari waited until the two were seated at one of the smaller tables and Ellen had cut a slice from her sausage before putting her first question. "Are we training to be witches or mages? I can't tell."

Ellen considered for a moment. "We are training to use magic. Women who use magic are commonly called witches. Several of the magisters here think they ought to be called mages, that what they do is no different from what men who use magic do."

"Women do different sorts of magic. Everyone knows that. Weaving magic and healing magic and things like that. Men are fire mages and earth mages and ..."

Ellen shook her head. "Everyone knows it. But it isn't true. At least, not completely true."

"How can it be both true and not true? I don't understand."

"That was part of what Magister Bertram was trying to explain" Ellen said. "Most weaving mages are women and most fire mages are men, but that doesn't mean a man can't have a talent for weaving or a woman for fire."

She looked around the refectory. It was getting crowded, but so far nobody had joined them at their table. "Which are taller, men or women?"

Mari gave her a puzzled look. "Men, of course. Jon over there is taller than I am and even Edwin is taller than you are."

"But you are taller than Edwin. So men are not taller than women. Not always."

"And men are better at fire magic, but not always?"

Ellen nodded.

Mari responded: "Well, of course lots of women are taller than short men. But I have never heard of a woman who was a fire mage. Not one."

Ellen thought a moment before answering. "Mages have to be trained. At best, an untrained mage cannot do much with his power. At worst, an untrained fire mage either kills himself by accident—that's what usually happens—or burns down a house or barn and kills someone else, and then, very likely, someone kills him. A boy who starts showing the talent is likely to be recognized before he does any serious damage and, with luck, sent for training. A girl... Everyone knows girls can't be fire mages."

"That's scary. But if women are hardly ever fire mages and the ones that are get killed, how do Coelus and Bertram know witches can do fire magic? How do you know?"

"I think Coelus figured it out from basic magical theory, but I'm not sure." Ellen gave the other girl a long, considering look. "How good are you at keeping secrets?"

"Quite. My brother tells me ... things. I never tell our parents." She stopped.

"Can you keep a secret for me too?"

Mari nodded.

Ellen turned in her seat, holding her hand, palm up, where her body blocked it from the rest of the room. For a moment her hand cupped a flame. "That's how I know."

Mari's eyes widened. She looked back at Ellen.

"May I join your table, noble lady?"

Both girls looked up. The speaker, a tall student, well dressed, was looking at Mari inquisitively. She nodded assent.

"Joshua son of Maas at your service. How have you been enjoying your first week in this temple of wisdom?"

"Everyone is very kind but I find the wisdom somewhat opaque," Mari replied, cheerfully. "Ellen was just kindly explaining today's lecture to me."

Joshua glanced at Ellen then back to Mari. "I would be happy to provide any assistance you ladies may require. After a year and a few weeks I think I have most of it down and I am looking forward to getting out, come spring. My father thinks a trained mage would be very useful in his business. What was it that was puzzling you?"

Mari gave Ellen a rueful glance, turned back to Joshua. "I am still puzzled by Magister Coelus' explanation of how magic can be entirely elemental, entirely humoral, entirely natural and entirely combinatorial, all at the same time."

"That I can explain. The elemental points are, of course, the elements: earth, air, fire and water. The natural points are the natures: hot, cold, dry, and wet. Hot is a mixture of fire and air, cold of earth and water, and so on."

"But didn't he also say that fire was a mix of hot and dry? If hot is fire and air, and dry is...," she looked at the others.

"Fire and earth," Ellen responded. Joshua looked momentarily annoyed.

"Fire and earth. That's right."

Mari continued: "Then a mix of hot and dry ought to have fire and air and fire and earth. That's two fire and one each air and earth. So how can it be pure fire?"

Joshua looked puzzled. "Say that again?"

"A mix of hot and dry ought to have fire and air and fire and earth. That's two fire and one each air and earth. So how can it be pure fire?"

He thought a moment before answering. "That does seem puzzling, but it must be true. I am afraid the explanation is a little complicated for students in their first year but by the time you finish Magister Coelus's theory course next spring it should be clear enough. That's the bell for the fourth period; my tutor will be expecting me. I hope we can talk more later."

He gave Mari a formal bow, nodded to Ellen, went out the door.

Mari turned with an arched eyebrow back to Ellen. "Well, perhaps you understand it?"

Ellen nodded. "But I don't think he does. Mixes are a loose way of putting it and misleading for just the reason you saw. The superposition has phase as well as amplitude; the air and earth cancel when you put hot and dry together with the right phase to get back to fire. How much mathematics have you learned?"

Mari looked at her helplessly. "When I add up numbers I can usually get the same answers twice running."

"There is a class next semester that you could take to get the basics — the math, not the magic theory. Then the real math class next fall. And then Magister Coelus' advanced theory class in the spring. He is supposed to be very good. Mother says he has been responsible for more progress in basic theory than anyone else in the past twenty years."

"Your mother is a witch? Or," Mari corrected herself, "a mage, I suppose I should say?"

"Mother is a weaving mage, which, outside the College, is a witch. She finds theory fascinating. She taught me as much as she could and then sent me here to learn more. When I'm done I expect she'll want me to come back and teach it to her."

"No wonder you know so much already. It would be a great favor to me if you would keep on explaining things to me. You are so much easier to understand than the magisters."

"Of course." Ellen looked down, back up, and smiled. "Mother says teaching is the best way of learning things, so it isn't really a favor at all. Besides … I'm happy to be your friend. But I must go now to prepare for my next class."

Mari watched her go. One problem solved. The next would be how to politely discourage Joshua. Not that there was anything wrong with rich merchants or their sons. But she did not think that was what her father was planning for her. And, in this case, hoped not. She wondered if the boy had forgotten that the schedule for all three years — with tutorials in the fifth and sixth periods, not the fourth — was posted on the corridor wall outside the refectory, or if he simply assumed she had not bothered to read it.

Chapter 3

Magister Bertram waited until the room was silent before beginning.

"You are here to learn to make use of magery. To that lesson there are three parts.

"The first is to gain understanding of how magery works. This training you will receive from Magister Coelus, whose first lecture you had yesterday morning. I hope you are all continuing to ponder the wisdom it contained.

"The second part is how to do magery, how, with the power within you and through the knowledge of the names of things, using spells constructed by wise men of old, to cause effects in the world. Before I teach you that you must first learn from Magister Simon an understanding of names in the true speech, which is the language in which the world is told, the language in which spells are spoken. Or written. Or thought. Not in our common tongue.

"The third part is how to use your power. That is our subject today.

"A spell has a direct effect and an indirect effect. The direct effect is commonly called magic. It is what the spell does. The indirect effect is what you do with the spell. The direct effect is to set one stalk of straw alight. The indirect effect, of which the direct is the cause, is that stalk setting a field ablaze.

"As you grow wiser you will see further, to effects of which the burning field is itself a cause and beyond. To do magic is only the beginning. Beyond that you will be using wisdom, knowledge, in order, by the use of magic, to alter the world.

"Magery is a tool. The first step to wisdom is to learn what sort of a tool it is."

He stopped a moment, looked up at the faces then down at his notes, and continued. "Magery is not a battering ram or a stroke of lightning; nobody ever smashed a castle wall with a spell or split an oak tree."

Magister Bertram lifted up his hand, turned it, and flexed its gnarled fingers. "Consider a hand. It cannot knock down a gate like a battering ram. It cannot split an oak in an instant like a stroke of lightning. But it is more useful than a battering ram or a lightning bolt because it can do more and more useful things. If you exchanged your right hand for a battering ram and your left for a lightning bolt you would, no doubt, be a very impressive figure. But you would regret the change the first time you needed to eat dinner."

He stopped, looked into the silence, and recalled hearing the same words, in the same lecture hall, when he was a student. He had thought it a striking figure of speech at the time.

"Nobody can knock down a castle wall with his hand. But when walls come down, it is hands that do it. Hands build siege engines, dig mines, bribe traitors. The greatest hero cannot split an oak tree with a blow of his hand. But human hands split the oak to make the benches you sit on.

"You have had hands your whole life long, so they no longer seem wonderful to you. But try to imagine what it would be like if you had to figure out for the first time how five fingers could bring down a tree, or dig a hole, or start a fire, or draw water from a well.

"A mage must learn to use magic as a child might learn to use his hand."

He again looked down at his notes, let silence build before continuing. "We start with a simple problem. The Forstings have seized Northpass castle and the king is sieging it to get it back. The Forsting defenders have succeeding in sending a messenger off. He is several miles down the road, too far for pursuit to catch him. If he and his message get safe to the enemy army on the far side of the pass, they will come to the rescue of the defenders and the siege will fail. Perhaps the war will be lost.

"You are a fire mage. You do not have a great deal of power—no mage does—and the greater the distance over which you must work the less the power you can apply. How might you stop the messenger? How use fire to keep the message from reaching its destination? "

The lecture hall was silent as he looked out over the room. Eventually one of the students raised his hand. "Burn the messenger up?"

The magister shook his head. One student who had not been listening. "That requires a great deal of fire, more than any mage has."

"Burn just his head or his heart—that would be enough to kill him."

"Better; if he were standing next to you and you were strong enough it might do. But if he were standing next to you there would be no need of magery. At a distance of some miles, no. You are trying to knock a castle wall down with your hand."

Another student raised his hand. Magister Bertram recognized him, by his dress and rawboned height, as the farm boy Magister Dag had discovered and recommended to the college. One of the stronger mages among the new students, whatever his other limits.

"Follow after the messenger, quick as you can. First night on the road, set fire to the hay in the stable where his horse is. Hay's dry, won't take much to kindle it."

"Much better. But the messenger might buy another horse."

The third hand raised was a tall girl, very well dressed. Also strikingly good looking. "Eight miles past Northpass Keep the road forks at Fire Mountain. The main road goes on to Berio, which is where the enemy army probably is, or at least its commander. The other branch ends at the village of Efkic, fifteen miles away, where the old road to the pass was blocked by lava flows a century or so back. There are wooden sign posts at the fork with the names of the towns burned into them.

"It should take the messenger at least an hour to reach the fork. That gives you plenty of time to burn a few extra lines, changing EFKIC into BERIO, and BERIO into BERTOL. Send a squad of cavalry to the fork to intercept the messenger when he finally discovers he has gone the wrong way and turns back."

There was silence, half the class looking at the girl, half watching the magister for his response. He had to think a moment; it was not an answer he had heard before. "An adequate solution, provided that the wood of the sign is dry and the messenger does not know the road."

The magister turned to the class. "Consider the lesson. There is no one problem you will face and no one answer to be learned. It is up to the mage to find the best way of using his talent to achieve his goal. It does not take much to startle a horse. There might be a bend at some place in the road where a rider who loses control for a few seconds goes over the edge of a cliff. To a mage, knowledge is power. All knowledge."

He hesitated a moment, then realized that the girl's answer fitted neatly into his prepared closing. "Even knowledge of how the road signs read in a fork in the road eight miles north of Northpass Keep."

He gestured to the slate; spoke a Word under his breath. "Knowledge. Always knowledge," appeared on it.

As the students drifted out of the lecture hall into the corridor, Ellen and Mari were joined by a third girl, named Alys.

"Did you make it up? Is there really a signpost eight miles north of the castle?" Alys asked.

Mari smiled and said nothing, then relented. "As a matter of fact there is. My horse went lame there last year, when we were guesting with the Castellan. I had to walk him back. Eight miles."

"I was hoping you had made it up. Magister Bertram would never have caught you; he's an old stick. Coelus and Simon are much cuter."

The boy who had suggested burning down the stable joined the three girls, introducing himself as Jon. "Very clever of you, m'lady–changing the sign. Would never have thought of it."

"I would never have thought of setting fire to the stable. Mine only worked because I happened to know that place, by accident."

Ellen shook her head. "Nothing works everywhere. Jon's solution works more places than yours does. But yours was very clever because you had to see that one word could be changed to another. It wouldn't work, because no fire mage could burn lines into the sign from miles away, but it was very clever. Which makes it a good example of Magister Bertram's point."

Alys looked puzzled. "What do you mean? What point?"

"That the successful use of magic depends not only on arcane knowledge but on knowledge of everything. Mari happened to know something about the road north of Northpass keep. Jon knew about the risks of fire in a stable. A great mage will figure out how to use what he happens to know."

Alys interrupted: "I know that messages are usually written on paper and paper can burn. But that seemed like too easy an answer."

Mari nodded. "I expect that it is harder to light a bundle of folded paper in the wallet at the messenger's side than a wisp of straw. And it only works if the messenger doesn't know what is in the message he is carrying. But if there are guard posts the messenger may need a letter of passage to get through them, and that burns too."

* * *

Three days later, Mari and Ellen were seated in the small orchard at the south end of the College, sharing a luncheon platter of bread, apples, a sausage, and a chunk of cheese. Edwin passed by but seemed hesitant to join them. Mari whispered to Ellen, who turned and waved him over. "Come share with us; Mari brought more than we can eat and this cheese of hers is really good."

Edwin smiled a little shyly, hesitating. "Yes, do come," Mari chimed in, "it's much nicer here than back in the refectory and we do have plenty." Doubly invited he gave in, walked over, and sat down. The southern boundary of the orchard was a low brick wall, just beyond it the inner surface of the containment dome. Ellen, turning back to Mari, pointed to it as Edwin cut himself a slice of apple. "What do you see when you look at it?"

Mari thought a moment. "A wall of bright mist. How can the apple trees grow so well? Doesn't it keep them from getting enough sunlight?"

Ellen shook her head. "It doesn't stop the light, just the seeing. The dome is a barrier against magic. Some theorists think seeing is magical, for how else can we know what is happening far away just from the light that reaches our eyes? That's one of the arguments for the theory that even animals have a tiny bit of magic, since they can see too. If the light gets through and the magic doesn't, the trees are fine."

"So if something sucked all of the magic out of you, you would be blind?" That was Edwin, talking through a mouthful of bread and apple. Ellen hesitated a moment before responding:

"Maybe. There isn't any easy way of sucking magic out of a person, or any way of getting all of it. If seeing is magical, it must be a very deep kind. I'm not sure it is magic, anyway. Mother says the dome just scrambles the light and magic has nothing to do with why we see it that way."

"How do you see it?" That was Mari.

Ellen hesitated a moment, closed her eyes, opened them,

squinted. "Mostly as a wall of woven fire, but if I try hard to block my perception and just use my eyes, it's a wall of mist, just as you said."

Edwin finished chewing his current mouthful, spoke. "I like your explanations, Ellen. They're very clear. Tell me, do you think Magister Coelus believes in elementals, or not. From what he says, I can't tell."

Ellen considered the matter briefly. "The first question is what you mean by elementals. There are three answers. One of them Magister Coelus doesn't believe in, one he isn't sure, and one he believes in absolutely."

"You are talking in riddles, just as he does." Mari lifted a reproachful finger at Ellen. "Explain."

"The first kind of elementals are the ones in stories, magical beings associated with the four elements, sometimes friendly, sometimes not. Little creatures the clever mage tricks into helping him and the stupid or evil mage gets tricked by, or angers. Salamanders are supposed to live in fires, and every hearth has a little one that the clever child learns to talk to. Sylphs in the air, gnomes in the earth, undines in the water. Coelus would regard these as stories. So do I. Anyway, no mage has ever provided a reliable report of one, even though the stories say they are everywhere."

"What of the elementals that do exist?" That was Mari.

"The third category exists, but only on paper. For the sort of material covered in Coelus's advanced theory course, it is useful to have a symbol for pure fire, pure earth, or whatever. It's cleaner and makes the calculations easier, and all modern theorists do it."

"So there aren't really any salamanders, any more than there is really a minus three, they're just useful in doing accounts?" Edwin sounded disappointed.

Ellen shook her head. "There is a theorist, Olver—not at the college, but supposed to be very good—who has been working for decades on an overarching theory of magic, the sort of theory that would explain why there are four elements and four natures and why the whole pattern of magic works the way it does, and maybe the pattern of other things as well, all other things. His idea is to start with very simple basics and build everything else up from that. He hasn't quite managed to do it, but some smart people think he may have something. I expect if you asked Coelus, he would say so. A lot of what Coelus teaches comes from Olver's early work.

"Olver believes the elementals are real and part of the structure of the world. But his are of the mathematical kind rather than the storybook kind. There is only one of each, of unlimited, if narrow, power. All the air magic in the world is based on the sylph; all the earth on the gnome. They may be beings, or perhaps more like forces of nature. And whatever they are, they are probably very dangerous."

Edwin motioned to speak and Ellen paused to let him. "When the Founder, Durilil, went looking for a salamander, what kind did he seek?"

"Durilil and Feremund were followers of Olver. Durilil went in search of the Salamander, Feremund in search of the Undine. They found Feremund's body—drowned, on high, dry ground, or so they say. Durilil they never found at all, not even a pile of ashes, and after that no one else went looking."

They were all three quiet for a while after that, Mari and Edwin looking thoughtful, all three absorbed in finishing their lunch. When they had, Edwin thanked the two girls and excused himself to prepare for the fifth period lecture. After he had gone, Ellen turned to Mari. "He seems nice."

Mari nodded. "Not clever enough for you or high born enough for me, but a nice boy, and pleasant company."

"You mean to marry? Is that what you think about when you meet boys?"

"One of the things. College is pleasant but life is out there waiting for me."

There was another long silence; Ellen broke it. "Why are you here?"

Mari gave her a curious glance. "You think I shouldn't be?"

"You aren't really interested in magic, except that you find it as interesting as you find everything else. You aren't at all interested in the mathematics you need to properly understand it. You don't need it to make a living—you don't have to make a living. And this is not the best place to meet the kind of husband you want. I am glad you are here; you are the nicest person I have met here so far and one of the two most interesting. But I do not understand why you came."

"You remember," Mari asked, "the first time we talked, I asked you about witches and mages?"

Ellen nodded.

"Well, father is very up to date and witches are useful, especially healers. My brother would probably have died two years ago, or, had he lived, been a cripple, were it not for ours. But they are not entirely respectable. I don't mean it as an insult to you or to your mother, but if a noble admitted his daughter to be a witch he would be daring others to make something of it.

"Mages are different. The kingdom was founded by a mage king. His Majesty's younger brother trained at the College and is supposed to have helped the King with all sorts of things. So when word spread that the College was training women as mages …"

"Your father decided that was a respectable thing for his daughter to do?"

"Not just respectable. And not just useful; father can always hire mages, after all. But it was a new thing and he wanted to be part of it. And our healer told him that I had talent…"

"What did she say about your talent?"

Mari shook her head. "That I had it. That I could be trained as a mage."

Ellen considered the matter briefly, decided that truth was, as usual, better than the alternative. "You do have talent. But you do not have very much. If you learn to be very clever at using it—which will take a lot of work, but you are clever—you can do things with what you have. Joshua has more talent than you do but he's a lazy fool who will never bother to learn to use it properly. He just wants to go back home and tell people he is a mage. And he is not clever. You could be better than him. But you can never be very good. I'm sorry, but it's true."

Mari looked down a moment then up, smiled at her friend. "Do you always tell people the truth?"

"Almost always. It's easier. If I were cleverer than I am and understood people the way you do, perhaps I could do better than that, but I'm not. There is too much complication in the world; I don't want to make any more."

"Thank you, at least this time. Being a powerful mage out of a storybook isn't what I care about, even if it is fun to imagine. After all, a mage is not what I am really going to be. But I would like to be able to do something with what talent I have, enough to be useful at least to me and maybe to my family. Something that I did, not just something I was."

The two were silent for a while. "You seem very sure about how much talent people have," Mari said. "Can you see it, the way you see the barrier down on the other side of the wall?"

Ellen nodded.

Mari looked around; the orchard was empty. "The magisters must be able to see it too, I suppose; that's how they know who to admit. Can they see what kind of talent you have? You seem reluctant to show it."

"Mother warned me that some of the other students, if they knew what I was, would be jealous and would make it unpleasant for me."

"Because you are a fire mage?"

"Yes. Partly that. Women aren't supposed to be fire mages."

"Can't some of the students, at least some of the older ones, see what you are, the same way you can see what I'm not?"

"I don't let them. I veil—like putting a globe of dark glass around a candle. Just enough so I seem like everyone else here, with a glimmer. It's hard. For me to pretend not to be a mage at all would be easier."

"What about the magisters? Can they tell?"

"If I veil, I veil against everyone. Some of the magisters are probably skilled enough to see what I am doing if they looked closely. I think one of them saw the first day, before I got in the habit. "

"If the magisters are more powerful, have more talent, couldn't they just see right through your veil?"

Ellen hesitated, and again decided in favor of truth. "They aren't more powerful. I think I'm the strongest mage in the college. That's the other half of why I veil."

"Stronger even than Coelus?"

"Coelus is not that strong. The magisters are not here for their strength. There are more powerful mages outside the college than any of them. What is special about the magisters is that they understand magic and can teach it. A lot of mages know how to do magic but don't really understand what they are doing. Most of them, I think. That is why we are here.

"What is special about Coelus is not the strength of his talent. Even in the college there are stronger mages. But he can find out things nobody knew before. Most of the spells mages use they learn from other mages; he is one of the few who create new ones. Even fewer invent spells they cannot themselves do—Coelus may be the only one. That is the beauty of theory. It lets you figure out what you could do if you were a water mage, even though you are a fire mage. Then you show it to a water mage and he goes and does it."

The two girls sat quietly for a while, Mari thinking, Ellen watching a pigeon snatch crumbs then retreat to a safe distance to eat them. Finally Mari spoke. "How do you think that pigeon got in? Do you suppose he pecked at the entrance chime and Magister Gatekeeper opened to let him through the sphere?"

Ellen smiled at the image. "He must have come through with some of us; this isn't the first time I've fed him."

Chapter 4

B_y the third month their regular lunch gatherings in the orchard or, if it was raining, the cloister next to it, were being referred to as Ellen's tutorial. Edwin, Jon, Mari, and Ellen were the regulars, with Alys and several other first years dropping in from time to time.

Mari continued to provide cheese; Alys accused her of doing it to remind the others of just how bad refectory food was compared to the real world. Conversation almost always started with something one of the others wanted Ellen to explain then drifted in almost any direction, from Jon's precise, professional explanation of what was in the sausage they were eating and how it got there, which put Alys off sausages for two weeks, to Mari's well informed and irreverent view of the upper reaches of kingdom politics.

This afternoon the questioning started with Jon and dealt with a topic of practical concern to all of them.

"I know the elements, and natures, and that they are basis stars, along with some other things. Don't understand how each provides a full description of magic but if you and Magister Coelus say so, must be true. Also don't understand how this fits into mage types. Fire and water are elements. But there are also healing mages, used to be called witches, and war mages. Are healing and war elements as well, or points of another star magisters haven't gotten round to confusing us with yet?"

Ellen thought for a moment before answering: "It's complicated."

"It's always complicated." That was Edwin; Ellen, ignoring him, continued: "Mages get described both by what they do and by how they do it. A weaving mage is one whose power is mostly in the weaving point of the combinatorial basis star. A healing mage is one who uses power to heal people. One way of healing people is by weaving, not cloth but damaged flesh. So a healer might be a weaving mage.

"But she doesn't have to be, because there are other talents that can be used to heal—including all of the points of that same star. A mage with power to refine could filter poisons out of blood or fuse the poison with something else to render it harmless; fusing is refining done backwards, like weaving and untangling. So a healer is one who has learned ways of using magic to heal. A weaving mage or a refining mage is someone who uses that particular kind of magic."

Jon cut into the conversation: "Just as some farmers good with animals, some at spotting weeds and pulling them, some strong, some clever what crops to plant where."

Ellen nodded. Edwin joined in. "So a war mage is one trained to use his skills for war? A fire mage would burn the enemy up, a water mage flood them, or a damp mage make their tents mildew?" The last got a laugh from Alys, a smile from Ellen. She responded:

"Mildew might even be more effective than the rest, over time. A war mage uses his talents for war, some more effective than others, but practically anything can be used if you are clever. Mari's changing a road sign could be effective if it sent an army off in the wrong direction. We are born with talents that we can't change, but we can decide how we use them. That is what the third year tutorials are mostly about, for those who choose to stay for the third year."

"But how much choice do you really have?" That was Mari. "If you are a fire mage," she deliberately kept her tone level, "healing, or farming, or most other things are not really an option, because they are not things fire can do."

Ellen shook her head. "Powers are hardly ever pure. A fire mage is not someone who can only do fire but one who is better at doing fire than at doing other things. Combine fire with refining and you can draw gold out of the ground, if you are good enough at it. And if you are mostly fire but a little refining, your fire can provide the power and your refining control it.

"Most mages are a mix of talents, strongest at one but with some power in others. A pure mage can't do much; there is a limit to what you can build out of pure fire or pure air. A fire mage with a little earth talent, or an air mage with a little earth, can do a lot more, get most of the power for a spell or a construction from one point then structure it with the talent from another, or several others."

Mari nodded. "So the strongest mage of all would be one with all four points of a star, or all four points of all the stars?"

"Not the strongest." Ellen paused a moment, trying to see how to explain. "A mage with all four elements would be the most flexible. He could do more things, but since he wouldn't have much power in any element, he couldn't do much of anything. And one star would be enough. If you have all four elements, then you have everything; you just have to learn how to combine them. That's why the theory Magister Coelus teaches, which some of you think doesn't matter, really does. It is the theory that tells you how it all fits together, how someone with the right elemental talents can learn to do spells out of natural or combinatorial magic."

Edwin shook his head. "Theory matters to you and to Magister Coelus. It doesn't matter to me, though I do my best to understand it. I am going to learn the spells to do what I want with the talents that I have. Someone else can figure out what those spells are. Magister Bertram is my guide to how I can use my skills to get the results I want. That isn't magical theory at all, just the same problem everyone faces, mage or not. Mages merely have extra ways of solving it."

Ellen nodded. "That you know you need to learn how to use spells is precisely why you and Mari will be better mages than those who only learn how to cast them. Learning spells may make you a mage. But not a very useful one. That's why there were very effective mages a hundred years ago, back when how a mage could use air and fire to do the same spell as a mage with heat was still a puzzle."

The students were silent for some minutes, thinking about this, till the front gate bell sounded time for the afternoon lecture.

* * *

"Come in."

It was the girl student, the special one. Ellen.

"You wanted to speak to me, Magister Coelus?"

He looked up at her. A little short, a little broad, simply dressed. Not a woman who would stand out in a crowd. Face plain but not ugly. And, as had become increasingly clear, a mind easily matching her carefully concealed talent.

"I have a project. A very important project, I believe. It

requires the help of several mages; I would like you to be one of them."

There was a long silence as she considered the matter.

"Would not one of your colleagues be better suited to help you?"

"Most of my colleagues can see nothing new in magery for the past fifty years and look for nothing new for the next hundred. I expect to have Maridon's help, and perhaps I can get one of the others. But to do the project properly requires four mages, one for each of the four elements. Or the four points of one of the other stars, but the elements are easiest. I am Air, Maridon is Earth. We need Fire and Water, and you are Fire.

"Besides, even if I could get help from another magister, you, student or not, are the strongest fire mage in the College. I think you know it. If you did not why would you choose to veil?"

She was silent for a space, then asked: "What is your project?"

"You know that two mages can pool—we discussed it in class last month."

Ellen nodded.

"Mostly, pooling is done by two mages of the same sort, two fire mages or two refiners. It is possible but much less common and more difficult for two mages to combine different talents for a single work. I believe it is how the containment sphere was crafted, fire and weaving together."

She looked up startled, started to speak, stopped.

Coelus continued: "The records are not clear on how it was done, but that is the only explanation I can see, and I have examined the sphere closely.

"I believe I have discovered a way in which four mages, one for each point of a basis star, can pool. The pool then spans all magery. Better still, it can be used to pull more and more magery into the pool, from mages of all sorts and even from ordinary people.

"Think how much we could do with the pooled talent of fifty mages and five hundred, or five thousand, or fifty thousand ordinary people, each adding his trifle of talent to the pool, pouring it through a trained mage. Almost unlimited power to end a plague, to heal even someone at the point of death, to build a road or monument, to do things that no single mage, whatever his talent, could do before. And since the pool would span the whole range of magery, the power could be used for anything.

"Half the courses in the curriculum are a waste of time for you; you already know them. That has been clear for months. I could set up a course of independent study to teach you the theory behind the Cascade Effect, get your help with the research…"

She interrupted. "The people you pull in; must they give their consent to lend you their magery?"

"How could they? We are not talking about a group of four or five mages but about hundreds or thousands or tens of thousands of people, most not mages, and the mages among them would be mostly half-trained. Not one mage in ten is a graduate of the College. How could I ask all of them, and, if I could, how could they understand what I was asking them to do?"

"I thank you for the offer, Magister Coelus. If you wish to instruct me in theory, I will be happy to learn. But I will not aid you to take what is not freely given."

"You will not …"

"I will not help you to take from mages their power or from common people the magery that aids them in growing their crops, hunting their game, without their consent, whatever purpose you propose to use it for."

He looked at the girl in astonishment, felt for words to explain. "You don't understand. There is so much to be done, so little power to do it with. A river floods. With enough magery in the hands of a water mage with proper skills, we could divert the water to where it would be harmless. A plague kills hundreds, mothers and fathers"—his voice faltered—"leaving behind orphaned children. Enough power in the hands of a healer could see the plague when it first struck, cure everyone before the sickness spread farther. So much to do, and we are so weak.

"You are young, sheltered. If you had seen… I cannot make you aid me. But consider the needless deaths and misery that might happen if you do not."

She shook her head. "My mother is a healer; I have seen sickness enough. Men with gaping wounds that she has closed. When you have seized her power to shift a flood, on whose hands will be the blood of those she cannot heal?"

There was a long silence. Ellen nodded to Magister Coelus, turned, left the room.

* * *

"She won't help."

Maridon looked up from his desk. "Come in, sit down, tell me about it. Was she afraid she might get hurt if something went wrong?" Coelus sat down, shook his head slowly.

"That wasn't it. She thought what we wanted to do was wrong."

Maridon looked puzzled. "How can it be wrong to gather the power needed to make the world a better place?"

"She was unhappy over using power without the mages' consent, even though I explained why we couldn't possibly ask everyone. She ..."

Maridon cut in before Coelus could finish. "Some youngsters are like that, especially girls. They worry too much about following rules, not enough about what it takes in the real world to get anything done. High and noble principles sound very well, but they do not count much in the balance against what we can accomplish once we have the Cascade working.

"It is something we will have to watch out for; youngsters are not the only ones who miss the bigger picture. I would not be in the least surprised if Dag reacted the same way; you know what an icicle he is about keeping to the bounds. Good thing he is off looking for more talent.

"In fact, it might be better if you leave out the Cascade when talking to the others. Just describe what we want to do as a pooling of four mages to span all of magery and make possible all combinations. That is impressive enough to get their attention but not enough to start the more rigid of our colleagues nattering at us."

Coelus still looked worried. "You don't think she's right? She is worried about what might go wrong while we were draining off mages' power into the Cascade."

"So they stop killing off bedbugs for rich innkeepers or healing sick cattle. You know as well as I do that most mages outside the College aren't doing anything that really matters—not to mention those inside. With this pooled power, we can do things that do really matter. There is always something that could go wrong in whatever you do. Every hunter knows his arrow might miss the deer and hit a man who happens to be on the far side. That doesn't stop him from hunting. Healing someone today may mean he might kill someone else tomorrow. That's no reason not to heal people.

"Your Cascade is the biggest breakthrough in generations. It will make you famous. It will make it possible to do things no mage could ever do before."

Maridon paused a moment, then continued speaking. "Is the girl a gossip? Will she be telling everyone in the college about your project and how wicked it is? If so..."

Coelus thought a moment. "She doesn't talk much with the others and veils her power all the time. As far as I know you and I are the only ones who see her as anything more than ordinary. Hal didn't at the interview. Considering what I went through as a student, I can see why she keeps her head down. At least she won't have half the class looking for ways to make her life miserable."

"Would it help if you spoke to her, just to make sure, told her it would be breaking a confidence to babble about your work? Suggest that you will be happy to teach her, but only if her confidentiality can be trusted? It is not every student who has the chance of personal lessons from a mage of your ability."

Coelus looked doubtful. "Let me think about it."

"You think. I will listen for rumors and consider what to do if need be. Both of us can think about where to find two more mages for the real experiment, once you finish the preliminary series. But this time, before you ask anyone else, talk to me first."

"I will. I suppose I should have earlier. But she was the obvious choice, once I thought of it, and it never occurred to me that she might object."

* * *

As the notes of the evening bell died away, Ellen looked around the small orchard then down at the message in her hand. Coelus wanted to speak with her again. The orchard had a pleasant smell to it that she did not remember from earlier visits, green mixed with the rich odor of the earth. It was getting late; another hour or two and she would be in bed. Already she felt sleepy, sleepy enough to lie down on the grass by one of the trees, nestle her head on the warm earth and close her eyes.

A searing pain on her right hand woke her, as if someone had blown a flame across it. She opened her eyes and tried to lift her hand to look at it. It was almost dark. Something, cold and strong, was holding her arm, keeping it from moving. Her body, lying flat when she fell asleep, was now almost vertical.

She bent her head, looked down, and saw grass just below her chin. Somehow she had sunk into the earth. Her head, neck, right hand and part of the arm were still above ground and she could move her toes, but not her legs. She felt herself being sucked down, farther.

She drew in a deep breath. Fighting the pressure of the earth against her chest, she looked up. Just above was the apple tree she had fallen asleep against, its thick old trunk motionless, branches moving slowly in the wind, one low one almost within reach if only her arm were free.

What else could she use? The grass around her was long. With a thought she bent it down and wove it into a thick mat just below her right hand. Pushing down as hard as she could, she levered her arm up. The ground was soft but the mat of woven grass held firm. Her right arm pulled free. Straining upward, she grasped a twig on the branch above her and held it.

Just above that branch was another; under her stern gaze the two began to twist together, pulled in a third, forming a thick triple braid of woven branches that dipped to twist around her wrist. More and more branches bent down and added themselves. The mat of grass became a green sleeve, cradling her arm, its ends weaving in and out of the braid.

She pulled down with her right arm against the woven branches, up with her left, trying to break it free. Not enough. She stopped, breathed deeply against the pressure of the earth, and thought her way back into the pattern of the tree, downwards. A root moved against her foot, another. She felt something move against her imprisoned left arm. Again she pulled down with her right arm on the braided branches, straining to lift herself.

Her left arm broke free; the hollow where it had been was so thick with woven rootlets she could see only a bit of earth beneath. She reached her freed arm up, caught the branches, and pulled, now with both arms.

Eyes closed that she might better see, she looked down her body, still buried in the ground. Small roots were running up her legs, sending out rootlets, weaving together a loose fabric which guarded her from the earth that had tried to swallow her. But most of her body was still trapped. Against the pressure of the earth even to breathe was hard.

There was only so much one tree could do for her.

The edge of the containment dome flared, more brilliant than she had ever seen it. There might be an answer; she felt her way into its woven fire. Power, more than a dozen trees, a hundred. With the fingers of her mind she teased out one strand, two, three, more, wove a garment of flame about her body.

She felt the ground shudder, release her. Letting go of the branches, she put her hands against now solid ground, heaved herself out of her half formed grave, and stumbled over to the apple tree. She leaned against it gasping for breath. A few minutes were enough to unweave branches and grass. The gaping hole in the earth was no work of hers. She would leave closing it, or not, to whomever had made it.

Ellen looked down for the note she had been holding when she fell asleep. Hard to see in the faint moonlight, but it seemed to be gone. She brought a tiny flame from one finger tip; still nothing.

In its faint light she could see the sorry state of her over robe and the tunic beneath, both filthy and torn. The rips she could fix, but... She let the flame go out, reached into the dark, and wove a thick cloak of shadow about herself.

Back in her room she closed and barred the door and set the small oil lamp aflame, then stripped out of her robe. Her right hand hurt. The palm was red and a few small blisters had begun to form. Something had burned it. Something had awoken her just before she was fully buried.

Two puzzles then, perhaps two mages, if this had not been merely a bizarre accident. She would think about them tomorrow. For tonight, she reached into the lamp flame, pulled out a thin strand of fire and formed about her wrist, arm, and body a pale garment, an armor of woven flame. Paler and still paler, until it vanished to a ghost even she could barely see. She put out the lamp, went to bed, closed her eyes and, in time, slept.

Chapter 5

The next day Ellen awoke to the pleasant sound of rain on the slate roof above her bed. Judging by the amount of water on the paving stones, it had been raining for some time. She lay in bed, stiff and sore from the previous evening's struggle, wondering what condition the orchard was in. The rain should be good for the apple tree; she thought briefly about what if anything she could do to compensate for diverting so much of the tree's stored resources to her use.

Last night's clothing she could wash in her wash basin, then repair the damage. No need to start talk by involving the College servants or anyone else. Best to take her own precautions, keep her eyes open, and wait for her hidden enemy to make his next move.

The breakfast bell broke into her thoughts, and brought her out of bed.

By lunch time the rain had gotten harder, the first real storm that fall. Mari met Ellen at the entrance to the refectory. "The orchard will be a swamp by now and the cloister damp. The dining hall is packed. I've been telling the others to get their food then head to my rooms for an indoor picnic."

Ellen fetched a plate and bowl, filled them, and followed her friend. The desk in Mari's sitting room had been pulled out, the three chairs around it occupied by Mari, Alys, and Edwin, who offered his to Ellen. She declined in favor of the floor, back against the door to Mari's bedroom. Jon joined her there and put the first question:

"Magister Simon has had us memorizing names in the true speech for a month now, still don't understand what it's all about. Nobody speaks it, not even the Doray, so why learn it for spells?"

Ellen, as usual, thought a moment before answering. "What's special about the true speech is that spells done in it work. Lots of people say they know why, but most disagree with each other. The Dorayans claimed that our world was a story told by the creator God and the speech was the language that story was told in; the surviving Doray sects, here and in what's left of the

League, still believe that. The orthodox sects, or at least some of their mages, say names in the true speech are those the first man gave everything on the day of creation."

"What do you believe?" That was Mari.

"That spells done in the true speech work. I don't know why, but it might be because the names aren't arbitrary, the way names are in other languages."

Edwin looked up, spoke. "You mean that confusing business about the component syllables from the first lecture that Simon has hardly mentioned since?"

Ellen nodded. "Yes. A name in the speech isn't just a name, it's a definition. If you break up the word for "horse," the pieces come out as "hornless quadruped with mane." And of course "mane" itself isn't a single syllable; it means "neck hair." And there are long forms for both "neck" and "hair" that get squished down to single syllables for building other words out of."

Alys put down her piece of bread, joined the conversation. "But none of that really matters, does it? We're learning the names; there's no need to make it even harder by learning why they are the names. I don't have to know the word for 'mane;' I'm not enchanting horses' manes."

Ellen shook her head. "It matters for two reasons. The first is that the definition tells you what the name you are memorizing means. If you do a spell on horses, you only expect it to affect horses. But if you are using the true name for "horse" — and you will be if you want the spell to work — it will affect any other hornless quadruped with a mane that happens to be in the area. The true name for "horse" doesn't really mean "horse," it means ..."

Jon cut in. "Hornless quadruped with mane. Could be a mule, even a donkey."

"Yes. And the same is true of every name you use in a spell. If you want to affect only the horses, you have to say something that amounts to 'horse but not mule.' It's really very much like mathematics, especially mathematical logic." Ellen stopped a moment to take a bite of bread.

Mari reached over for the wine bottle. "Which explains why I don't understand it. I'm with Alys this time. Word for word translation may not get it exactly right, but if the alternative is mathematical logic I will have to be content with almost." She half filled her glass, put the bottle back.

Ellen looked up at Mari. "I said there were two reasons. The other is that if you understand how true names are built you can build one. You don't have to say 'horse but not mule' — which expands into a lot more than that in the speech. You can say 'fertile hornless quadruped with mane' instead."

Jon grinned: "Not if you want your spell to work on geldings."

"I hadn't thought of that. But it shows why you have to understand how names are built. Someone might construct the name I just offered and teach it to you as an improved version of 'horse' and if you didn't understand the pieces of it you would never figure out why some of the horses were still coming down with worms after you had spelled all of them not to."

Alys wrinkled up her nose. "Do you think you could keep worms out of it until I'm finished eating? Jon's account of sausage last month was bad enough."

Ellen looked at her, puzzled. "I thought it was very interesting. If you don't like worms, make it something else."

"Cracked hooves and splints. That is what our horses are always coming down with. If Alys doesn't like worms and sausages, she can always eat bread and cheese." Mari passed what was left of the small wheel of cheese across the desk.

"Haven't told you about making cheese?" Jon was grinning.

Mari gave him a stern look. "And you shan't. Not today, at least, or poor Alys may starve to death. Anyway, I have another question for Ellen. About names."

She paused, turned to look at her friend. "Why do mages never change their names, even when pretending to be someone else? Why do they avoid giving their names, and use nicknames, and confuse people in other ways? Why not just take a different name? Is it only in the stories, or is it real?"

"It's real."

Edwin looked up from his plate. "Do people have names in the true speech? Do you have a name? 'Short dark haired lady who knows everything about magic?'"

Ellen shook her head. "That's not how it works. The Speech has a word for 'person,' and 'woman,' but not for particular people. Though I am sure you and Mari can have fun making them up. My name is 'Ellen' — 'Elinor' in long form. It is what I've always been called. Spells cast on me are anchored to that name. If I didn't want to be spelled I could change my name to weaken the connection.

"But a spell is anchored at both ends and a mage cares more about casting spells than about stopping others from casting spells on him. If I changed my name, my spells would stop working, or at least working as well. The more and the longer people called me by the new name, the weaker the old name would get, the less it would be me, and the weaker any spells I tried to anchor to it.

"I could have changed my name when I was two, I suppose. But if I changed my name now and tried to shift everything to it, I would never be as strong as I am now. That's why mages in the stories keep their own names even if they are doing their best to hide who they are.

"The only words you can read in written spells and amulets are people's names. The rest are in glyphs, the written form of the true speech. Each word is a symbol, almost a little drawing, not a drawing of the thing but a graphic definition made up of little bits each of which corresponds to an element in the definition. I expect Simon will get to that next semester."

"After he gives up on teaching us the spoken version?" Mari ate her last bit of cheese, pushed back the plate. "He will teach us to try to draw words?" She stood up, opened the window that opened on the College's kitchen garden, looked out. It was still raining.

"Isn't it wonderful to have something to look forward to."

The others snickered; Ellen stared at them, head to one side, perplexed.

Chapter 6

A room, scantily furnished. At the end by the door a desk, an untidy pile of codices, a few scrolls. Along one long side a work table, its wooden top scarred and scorched. Two mages, earth and air.

Coelus carefully arranged the small brazier on the table over the chalk mark for fire. Over the other mark, part way down the table, a glass goblet, clear as water, beside it the sealed flask. He motioned Maridon over to the fourth mark.

A knock on the door.

"Come in."

"Am I late? Magister Maridon said at the sixth bell." The student looked a little uncertain.

"No. Just in time. Sit over there, facing the wall. This should not take very long."

Joshua took his seat. Coelus went to the far end of the table, opened the clay fire box, used a small pair of silver tongs to remove one glowing coal. Into the brazier. He blew gently on it, was rewarded with a trickle of smoke, a pale flame.

Next the flask, unstoppered, a thin stream of water into the goblet.

"Galfred sent it; with luck there's enough."

A wide silver spoon filled with grey powder; he sprinkled it onto the brazier. The charcoal burst into brilliant flame. Back to his own place, the fourth point of the star.

Coelus spoke a Word. For a moment nothing happened. He raised his hand, spoke again. From his hand to Maridon, a faint white line. Maridon raised his hand, spoke a Word; their two hands were linked by a double thread, white and black. Coelus lifted his left hand; as he let it fall the two spoke the third Word together.

From Coelus the double thread leaped to the brazier. Triple now, the black and white lines clear, the red line barely a thread. To the goblet.

The four—two mages, the brazier, the goblet—were the corners of a square, its edges traced in four-fold lines, the mage's colors bright, the other two, blue and red, spiderweb thin. Coelus spoke a final Word.

From Joshua to Coelus' hand another thread of light; to Coelus it seemed a turning twist of white and blue. For a moment everything froze, the square outlined in fourfold light, the fifth line.

With a sharp crack the flask broke, spilling steaming water and fragments of glass onto the table. The threads of light vanished, the blue an instant before the others. Joshua cried out, stood, tried to turn, and fell face forward onto the floor.

"Did it work?" That was Maridon. Coelus, bent over the fallen student, took a moment to answer.

"I think so. The elemental water must have run out. The boy is still breathing; I think he'll be all right. If it hadn't worked, how could he have reacted as he did; that's the clearest evidence. I can hardly perceive any magery at all in him now. Besides, I saw the fifth line, even if only for a second.

"But I have the geometry wrong; it's unbalanced, with me as both starpoint and focus. It needs five mages, four for the basis star, one for the focus. I suppose four mages might work, but not as well and it might be dangerous. I think the other part of what unbalanced it was using substitutes, elemental reagents to stand in for their mages. But five would be better."

Maridon gave him a skeptical look. "So it works in theory, but not yet in practice."

"It worked in practice, just not for very long. I could feel power coming in from the boy. Just a trickle, but more than we were getting from the workbench alone and it felt different from ours. With five mages, maybe even with four, we could do it."

Maridon had another question. "The boy we pulled from is a mage, even if he is not trained. What about the rest of the Cascade?"

"I don't think we can pull from plain people yet, not with half the star filled with tokens instead of mages. Even with four or five mages it would be hard. If my calculations are right, the best way is to cascade over a dozen mages or more, then use the pool to start pulling in plain folk."

Maridon walked over to the unconscious student, nudged him with a toe. "What about him?"

Coelus bent over Joshua, examined him carefully. "His breathing is fine, his heart is beating, I can even see a faint glow of magery, so that is coming back all right. We drained him too much; I need to find a way of keeping the flow down to what the source can keep giving. I expect he'll wake up in a bit. With luck he will be willing to help again; we need an outsider with at least a little power to test the Cascade. But we ought to send for a healer for him now, just to be safe."

Maridon shook his head.

"The fewer know about this the better; we do not want to start rumors, whether among our colleagues or the students. I will trust your judgment that he is all right. I talked to him this morning; I do not think there will be a problem getting him to help again. You do the calculations, work out the next test. I will see about getting us two or three more mages for when you are ready to do a real Cascade. Not from the College; the fewer rumors the better until we are ready to show our colleagues what real magery looks like."

Maridon gave the unconscious student a final glance, turned, left the room. Coelus took the student's folded cloak off the back of his chair, spread it over him, folded up his own cloak to make a pillow, sat down in the other chair to wait.

A mage's workroom. A body on the floor, a mage sitting watching it. Slowly the image faded.

* * *

"Have you done the work I assigned?"

Ellen nodded. "Yes. But before I hand it in, I have a question."

Coelus looked at her quizzically. She was holding a thin stack of neatly written sheets.

"Do you know the answers to all those problems for ways of building a pool to span all of magery?"

He thought a moment. "Almost all. The last one, the combinatorial star, I have not actually calculated, since we have none of the mages it requires, but it is straightforward enough. I don't expect to have any difficulty judging your answer."

"Any right answer will do? It does not have to be the best?"

That got his attention. "Is finding a better solution too much work for you, once you have one?"

37

She shook her head. "I told you; I wish to learn, but I am not willing to help with your project. If you tell me you have solutions, I will be happy to show you mine. But I will not work to make it easier for you to drain mages, or others, without their consent."

"So you want me to help you learn but you will not help me?"

"I have done my best to offer you the one thing I have to give that matters. So far I have not succeeded. If one of the other magisters asked you to help him devise a better love philtre, would you do it?"

"Of course not. Compulsions are …"

"Compulsions are beyond the bounds of proper magery. So Magister Henryk told us the first day of class, and I believe it. To pool the power of," she hesitated a moment, "of four mages with their assent, and in so doing span all forms of magery, is indeed a fine thing. To calculate out how one mage can use the pooled power to do, in the limit, everything that a mage of any sort could do, is a puzzle worthy of your ability. Further than that is compulsion."

He looked up, struck by something she had said. "If you were doing it, how many mages would you use?"

She said nothing.

"I see. Let me look through those papers and I will think about whether I can accept your terms and still teach you."

Ellen handed him the stack, turned and left. He looked after her for a long minute before looking down at her work.

The next day when she returned, he was the one with a question: "What you handed me. Was that all of your work or only the final result?"

She looked puzzled. "All of the written work. Paper is expensive and it is hard to work clearly on wax. Things are tidier inside my head."

He smiled. "For me too. I am not sure I have met anyone else who feels the same way until now. You worked out the answers in your head, then wrote them down on what you gave me?"

"Yes. It's easiest at night, in bed with my eyes closed."

"And you wrote down only the first answer you found?"

She hesitated. "Sometimes. Sometimes the second answer was

simpler, so I wrote that down instead."

"I am sorry I cannot persuade you of the good I hope to do. I have here," he handed her a single sheet, "six more problems. None are part of the Cascade project, I promise you. Five I know the answers to. I will let you decide which five, if you can."

Her sudden smile was brilliant, lighting up the face he had at first thought plain. She took the sheet, dropped a brief curtsey — it felt more like the bow before a duel — and left the room.

* * *

She returned the next morning, papers in hand. He looked up from his desk. "You look tired."

She nodded. "The first three were easy. The fourth … I found an answer, but it's hack work, clumsy. I gave up on trying to find a better one when I got too sleepy."

"So you didn't do the last two?"

"I did them, then went back and tried to do the fourth better. Then I gave up and went to sleep."

She handed him the sheets, covered with her precise script. He started reading, stopped and looked up.

"This will take a while. Sit down before you fall down." He went back to the papers.

He handed her back the stack when he was done. "Your solution to the fifth problem requires a mage who spans fire and weaving and another who spans air and fusing. Where do you plan to find them?"

"It also requires most of a gallon each of elemental earth and water. You put no limits on the materials I could use."

He nodded. "True enough."

"I did find a more elegant solution to the fourth problem but it required the assistance of two of the elementals. Since nobody knows if elementals are more than a convenient mathematical device, I decided it did not qualify."

Coelus nodded. "Not to mention that nobody has found even one, and the last mages who went looking disappeared forty odd years ago."

"I also found a way of doing what you want that involves no compulsion at all, at least I don't think so. Unfortunately…"

For a moment he thought she was serious, then he looked at her face.

"It also requires all four elementals, one at each point of the star. Unlimited power, so no need to drag in anyone else. And however much you use, there is as much and more left for the rest of us."

His smile answered hers. "An excellent solution in theory but I am afraid there may be some small difficulties putting it into practice."

* * *

"How old do you think Magister Coelus really is?"

Ellen responded to Alys with a puzzled expression; Mari put it into words. "What do you mean? He's older than we are but younger than the other magisters. Thirty, maybe, or a little under?"

Alys shook her head. "That's how he looks. But everybody knows mages can make themselves younger. That's one point of being a mage. For all we know, he could be a hundred and thirty and been teaching the same course for the past hundred years."

Mari looked at Ellen helplessly. Ellen took a bite of cheese before answering. "He can't have been teaching here for the past hundred years, because the college isn't a hundred years old. Most of what he is teaching wasn't known a hundred years ago. The library has records of faculty and curriculum going back almost to the founding; if you are curious you could check them. I would be surprised if he has been here as long as a dozen years.

"And he can't be a hundred and thirty because no mage is strong enough to hold his physical age down by a hundred years for more than few minutes."

Alys looked unconvinced. "Records can always be changed, especially by mages. The Mage King was still fighting battles when he was past a hundred, wasn't he?"

Mari nodded. "Theodrick fought his last battle at a hundred and twenty-three. I don't know what his apparent age was then, but I doubt it was thirty. Don't you know how Theodrick died?"

"Didn't he die in his last war with Forstmark? The one we won."

"But do you know how?"

Alys shook her head and waited for Mari to continue.

"Ellen probably knows the story better than I do, but as I understand it he was using a team of mages to keep him young enough to rule the kingdom as well as command the army in the field. By the final war it was taking a lot of the best mages to do it. The Forsting were winning. At a hundred and twenty-three, Theodrick named the ablest of his grandsons heir, had him crowned, then sent the mages supporting him to help the army instead. He was buried in a closed coffin with a handsome statue on it representing him when he took the crown."

"Why couldn't he just spell himself younger or have his mages do it, then send them off to fight the war?"

Mari looked at Ellen, who took the hint. "It doesn't work that way. A mage with suitable training can make himself younger, but it isn't a spell you just do and it stays done. You have to keep maintaining it. The older you are, the more power it takes. I expect Coelus could push his age down by a year or two without much trouble, but more than that wouldn't leave him a lot of power to do anything else with. If he tried to hold to thirty, in a few years it would be taking all his power to do it and at some point his age would have to start going up again."

"So even if I study hard, pass the second year exams and learn all they teach me, I still won't be able to be nineteen forever? That's terrible! What if I get a powerful mage to fall in love with me? Could he do it?"

"If he were close enough to the same kind of mage that you are and sufficiently skilled, he could combine his power with yours and the two of you could hold the age of one of you for a few more years. But, again, you would have less power for anything else. Theodrick was holding a difference of about forty years at the end and it took a team of mages to do it."

"I knew you knew more about it than I did, if I could just get you to talk." Mari turned back to Alys. "If you came here in the hope of perpetual youth, I am afraid you are in the wrong place."

Alys pouted, but her eyes were merry. "Neither of you are any help at all. If I can't stay young forever, I suppose I'll just have to enjoy myself while it lasts. Speaking of which…"

She nodded in the direction of the next table, where Edwin and Jon were sitting, and winked at her friends. "I'm thirsty," she said, raising her voice. "If I fetch another pitcher, will you boys help me drink it?"

Chapter 7

The two girls were in the cookshop starting dinner when Joshua came in and walked over to the table where they sat. "May I join you, ladies?"

Neither spoke; he took their silence for assent.

"Do either of you care for anything to drink?" he said, looking at Mari. "The wine they got in last week is better than you might expect."

She nodded. "Thank you."

Ellen said nothing. In a few minutes he returned with a bowl of mutton stew in one hand, two clay cups and a small pitcher. He poured wine into the cups, handed Mari one, spoke over the background of voices and clattering dishes.

"How have you been enjoying the lectures? Is Bertram as dull as he was my year? I got more sleep in that class than in my own bed."

Mari took the cup and looked up at Joshua. "He is rarely entertaining, but at least I can understand most of what he is saying. Sentence by sentence Magister Coelus sounds very interesting, but when he finishes I feel that I know a little less than when he started. I have no doubt that he is as brilliant as Ellen says, but unfortunately I am not." She drank a sip of wine, then put the cup down again.

"Coelus? I don't know about brilliance, but he is not teaching anything useful. I don't want to know about basis stars, I want to know how to do magery. All the lectures are mostly a waste of time anyway; it's not until you get to the tutorials that you learn anything you can actually use." He watched Mari as he spoke.

"I … I suppose so."

Ellen looked at her friend in surprise, then back at Joshua. Mari's face was faintly flushed.

"And a boring waste of time. There are so many more interesting things to do." He was speaking to Mari; Ellen might as well not have been there.

"Yes, yes, I suppose there are."

"Down by the river bank it is very pleasant this time of the evening."

Mari rose from the table, her wine cup still half full. "It was pleasant speaking with you," Joshua said to Ellen. "I will see the lady Mariel safe back to college."

Ellen hesitated a moment, stood up, and spoke to Mari. "You look unwell. Do you have a fever?"

"A fever? No. I don't think so. Not exactly." Her eyes never left Joshua's.

"Let me feel your forehead." Ellen put her hand against her friend's forehead, closed her eyes.

"Shall we be off?" Joshua started around the table, tripped, and came down heavily. In a moment he was up again, stepped forward, and stumbled again. He looked down.

"Damn, the laces have tangled." He leaned over, carefully undid and redid his bootlaces, then stood up again. Mari gave him a look. "Shall we go now?" he said, a bit impatiently.

"Go where? I haven't finished my dinner yet."

"We were going to take a walk down by the river."

Mari shook her head. "I think not. Perhaps some other day." She sat down again.

Joshua glanced down at the table, up again at Mari. "We still have some wine left. Before I go, a toast to fewer boring lectures, to successful spells, and your graduation as a wi… as a mage of the college." He lifted his wine cup, drained it, still staring at Mari.

Ellen picked up Mari's cup. "Since the toast is to Mari's success, we two should drink it, not she." She sipped from the cup, put it down, and looked up intently at Joshua.

"Of course. Well, back to prepare for my next tutorial." He fled. Ellen sat back down again. Mari looked at her curiously. "That was very strange. What are you laughing at?"

Ellen took a bite of her stew and, still smiling, chewed it thoughtfully. "It wasn't supposed to show." She swallowed and said, "I was laughing at Joshua trying to get out of the room before I fell in love with him."

"Before you what?"

"Before I fell in love with him."

Mari inspected her friend's face. This was not her sort of joke. "There was something in the wine?"

Ellen nodded. "A love potion, I think. I'm not properly trained as a healer, but mother taught me some useful tricks. Dealing with potions was one of them."

"So that was why I felt so odd. I don't think love is quite the right word. I wasn't in love with Joshua. I just ..."

"Wanted to walk down by the river among the willows, pull him down and tear his clothes off?"

Mari nodded. "Two years ago I had a crush on one of my tutors. It was a little like that, but with parts missing. I wonder what he wanted."

This time it was Ellen's turn to look surprised. "I thought that was obvious."

Mari shook her head. "There are two whores in the village that I know of, one of them quite pretty. With easily a hundred single men in the college, they must get a lot of business. Joshua might enjoy seducing me, but in the long run there would be consequences. He can't be that stupid." Her face had gone pale, but her voice remained calm.

She thought a moment. "Perhaps he thought if he could get me pregnant my father would let him marry me. He doesn't know Father! Lucky for him it didn't work; he should be more grateful to you than I am. I can't think what might have happened if you hadn't been here. I didn't think potions like that were included in what students here got taught. Didn't Magister Hal say something about them?"

"They certainly are not included in what we are taught; love potions are a compulsion, in violation of the bounds of magery. Magister Hal discussed them in one of his first lectures. And if they were taught here, I wouldn't trust Joshua with making one; he'd be as likely to poison as seduce you."

"He must have bought it. Lots of money and no morals—the perfect customer. It probably isn't the first time; he seemed so expectant."

Ellen nodded. "I expect they're also against royal law, at least for what he was trying to do. Should we speak to Hal or one of the other magisters?"

Mari shook her head. "Better not to have my name in a scandal. I will just have to be careful about drinking anything he offers me in the future."

"That may not be enough. Potions are not all he can buy. You said you wanted to show me some trinkets you were thinking of purchasing from Master Dur's in the village. Will he still be open?"

"I expect so. It's still light and I don't think he closes until dark. But what …"

"Show me whatever you like, but I want you to buy an amulet case. And let me look at it first so I can see if it will do."

When they got to the jeweler's shop it was indeed still open. Inside they found Alys, pondering several necklaces and bracelets. The jeweler was in the back room of the shop tidying up after his dinner, having left a mug of beer behind him on the counter. Ellen and Mari looked over his wares; Mari commented in a low voice. "Mostly silver, and none of the stones are very valuable, but it's lovely work."

"There can't be much of a market here in the village for expensive pieces."

Mari nodded agreement. "He keeps a few in the back, for customers who look as though they can afford them. But I don't see why he is here working in silver and garnet when he could make far more in the capital doing the same work in gold and rubies instead. He's at least as good as mother's jeweler, maybe better. I must bring her here — perhaps she can commission something."

Alys addressed Master Dur as he came back into the front part of the shop:

"Could you help me with this amulet case? It seems to be stuck."

He picked up the case, tried to twist off the lid; nothing happened.

"It is stuck; I wonder how that happened. Let me see…"

He walked along the counter to where a small anvil was sitting, next to it an iron hammer.

"This might do it." He tapped the amulet case gently on the anvil, turned it, tapped it again, again. This time the cap came off with a gentle twist. Alys gave the jeweler a startled look.

"If it gets stuck that easily, I don't think I want it. Have you a sapphire pendant I could look at? I think the color would go with a dress I have."

By the time the jeweler returned with a tray and several pieces, Mari and Ellen had agreed on an amulet case. Dur left the tray with Alys and came over to speak to them.

"You plan to enchant it?" The question was put to Ellen. She nodded. "I assume that is its intended purpose?"

"Yes. Virgin silver; I refined it from the ore myself."

Ellen took the amulet case; Mari paid the jeweler, turned back to her friend.

"Now I'm going to see what else I can find. You can stay and advise."

Ellen shook her head. "I should be getting back. I have work to do." She glanced down at the amulet case. "I'll come by your rooms later this evening; you can show me what treasures you have bought then." Mari nodded farewell and turned back to the jeweler's wares.

It was a good hour past vespers when Ellen knocked on Mari's door. Mari was at her desk inspecting her purchases. Ellen handed the amulet case to Mari, then sat down. Mari examined it curiously.

"It looks just the same."

"It is a pretty piece, but you won't be wearing it for looks. Wear it where it does not show, next to your skin. If you feel it getting uncomfortably warm, someone is trying to enspell you; if I am not too far away I will know. There is no way to protect you from everything but at least we can be warned if Joshua tries a spell rather than a potion next. Now show me what other treasures you have acquired."

"I must tell you what happened after you left. You remember that Alys asked the jeweler to show her sapphire pendants?"

Ellen nodded; Mari went on, "I was a bit surprised. She doesn't wear anything that expensive and I wouldn't have thought she could afford to. I wondered if she might be wanting to drop a hint to one or two of the young men she has running after her. But now I'm not sure."

"What happened?"

"After Dur got a few things for me, she called him over to complain of something wrong with the pendants. I went to look. They were nice work, mostly gold. You would expect to see valuable stones set in, but they weren't sapphires; two were clear, like rock crystal, and one dark. Dur looked annoyed, as if he made a mistake in what he had brought out. He apologized, picked up the tray, and suddenly Alys screamed. I looked at her and her hair had caught fire. She was standing with her back to the fireplace at one end of the shop and I suppose a spark must have caught it; you know how fine it is.

"For an old man, Dur moved pretty fast. He dropped the tray on the counter, picked up his beer mug, and dumped it over her. It put out the fire but she was a mess—soaked with beer and half her hair burned black. She'll need a scarf tomorrow and a haircut. But something felt strange about it all; first the stuck amulet case, then the sapphires that weren't, then the fire."

"Yes." Ellen thought for a moment. "It must have been an accident but I think Alys got what she deserved."

"What do you mean?"

"The stuck amulet case was her doing; I saw it. Before she put the cap back on she sprinkled something onto it and said something under her breath. I suspect it was the spell Magister Bertram told us about two days ago as a simple example of a union of similar materials. She probably got the powder from one of her older admirers with access to lab supplies. She must have been practicing it by trying it out on master Dur."

"Why didn't it work?"

"It did." Ellen was smiling.

"Not for long. He got it loose with almost no trouble at all. Just a couple of taps."

"It wasn't the taps, it was the anvil. The spell depends on the similarity of one piece of silver to another. The amulet and the top both tried to identify with the iron, so the spell collapsed. But I don't know why Alys was doing it. Did she think the jeweler would give her a discount if there seemed to be something wrong with it?"

Mari shook her head. "I expect she was just trying to play a joke on the old man. After he gave up trying to open it she would have said the counterspell and left him wondering why it hadn't opened for him. She's mischievous, but I don't think she would cheat someone."

"Well, the joke didn't end up being on him then." Ellen looked down at the amulet, back up at Mari. "I wonder if it was an accident. He must have been dealing with students from the college for a long time, maybe guessed what was going on years ago and asked one of the magisters how to counter such tricks, then amused himself by turning the tables on students like Alys. That's why I wonder — but I don't see how he could have..."

"Were the sapphires another trick?"

Ellen nodded. "Last week in Simon's language class, remember? One of the names we had to memorize was the true name of sapphire. She must have gotten someone to teach her an illusion spell. With that and the true name it would be easy to make the stones look different, at least for a while. I expect by now the spell has worn off and Master Dur, if he's had another look, is relieved."

"And if he's used to students doing pranks...?"

"He might have suspected what she was up to. He's probably at least as good as you are at guessing what customers can and can't afford to buy; it's how he makes his living, after all. But unless he happened to have a friendly fire mage in the next room, I don't see how he could have made her hair catch fire. Accidents do happen. Now, show me what you bought."

Chapter 8

Coelus handed back the papers and gestured Ellen to the chair. "One careless mistake, two places where there is a more elegant solution than the one you found. I have marked them. See if you can improve your answer. One place where you found a more elegant solution than anyone I'm aware of ever has. I marked that too.

"The question is what to do with you beyond lectures at the College. I will be happy to continue teaching you what I can. In particular, I would like to work through Olver's first treatise with you. It is a tantalizing piece of work, a signpost to the future of magical theory, and I would be happy to have your view of it.

"But doing problems I set, reading treatises that I assign, is not enough. It is time for you to start on your own work, learning things I cannot teach you because I do not know them.

"Independent research is for select third year students. You are not yet at the end of your first year but, at the level of pure theory, you already understand more than half my colleagues. There is much you can still learn but less and less left that I can teach you. At your age I too was a student but it did not stop me from starting my real work. There is no reason you should not do the same.

"You do not wish to help me with my project. I do not agree with your reasons but I accept them. So you should have a project of your own, and perhaps more than one."

"What sort of project, Magister?"

He hesitated a moment, opened his tablet, looked down at the first leaf. "It is your decision but I have a few ideas. It could be either research in understanding something that already exists. Or research in creating something new. My advice would be to start with the first and perhaps go on to the second later. I have a short list of puzzles here; you could choose one of them or find another for yourself."

"What sort of puzzles?"

"We have spoken a little about the stability problem—the tendency of constructions, static spells, to decay over time. One of the problems you did last week involved calculating the rate of loss for a simple static spell and, from that, the time to collapse."

The girl nodded, said nothing.

"I have long been puzzled by the stability of the containment sphere. I did some rough calculations a few years ago and concluded that either it was much stronger when it was built—and I could find no evidence of that in the records—or it should have collapsed years ago. You are better fitted than I to examine it, tease out its structure. So one project would be to redo my work more carefully and precisely, calculate how fast the sphere ought to be losing its fire and, if you can, determine how fast it is fading, either now or using any old records there may be from which its past strength can be deduced.

"It is a puzzle that should test your abilities. If it turns out to be too easy for you there is another sphere of fire, a somewhat brighter one, whose continued brightness may pose a still more difficult problem."

She looked puzzled for a moment, then smiled. "You mean the sun. I have wondered about that."

"Yes. By Olver's calculation, it ought to have burned out centuries ago; that's one of the six puzzles he starts the thesis with."

"Does Olver have a solution?"

"Some day you might go and ask him. When I did, he told me that he wasn't willing to publish half finished work. Perhaps you would have better luck."

Ellen shook her head.

"The containment sphere will do for the moment. Do you want me to work it all out myself or am I free to look for information from others more familiar with the construction?"

Coelus shook his head. "It won't do you any good. Nobody here knows anything useful and I searched through the library years ago. If Durilil left any description of how the sphere was constructed, it is long lost.

"But you are welcome to look. This is a project, not a test; there is no need for me to test you any more. In seeking truth, one uses what one can find."

* * *

"You are sure you want to risk it?"

Maridon nodded. "You invented the Cascade effect and you are the only one who really understands it. If something goes wrong, you have to be here to fix the schema and try again. I do not.

"Are all the preparations made?"

Coelus looked around the lawn. Maridon had taken the center position with three mages arrayed in their appointed places around him. With himself in the fourth position as air, all four elements were there to start the Cascade. It should be easier than the earlier experiments, with the improved geometry and with all four positions held by elemental mages instead of some only by material symbols. Coelus was in reach of the core line of the first stage; his athame, newly sharpened, lay on the table by his right hand, its silver blade gleaming. With luck, if something went wrong...

Maridon glanced at him; Coelus nodded. Everything had been rehearsed; this was it. One side of the lawn was the wall of the magister's wing, windows shuttered against the late autumn chill. The other was the inside surface of the containment sphere; at least if something did go wrong only the college was at risk. His colleagues, having advised him confidently that his absurd pooling schema could never work, would have no business complaining if it turned out to work too well. Idiots. He turned back to his colleague.

"Ready."

Maridon began the first invocation of the schema. Coelus chimed in on cue, then the other three. With eyes closed, Coelus could see the web building, woven with mixed lines of the elemental colors. For a moment it trembled, then froze, a solid four pointed star centered on Maridon, drawn everywhere in the Four Colors.

Maridon spoke the Word. The Colors poured through him, up his right arm, out the outstretched hand from each finger in a spreading web, further and further. One line pulsed, froze, a bright line of cold blue—a mage pulled into the web. A line twisted of blue and white. Again, this time a hair thin line—not a mage, but every drop of power mattered. Again. Again, until the air was filled with a spiderweb of lines.

Maridon's face held triumph in part, in part something else.

He half turned, pointed with his left hand. Coelus looked down; the silver blade of his athame was sinking into the grass, vanishing, only the handle visible. He tried to turn, willed the link broken. Nothing.

Maridon pointed, one after another, at the other three. Cold lines from his fingers to them. They too froze. For a moment time stopped, save for Coelus's mind racing. No answer.

Coelus watched, unable to move, as the most powerful mage in the world, the most powerful mage that had ever lived, walked slowly over to the wall of woven fire bordering the garden, the inside surface of the sphere protecting the college from the world, the world from the college. Maridon reached out with both hands, caught strands of fire, pulled.

For a moment the weave held. Maridon said another Word; Coelus felt the shock and saw the others sway. For a moment the world darkened. Slowly Maridon's hands pulled apart. Through the widening gap, Coelus could see the elm tree just outside the dome, the barrier that no mage in the world could break. Until now.

Maridon said a final Word. From his fingertips new strands spread, beyond the sphere. A million ordinary folk, each with his little magic to tap, thousands of mages.

One of the new strands pulsed, hair thin, froze. Another.

The third was a column of red as thick as the mage's wrist. For just a moment Maridon was outlined in fire.

The fire died. The gap it had poured through closed. Where Maridon had stood was nothing but floating ash.

Chapter 9

"You look tired; how is your project going? Have you solved the puzzle of the containment sphere?"

Ellen had been up most of the night finishing the work she was about to hand in to Magister Coelus, but she was sure she looked better than he did, after the death of his colleague and the tense inquiry that had followed. She sat down without being asked, knowing he would follow suit.

"Not exactly solved. This—she handed him a single sheet of paper—is my theoretical calculation of the rate of loss. It is not precise because I do not yet have the full structure of the sphere, but I do not think it can be high by more than about a factor of two. I assume no loss from the bottom half, earth being a good insulator against fire, and no net loss from the interior surface."

"This," a second sheet of paper, "summarizes my empirical test of the theoretical work. I constructed things similar to the sphere on a much smaller scale—the biggest was four inches across—and timed their decay. The results fit within my estimated range of error.

"This is the other half of the empirical work. I measured the actual loss from the sphere through a very small solid angle and then scaled it up accordingly. It comes out lower than my theoretical estimate but within my margin of two."

"This is my calculation of the pattern over time, assuming no additional support after the sphere was created. It shows how strong the sphere would have had to be forty-seven years ago, when it was created, in order to be at its present level now."

"And this"—she handed him the fifth and final sheet of paper—"shows what it would have taken Durilil to construct that strong a sphere. If we assume he was three times as powerful a fire mage as I am and doing nothing else, it comes to about twelve years; that is how long it would have taken to generate that amount of power. I assume that if he had spent twelve years constructing the sphere and doing nothing else, someone would have noticed and commented on it. And, of course, there is nothing in the early records to suggest that the sphere was eight times as intense then as now. If it was more intense it should also have been thicker. The stone footing at the entrance gate was built then and its depth matches the current thickness of the sphere. Not a likely accident."

She pushed the stack of papers across the table to him. "The conclusion, as the treatises sometimes put it, is left as an exercise for the reader."

He stared at her for a moment, looked down at the papers, then up. "I fear I am not at my best today, and I have less time to review your work than I would wish. I am still trying to understand the accident that killed Magister Maridon. Until I solve that problem I cannot continue the project, even if I could persuade any more of my colleagues to risk participating, but I will try to get to your calculations in the next few days. Assuming I do not find any critical mistakes—and I do not expect to—what is your conclusion?"

"Either Durilil found a way of violating the laws of magic as we understand them or the sphere is being maintained by some substantial source of added power."

"Such as?"

"Such as us. The sphere contains the college, after all, and between magisters and students the college produces far more power than would be needed to maintain the sphere. Perhaps the makers found some way to tax us for our protection, to drain off a trickle of our power to keep up the sphere. I don't see how—but I thought you might."

He looked up, startled. "You are suggesting that Durilil anticipated my current work by more than forty years, but in the form of a construction, not a mage pool?"

"Your work is based on Olver's, on a treatise that was completed just two years before the sphere was constructed. If you think about it …"

"It is an odd coincidence. You are right."

"And we know Durilil knew Olver's work, because after he constructed the sphere …"

"He went off searching for the Salamander. Olver's salamander, one of the essential elementals. It fits together. It may even be true."

Coelus, to Ellen's considerable relief, no longer looked like death warmed over. He thought for a moment, eyes wide open and alert.

"It is a fascinating puzzle, but it is your puzzle, not mine. You discovered it, you solve it. I cannot afford to shift to another line of research just now, and although this one is important I do not see how it can provide a solution, or even a clue, to the problem of what went wrong three weeks ago.

He smiled at her. "I realize that if you do find out anything relevant to my main line of research you won't tell me, but I am willing to take that risk. Now go get some sleep and then get back to work and let me return to what I am supposed to be doing."

She hesitated a moment before getting up, and returned his smile. "Good luck, or bad, whichever you deserve. Try not to get yourself burned up as well." She nodded to him and left the room. It was a long moment before Coelus too rose, went through the door into his workroom. There, he scribbled a brief note on the wax of the tablet that was open on the long table and set to work.

* * *

Mari intercepted the others outside of the lecture hall. "That was the last lecture of the semester and I survived it entirely due to Ellen's help. I may even have understood a few bits and pieces. She won't let me buy her anything, so instead I am inviting all of you to dinner at the inn as my guests. We're meeting at the front gate in half an hour."

When the five students arrived at the inn they were shown to a private upper room and seated at a big table with room for twice as many guests. A waiter brought a bottle of wine, bowls of soup, and a first course, a made dish of eels. Mari gave Jon a stern look across the table:

"And if you know anything unpleasant about eels, please leave it until after dinner."

He shook his head. "Don't know a thing about eels. Never grew any."

Alys smothered a giggle and turned to Edwin. "I am going home for the break and have a place reserved in tomorrow morning's coach. Will you be keeping me company?"

"It will be my pleasure. What are the rest of you planning?"

Jon was the first to answer:

"Home's a long trip. This time of year, don't much need an

extra pair of hands on the farm. Plan to stay in College, catch up on sleep."

Alys gave him a sideways look. "Won't it be very dull here all by yourself, with nobody but the magisters? Or do you know something I don't about who else is staying?" She looked around the table.

Mari shook her head. "Not I. The family is spending midwinter a few days north of here and I will be joining them. Ellen?"

"I am going home with my head full of things to tell Mother about. I've arranged to rent a horse from the Inn stable."

"Isn't it terribly dangerous, riding all that way by yourself?" Alys looked almost alarmed.

Ellen shook her head. "I've ridden the horse they are lending me before and it seems safe enough."

"I didn't mean the horse. Who knows what could happen to a girl riding across the countryside with nobody to protect her?"

For a moment there was silence. Mari started to speak, but didn't. At last Ellen broke it. "I got here safely enough on a borrowed horse; I expect I can get home the same way. It is not as if there were a war going on, or a plague of bandits. It will be royal road most of the way, and the last bit is country I know. "

She turned to Jon. "It will be quiet here by yourself, but there is always the library. I expect they keep it open for the magisters. I gather that some of them stay through the break."

Jon nodded. "Yes. Between library and bed, expect to fill the hours catching up. Everything during term that I didn't understand.

He stopped a moment, then continued. "Spent part of last Seventhday reading history of the College. Did you know place was originally a monastery?"

Alys looked up from her plate. "I expect it's still haunted by the ghosts of the monks the mages murdered. I will have to stay awake tonight to listen."

Jon shook his head. "No monks murdered, least not by mages. Monastery belonged to declining faction of one of the Doray sects, back when they were losing out to the orthodox. Abandoned twenty or thirty years before founders took it over. Durilil and Feremund showed up with plan for a college, moved in with apprentices, magery, mops and brooms. Must've been a job to get it cleaned up, put back together. Started in front with two magisters, eight or ten students, over the years grew."

Alys interrupted him. "Our wing is in the front; I wonder if it's where the Magisters lived at the beginning. I might have been sleeping in Durilil's bed, for all I know."

Mari put down her glass, took a moment to prepare a suitable response. "I've heard plenty of rumors about students in magisters' beds, but that's a new one."

"Don't be silly; he's been dead for hundreds of years. Besides, most of the magisters are too old. The only one who might be interesting is Coelus, and the only student he is interested in ..." She stopped, in response to Mari's glare.

Jon stepped into the conversational breach. "Hundreds of years take you back to Breakup, when Theodrick tore Esland out of the Dorayan League, made himself king. Durilil and Feremund died less than fifty years ago. Think Olver still alive, must be very old. One of the magisters told me, back when he was a student, painting of Durilil used to hang in the lecture hall."

Alys would not be diverted: "According to the rumors, which magisters am I supposed to be sleeping with?"

Mari shook her head. "If I knew I wouldn't tell. The rumors were about second years using unconventional means to make sure they get to graduate. I doubt it's true though. When the magisters first decided to admit women to the College there was a lot of gossip from people who disapproved of the idea, didn't think women could be trained as mages. They suspected that the magisters had something else in mind. I expect this is just a remnant of that."

The door opened to let the waiter back in. He carried a tray with a roasted capon and several small bowls, each with a different sauce. Conversation vanished while the students devoted themselves to the new course. After a bit, Mari put down her knife, turned to Edwin. "I know Alys lives in the capital. Is that where you are headed too or do you go on farther? How long does the coach take?"

"Two days to the capital. We have relatives there. I'll spend at least the night with them, then go on; I expect they can lend me a horse. It's another twenty miles and a good road all the way, so it should be an easy day's ride. But of course," he turned to Alys, "it is much less interesting without a beautiful lady to keep me company."

Alys gave him a melting smile. "You could always stay a few more days with your relatives. There's lots to see in the capital. And do."

"It is a thought, but I expect my parents will want to see me, at least to make sure the college hasn't turned me into some sort of sorcerous monster. They were not all that sure they wanted me to go, but my uncle persuaded them. It might be easier on my way back. And then you can tell me all the latest court gossip."

Chapter 10

Magister Simon looked around the room, cleared his throat. The students fell silent.

"Last semester I taught you a little of the spoken version of the true speech; I expect you to learn more on your own. As you know, there are several word lists in the library as well as two copies of the canonical version of the syllabary. You will want to give some thought to what words, and what syllables for building words, will be most useful, considering your individual talents and your future plans.

"This semester you will be introduced to the glyphs that make up the written form of the true speech used for scrolls and other written spells. Just as a word is made up of syllables, so a glyph is made up of elements."

Simon waved his hand at the board; writing appeared:

Word(syllables) ↔ *Glyph(elements)*

"Just as the syllables represent a definition of the word, so the elements that make up a glyph define its meaning. Just as a word can be reduced to a single syllable and used in constructing another word, so a glyph can be converted into a simplified form and in that form function as an element in another glyph."

As Simon spoke, the outline of what he was saying continued to appear on the board. He gave the students a minute to get it into their tablets before again waving his hand; the board went blank. He picked up a piece of chalk, walked up to the board, wrote a symbol: three vertical wavy lines. "Can anyone tell me what this is?"

Jon, who had been watching closely, raised his hand; Magister Simon nodded to him. "Fire, sir. The element for fire."

"Correct. The element for fire, but also the glyph for fire. As an element it can be used in constructing other glyphs, as a glyph it can be used in constructing spells. It also has one other use, although I do not know if any of you would have encountered it yet."

He looked around the room. At last Ellen raised her hand. "In theoretical magic, it stands for the Salamander."

She was rewarded with a nod from the magister. "Correct. Most of you will not encounter the symbolic use of the elementals until later this semester or perhaps next year, but when you do there will at least be a few symbols you can recognize."

He turned back to the board, sketched a simple circle, turned back to the class. "And what is this?"

Jon again raised his hand, but this time Simon ignored him, gestured to another student.

"Earth. The element and the glyph, just like for fire."

"Correct." Magister Simon added to the board the symbols for air and water, writing the name of each underneath twice, the second time as a syllable in the true speech. "We start with these four elements, as mages have started for hundred of years. Suppose we combine them. What, for instance, is this?" He wrote two symbols: Fire and earth.

Again Jon raised his hand. Simon looked around, saw nobody else, nodded to Jon.

"Lava, sir. Burning rock. Or a volcano."

"Very good. Did you work that out yourself?"

Jon shook his head. "In something I was reading in the library, sir."

The magister gave him an approving look. "I am happy to see that at least one of you takes some interest in your studies."

He erased the symbols on the board, replaced them with the symbols for air and water. "And this?"

To his surprise, it was Mari who raised her hand.

"You have an answer, Lady Mariel?"

"Mist. Clouds. Something like that?"

"Correct. Both. Have you too been spending your spare time browsing the library?

She shook her head. "No. But it seemed to make sense, after Jon gave his answer."

"Very good. It does indeed make sense. It is the nature of the true speech, whether spoken or written, to make sense."

* * *

Ellen looked up at the sky. Almost dark; the gate would be

closing in half an hour or so. Finding Mari again might take longer than that; Mari could find her way home alone.

She was just passing Master Dur's shop when she heard someone calling.

"Ellen. Come in. Quickly."

Nobody was in sight, but the shop door was ajar. She stepped to it, looked through.

At the back of the shop a figure slumped in a chair; a second was lying on the floor barely a foot away. She thought she smelled a faint odor of burnt meat.

"Ellen." It was the figure in the chair.

"I've been stabbed. Pull out the knife and weave together the wound."

She hesitated.

"You are a weaver. Weaving can heal. You must be quick."

The voice was faint, but she thought she recognized it: Dur, the master jeweler who owned the shop and crafted its contents. He had spoken to her once or twice. But so far as she could remember, he had never heard her name.

"Be quick."

Coming closer, light from the open door showed her the handle of the knife protruding from Dur's side, the dark stain spreading below it. She put her hand hesitantly on the cloth.

"The skin. Working through woven cloth makes it harder."

That made sense, however he knew it. She slid her left hand in through the open front of the wool robe, up under the shirt, against the skin over the wound, fingers either side of the blade. She closed her eyes, felt her way into the wound. The pattern of the flesh either side was clear, and the abrupt break, iron where there should be flesh. Iron.

"You can't work with the blade in. When you are ready pull it out, and be quick."

She took a deep breath. With her right hand she groped for the hilt of the dagger, found it, pulled it out. One fair sized vessel had been cut; she knotted both ends. Crude but fast; knots were the first thing you learned. Then she worked her way along the cut, starting where it was deepest, weaving the flesh back together, matching the ends of the tiny vessels that the knife had severed. She reached the skin, felt it moving, knitting together under her hand. She let her perception sink back into the wound, undid the knots and wove the final vessel together. She stood up. For a moment the world spun around her, then came steady. She stepped back, almost tripped over the body on the floor. She bent down to look at it.

"Don't bother; no healer on earth could help him now. The idiot thief didn't see me sitting here with my eyes closed and the door open. The idiot me didn't see him either. Until he stepped on my toes, panicked, and knifed me before I could kill him."

There was a long silence. Ellen looked at the man she had just healed.

"You're a mage."

She hesitated a moment, sniffed the air again.

"A fire mage."

He nodded.

"Useful for killing people. Not so useful for healing them. Give me the knife."

She handed it to him. He slid down from the chair to a kneeling position by the corpse, drove the knife between two ribs deep into the body.

"I don't want people to wonder what killed him. You had best get back to the College before they close the gates. Come again when you are free and we can talk."

"And until then, you would rather I not …"

"Until then, I would rather you not."

He did not seem greatly concerned that she might go back to the college and inform the magisters that Dur the jeweler, unknown to them, was a secret fire mage. It would be easy enough for him to kill her and blame it on the dead thief; fortunately the idea did not seem to have occurred to him. She walked out the door, down the street in the direction of the path leading to the college entrance, and started to breathe again.

Dur pulled himself back into his chair, closed his eyes. For a moment Ellen was invisible to him. He found her, with a thought thinned the barrier she had built around herself. She showed to his sight as a pale tower of woven flame. His side throbbed but, looking back at himself, he could see no more bleeding inside or out. Her mother would have done it faster and better, but it was, so far as he knew, the first time the girl had used her talent to heal a serious wound. After a time, he saw her reach the woven flame of the dome, pass into it through the gate.

Opening his eyes, he pulled a strip of cloth from the top of the display counter, spilling several rings onto the floor. He dipped the middle of the cloth into the pool of blood by his feet, bound it tightly around his body with the stain over the wound. A minute to catch his breath and drop onto his knees on the floor, moving towards the hammer. Three sharp blows on the alarm gong. He considered trying to make it back up to the chair, decided against.

It took only a few minutes for the street watchman — Dur, as the most likely target of theft, paid the largest share of his salary — to arrive.

* * *

On her way to her room Ellen suddenly remembered Mari's account of Alys at the jeweler's shop. Not an accident after all.

A pity that she couldn't share the joke.

* * *

"You wanted to speak to me, Magister Coelus? One of the porters brought me a note."

"Yes."

Ellen looked at him in surprise. His face was white, drawn, angry; she had never seen it like that before.

"Did you do this?"

"Do what?"

He held out the wax tablets, open. They were blank. "My notes, observations from the past weeks of experiment, ideas for other approaches to take. I've been working on trying to figure out what happened to Maridon, how to keep it from happening to me next time I try the experiment. All gone, erased."

She shook her head. "I didn't even know you used a tablet for your lab notes. We've been doing theory; I knew you did experiments but I don't think you ever showed me one."

"Someone blotted them out last night. You are the only pure fire mage in the college. I doubt any of the others have enough fire, or enough control over it, to melt the wax without scorching the tablet. And you have told me enough times that you disapprove of my project."

"I do. Perhaps if I had known what was in your tablets I

would have erased them; I don't know. But I wouldn't have done it secretly then, and I wouldn't lie about it now."

For a moment Coelus seemed to relax, then something else occurred to him. "Where were you last night?"

"Asleep in bed, of course. Where else would I be?"

"I don't know, but you weren't in your bed a little after midnight. I went to your door and looked through it—not with my eyes—after I found the tablets. There was no-one there. You weren't in your bed. Whose bed were you in?"

There was a sudden silence; Ellen's face turned as white as paper, whiter than the mage's. "I do not think it is for you to put that question to me. As it happens, I was in my own bed."

"I looked, I tell you. I know you well enough by now, veil and all. You were not there. Nobody was."

Ellen reached out to the lamp burning on his desk, pulled out a thread of flame, drew it in a quick gesture down her body.

"Close your eyes, Coelus, and tell me where I am."

He looked puzzled, but after a moment his eyes closed. His voice was more puzzled still.

"You aren't there."

He opened his eyes.

"That's impossible. How do you do it?"

"With your eyes closed, how many people in the village—mages or not—can you see from here?"

"None, of course; they are outside the dome. I'm inside it. The dome is ... ."

He looked at her again, closed his eyes, opened them.

"You have a way of blocking magic, like the dome?"

"Very like. I've slept behind a barrier for three months now, ever since Maridon tried to kill me."

His mouth fell open; it occurred to her that, for an air mage, he looked strikingly like a fish.

"Since Maridon what?"

"Since Maridon tried to kill me. I was not sure at first who it was or why, but he was the only decent earth mage here and the attempt was obviously earth mage work. After he tried to seize the Cascade and use it for his own power, it was obvious why. You must have told him that you told me about the effect; he wanted to be sure nobody knew about it who might persuade you

64

not to give him control of the pool."

Coelus hesitated, torn between two questions.

"How do you know about the experiment and what happened to Maridon? All anyone in the college knows is that something went wrong with a spell."

"It was obvious you would try to test the Cascade; why else were there three outside mages here, all guest friends of Maridon? I was behind the strongest barrier I could weave, watching. Do you think you are the only one who can see with his eyes closed?"

Coelus shook his head, as if to shake off distractions.

"You said he tried to kill you, months ago. Why didn't you say something? Why didn't you tell me?"

"I did not tell because I had no way of proving it. I was a student, he was a magister; why should they believe me instead of deciding I was crazy and sending me home? I did not tell you because I did not know whether or not you were behind it. You and he were working together, he was an earth mage. You had good reason to want me silenced."

She fell silent, looking defiantly at him. Coelus was silent as well, speechless. He drew several long, slow breaths.

"You thought I would try to murder you to keep you from telling people about the Cascade?"

"It was one possible interpretation of the available evidence."

"I couldn't try to hurt you." He hesitated, the moment passed. He gave her a weak smile. "Killing you would be like burning a library or smashing the only instance of a precision instrument." He hesitated again. "For one thing, you are the only person in the whole college I can talk to without feeling as though I need a translator."

She nodded.

"I know. I feel much the same. It is one of the reasons I have not killed you, which would have been the simplest solution. And not unjust, considering the scale on which you have violated, and intend to violate, the limits of magery."

He looked at her indignantly.

"You. Kill me? How?"

"For a brilliant man you are sometimes very stupid. You know what I am."

She turned, pointed at one of the unlit candles on the shelf above his desk. It went up in a blaze of flame; an instant later, where the flame had been was nothing but a faint mist of grey ash.

* * *

The next morning was breakfast, Constructions, Ethics, a free hour, lunch. Two temptations: To skip Ethics or use it to hint at Magister Coelus' project in the hope of getting the other magisters to stop it. She resisted both. Two hours would be enough, and Master Dur's shop was a few doors down from the cookshop. She had been considering the puzzle of Magister Coelus' tablets and it had occurred to her that although she might be the only strong fire mage in the college, there was another one not far away.

Ellen spent the next two hours in a hard chair pretending to be interested in the lectures. Guydo preferred to put his questions to the students who didn't know the answers—but not to women. That suited her well enough, especially this morning. Hal, as usual, turned to her every time someone else stumbled. She was tempted to raise it as an ethical issue outside of class; was it just to make her a target of resentment in order to keep him from having to explain the answers himself? But she thought better of it.

Ethics over, she escaped from the lecture hall past Magister Hal's attempt to explain to an uncomprehending Joshua what was wrong with compulsions. She had no doubt what sort of compulsions Joshua was interested in, or why. Hal glanced up as she passed but she, looking intently down at the notes on her tablet, managed not to meet his gaze.

Getting out of the College presented its own problems; the Magister Gatekeeper knew her. He might wonder why she should run off to town in the middle of the day. Instead of following the main corridor to the gatehouse and the front gate, she turned right into the student wing past her own door to the end of the corridor, through the small door there into a corner of the college's kitchen garden. It was bounded by a low brick wall, beyond that the curve of the inner surface of the containment sphere. She stepped over the wall, hesitated, remembering again what she had done in the small orchard.

Ellen took a deep breath, walked up to the grey mist, closed her eyes, let her mind sink into it, stepped forward.

* * *

The shop door was closed, the sign leaning next to it read "out to lunch." As she turned away, disappointed, it opened. Master Dur looked out and beckoned her in.

Two chairs, his own from behind the counter and the one reserved for favored customers, had been placed at a small table set with a glazed bowl full of stew, two wooden bowls, two spoons, a plate with a loaf of bread and a knife. Dur gestured her to sit. Spooning food into the bowls, he slid the plate of bread over toward her.

Two sets of questions; she would start with the older one.

"Three months ago, when Maridon tried to kill me in the orchard. It was you who used fire to wake me?"

He nodded. "You were almost buried before I saw what was happening. Short of trying to get there with a shovel before you were swallowed up, I didn't see what else I could do."

"Do you know how it happened?"

Dur shook his head, waited. In a moment, Ellen continued. "I thought it might have been an accident, someone doing an experiment that went wrong. But I had gotten a note from Magister Coelus, who had offered to take me for independent study on a research project of his, suggesting we meet in the orchard at evening bell. I thought it a bit odd — why not the office? But he had said something about colleagues gossiping."

"More likely to start gossip if he's meeting with you in the orchard in the evening."

"He might not have thought of that. I didn't think..." She stopped, looked down, cut a slice of bread.

"That he had any improper intentions? Probably not."

"It isn't as if I was ..."

"A striking beauty, like your friend Mari? Men have been known to fall in love with a beautiful mind. I expect Coelus could, although it might take him a while to notice. Was he in the orchard?"

"No."

"So it was probably not an accident. Not what I would expect of Coelus, and I doubt within his power anyway. Did you show him the note and ask if he wrote it?"

"By the time I got free, it was gone."

The two sat eating quietly, as if they had known each other all their lives.

"Do you know about the Cascade project?"

He nodded. "Part of the reason I am here. Ever since Olver published his treatise it has been obvious to anyone paying attention that things were going to change and that some of the changes might be for the worse. The first big breakthrough in magery, three hundred years ago, gave the Dorayans the advantage they used to build the league and turn it into an empire; the gods know where this one will lead. Since the treatise Olver has published nothing important that is new and does not intend to until he has worked the whole thing out to his own satisfaction.

"If anyone else were going to make a breakthrough, Coelus was the obvious candidate, ever since his third year when he finished his work on the formal elementals and submitted it as a thesis. I saw what it meant, even if none of the magisters did; I have been watching him ever since. Once he worked out the Cascade… I don't want to live in a world split up among warring mages, each powered by his troop of mage slaves. Nor in one where all magic, large and small, funnels through one pair of hands, not even if the hands belong to Coelus instead of Maridon."

"So it was you who erased the tablets with his notes on them?"

Dur nodded. "And some other things. I've been trying to slow the project without being too obvious about it. It should have occurred to me that he might blame you."

"Yes. I thought by now he knew me better than that."

"He probably does. Men don't always think with their heads."

There was another silence, while Ellen finished the last of her slice of bread. Finally she looked up. "Who are you?"

"You know my name. For the rest … if you look inside yourself, you will find a knot, a lock. The key is my name. Use it. "

There was a long silence. Dur had finished the last of the stew and sat watching Ellen, who had closed her eyes. She opened them then, and smiled. He was the first to speak.

"I'm sorry, love, but it did seem the only way, and you agreed. Too many mages in the college and too hard to predict what they might do or how well you could protect yourself. Or what they might learn from you. Forty years…"

"I know — now. You and mother agreed, and of course I did too. I don't mind, I'm just remembering the parts that were missing over the last few months."

She got up, leaned over, gave her father an affectionate hug.

Chapter 11

There was a knock on the door. Coelus looked up from his tablet and a sheet of calculations, let in the college porter.

"A mage at the gate, with a note." The porter handed it to him. Coelus glanced down at it and smiled.

"Good. Show the learned Gervase to one of the guest rooms in the north wing, then escort him to me."

Half an hour later another knock; Coelus stood to open the door and greet his guest. Gervase was tall and middle aged, with a beard sprinkled with grey. Coelus was the first to speak.

"I think I have solved the problem, at least well enough to prevent another accident. Did you arrange for the others to come? I have heard nothing from either of them."

"Raynald was willing. Nikolas thought one life-threatening experience was enough."

"Then we are two mages short. I doubt that any of my colleagues or students would agree. Maridon was the only one who believed in what I was doing. Anyone else?"

Gervase smiled. "An old schoolmate of mine—and he has brought several more mages, all at the inn in town. We should meet there. It is less likely to cause talk than if they all come here."

"Of course. But we should repeat the experiment here to take advantage of the containment sphere. This time I will be the focus. I won't rupture it, however much power I have."

"Is that what you think happened? That Maridon burned up after he tore through the barrier?"

"Not rupturing the sphere is one precaution. But I have also modified the spell to limit the power pulled from any one source. I should have done that anyway, to better protect the donors from being overdrawn. But I think it takes care of the other problem too.

"I still do not know exactly what happened to Maridon. He seemed to be drawing from an impossibly large source of fire, hundreds of times more than any fire mage that ever existed, and it burned him up. I wonder if he somehow tapped the containment dome itself; it must have a lot of stored fire in it. Or the sun, if Olver is right. But whatever it is, if I limit the amount the spell can draw it should not matter how much fire is at the other end."

"Interesting, but you don't have to go into it now. Let's be off to the inn to meet your new assistants. You can explain it to us all there."

Business was good at the village's only inn: the stable yard was filled with horses, strange grooms, and travelers' servants. Gervase took Coelus through the front room to the staircase that led to the guest rooms above. There Coelus stopped cold. Two men, in armor and wearing swords, stood at the top of the stairs looking down. "Who are they and what are they doing here?" Coelus asked.

"Come with me and all will become clear," Gervase replied. The guards stood back to let the mages onto the landing. Gervase led Coelus to the door of one of the rooms.

Inside were three mages. The one in the center—tall, very well dressed, face a little flushed—was at least in part an earth mage. One problem solved. The other two were veiled, strongly enough that Coelus could not be sure what the veil was hiding. There was something else as well about them, some sort of barrier. In a moment the tall man nodded to the other two and they left the room.

Gervase spoke: "Your Highness, may I present Magister Coelus of the college? Coelus, this is His Highness Prince Kieron. He and I were students together. When you wrote proposing a second experiment, it occurred to me that he would be interested in what you were doing and could help with finding sufficient mages."

There was a long silence while the two men looked at each other. The Prince was the first to speak. "I am honored to make your acquaintance, Magister Coelus. I have read some of your work and heard a report of your recent researches from Gervase. The brilliance of your theoretical accomplishments is only matched ..." He paused a moment for effect.

"By the irresponsible stupidity of your practical actions. Did you think at all of the consequences of what you were doing?"

It took Coelus a moment to respond. "Could your Highness explain in what respect you believe I have erred? It is true that the first attempt to implement the Cascade effect went badly, but new research is always risky. I thought the precautions I had taken were sufficient but they proved not to be."

"Precautions? What precautions?"

"The first implementation was within the containment sphere, so that if anything went wrong no harm would be done outside; also, I had my athame at hand, in case the spell had to be cut suddenly. I intend to do the same with the second implementation. It did not occur to me that the mage the effect focused on would try to breach the sphere, let alone that he would succeed; I still do not entirely understand why that happened. Nor do I clearly understand what happened to Maridon after he breached it."

"You put in the hands of one of your colleagues more power than any mage had ever had — the combined talent of a college full of mages, students and magisters together, bridging all of magery. And it did not occur to you that he might have some interest in the matter beyond doing an experiment for you?"

Coelus shook his head, a bit stunned. "Maridon agreed with me about what could be accomplished by use of the effect and on the protocol for the experiment. It did not occur to me that he might change his mind after it started."

"Change his mind? Did you read his mind in advance to know what was in it? You offered the man a chance at unlimited power and you are surprised he took it. Whose idea was it to make him and not you the focus for the Cascade?"

Coelus thought a moment, spoke reluctantly. "His, your Highness. Since I was the only one who really understood the theory behind the Cascade, he did not want me to risk myself if something went wrong... At least, that is what he said."

He paused. "It did not occur to me that he might have another reason."

The Prince nodded. "You are, so far as I know, one of the ablest theoreticians in the kingdom, perhaps the world. But you should not be allowed to wander about without a keeper. Suppose Maridon had not been destroyed by whatever went wrong at the end of the experiment. Have you considered what he would have done next, after he had control of all of the magic of thousands of mages?"

"I have not, Highness. Tell me."

"Perhaps he considered it time for another mage king. My brother is, of course, defended by mages as well as guards. But, if I understand your contrivance correctly, their power would be useless against him. Maridon would be drawing not only their talent but that of every other mage in range of the effect. As he increased the power he used against them, the power they had to use against him would shrink accordingly. I do not see how His Majesty could be defended under those circumstances. Am I missing anything?"

Coelus shook his head. "I think you are correct, so far as conflicts between mages go. Had Maridon succeeded in expanding the Cascade to the entire kingdom he could have slain His Majesty. But that might not suffice to seize the throne. His Majesty's soldiers, his nobles, are loyal to him, and wars are not won by magery alone."

"And why are they not? Because there are mages on both sides, and because the power of a single mage is very limited. But you have changed all that, have you not? If one side has the Cascade then there is really magery on only one side. And with the Cascade, there is more magery on that side than anyone has ever had before."

"I confess that I had not considered that possibility. Your Highness may well be correct. I will try not to make the same mistake again."

Prince Kieron shook his head. "That is not the only mistake you can make or have made. Maridon, fortunately, is dead. But surely there are others to whom you have mentioned your plans. You told Gervase enough, and he told me enough, to bring me here. Who else? With which of your students, your colleagues, have you discussed your work? Which other mages outside the College?

"Very few, Highness. At Maridon's urging, I told my colleagues only that I had a schema for pooling four mages, not what I planned to do with it. None of the others expressed much interest in the project. I described it to one student whom I hoped to involve, but she was not interested. Another student was used in an early experiment; he did not know its nature, and the design of the experiment was such that he saw nothing. Of course,

Raynald and Nikolas were involved along with Gervase, and I suppose they know as much as he does.

"Raynald and Nikolas I know of, and am taking steps to deal with. We will have to do something about the students; what are their names?"

"I am not sure I understand your Highness. What peril do you fear and what precautions do you wish to take other than to select the focus of the pool more wisely the next time we do the experiment?"

"We can discuss that later. My present concern is not with your experiments but with what others might do. Have you considered the consequences should the Cascade be achieved and the pool controlled by a mage in service to Forstmark? Perhaps it has escaped your notice, but there has been trouble on that frontier for some years now; we have been recruiting both troops and mages and may need to use them. Your Cascade would be very useful to us — but equally so to the Forstings, should they happen to hear of it and succeed in duplicating your work."

"I understand your Highness's concern. But the core of the work, the theory and the mathematics, is known to no-one but me. Even the mages who assisted with the first experiment knew each only his part of it, not the whole, as Gervase will confirm. Maridon knew the most of any of them, and he is dead."

"Yes. Nobody but you knows how to do it — today. But how long do you think another mage would take, even one less brilliant than you, knowing what I do, to work out the rest for himself? You are not the only able theorist in the world, and not all of them are within the kingdom. I may be mistaken, but the hard part seems to be the idea, first of the pool and second of the Cascade. Once that is known and shown to be possible, can the rest be so difficult?"

Coelus was silent.

"So, I want the names of the two students you mentioned. Bring them here. I have mages who will see what can be done to assure their silence, or remove the knowledge from their memories, in hopes that more extreme measures will not be necessary. I have already arranged to have Nikolas brought here for the same purpose and Raynald is here already."

"That seems drastic, Your Highness. Neither student has

committed any crime against His Majesty or shown any inclination to. Surely a warning against speaking carelessly of what little they know should be sufficient."

"Perhaps. I will speak with them myself and decide. What are their names?"

Coelus hesitated a moment.

"The student who participated in an experiment is Joshua son of Maas. The student to whom I mentioned the project is Ellen. As Your Highness knows, all instruction takes place within the college, so I can hardly send them a message bidding them come here, and it would be odder still if strangers came into the college seeking them."

He thought a moment.

"Let me send each a message arranging to meet in the college, not too far from the gate; I can then escort them out. I sometimes hold instruction out of doors when the weather is good. That will make it easier to avoid any unnecessary fuss."

"Very good; several of my people will accompany you. Gervase, fetch paper and pen from my servants in the next room."

In a moment the mage returned. Coelus wrote two notes, folded each, wrote "Joshua" on one, "Ellen" on the other.

"If we return to the college now, I can give the notes to a porter and then meet them in the orchard."

Chapter 12

Ellen re-read the note. The hand was certainly his; she knew it well enough. The words:

"Meet me again in the orchard."

Why he had written it or at whose command, she could not guess, but the meaning was clear enough. She got up, went over to the clothes chest at the foot of her bed, and opened it. From the bottom she drew out a tunic, flame colored, of some odd shimmery material. She changed into it, over it a plain tunic, long sleeved. She reached into the chest again, drew out an amulet on a tightly woven silk cord, put it around her neck. She took her wallet from the peg it hung on, put the strap over her shoulder.

One more thing. She shut the chest, turned it on its side to expose the bottom, spoke a Word softly and pressed down on one of the planks. It slid smoothly to one side. From the cavity revealed, she drew out a small leather bag full of coins and put it into the wallet, then put the chest back upright. She glanced around the room for a few moments, thinking of whether there was anything she had forgotten, took her cloak from its hook and opened the door. The corridor was empty.

Clearly someone other than Coelus was involved. Considering what he was doing, it would hardly be surprising if rumor had spread even outside the college. If so, the entrance to the College might be watched. Instead of turning into the main corridor she crossed it, continued down the student wing, turned right at its end through a door that opened on a corner of the front lawn. Nobody was in sight. Just ahead of her was the surface of the containment sphere; she sunk her hands into its web, stepped forward.

A few minutes later Coelus arrived at the orchard accompanied by three of the prince's mages and one guard, armor hidden by his cloak. It was, to his relief, empty. One of the mages spoke briefly to the others, then the three spread out, leaving Coelus and the guard alone near the dome.

"What do you want me to do?"

"Nothing. When they arrive we will take care of it."

They waited in silence. In a few minutes he heard footsteps in the cloister. A moment later Joshua came in sight.

"Magister Coelus, you wanted to speak with me?"

Before Coelus could answer, the three mages moved together with practiced skill. Joshua had barely time to look around before he was enveloped in a grey mist. When it cleared he was standing perfectly still, his face frozen in its expression of a moment before. One of the mages spoke softly to him. He walked over to the bench a little rigidly and sat down, expression frozen.

The guard spoke to Coelus: "That was easy enough. As you can see, they know what they are doing. The girl should be easier still."

"Do you know if the spell does him any injury?"

The guard shook his head. "When he comes out of it he will be a bit confused, not knowing where he is or how he got there. Until then, obedient as a lamb. The Prince said he didn't want any trouble, anything to get the college talking. This seemed the best way."

Coelus paced nervously up and down, listening for another footstep. None came. The guard stood patiently, waiting.

Ellen, listening on the far side of the barrier barely ten feet from the two men, stood up and set off for the village.

* * *

It was full dark by the time the men got back to the inn with their captive. The Prince sent Coelus off to one of the inn rooms, Gervase back to the College to see what he could find out about the missing student. That accomplished, he sent for provisions and invited Alayn, the guard who had accompanied Coelus to the college, to join him.

"Did Magister Coelus expect the girl to show up?"

Alayn thought a moment. "Feared she might, hoped she wouldn't, would be my guess. He looked nervous when we heard someone coming, relieved when he saw it wasn't her, less and less worried as time passed."

The Prince nodded and took a sip of his wine. "Remind me not to underestimate academics," he said. "Coelus has no sense of what he ought to be paying attention to, but once he gets hit over the head with the need to think, I expect he is very good at it. Something in that note warned her."

"There might have been a warning from someone else; she may be a spy and have accomplices. Perhaps we were seen at the inn and someone drew the right conclusion. Short of a trumpeter and a banner, we couldn't have been more obvious. A town inn doesn't usually entertain a party of guests with armed guards."

The Prince cut himself a slice of mutton, chewing slowly before responding. "If she was a Forsting spy and not just a student who heard too much, we are wasting our time trying to catch her. Coelus did his last experiment almost a month ago. Her report on whatever she discovered about it will be over the border by now, and our only hope would be to get Coelus's weapon working for us before they get it working for them. It may come to that, but I am still hoping we can keep the information from getting out, secure everyone who knows anything, and have time to complete the project with more care.

"It would help if we knew what she looks like. If I were sending a girl to the College to get information out of a susceptible young scholar, I would pick a pretty one. When Gervase comes back, we'll see what he can tell us."

The next morning, Alayn brought Coelus into the room as the Prince was eating his breakfast. Kieron motioned them to join him, spoke to Coelus as he sat down. "Your missing student. How much do you know about her? Could she be a spy for Forstmark or the League, or for someone else?"

Coelus thought a moment. "If you are asking about her background, where she came from or who her parents are, I am afraid I cannot help you, although I suppose someone in the College must know. It never occurred to me to ask such questions. But I am quite sure she was not a spy."

"Because you could read her mind?"

"Your Highness persuaded me yesterday of the limits of my abilities in that direction. My conclusion is based not on mind reading but on logic."

Prince Kieron gave him a quizzical look, said nothing.

"I invited Ellen to help me with the Cascade project. She refused, in quite clear and unambiguous terms, on the basis that it ought not to be done, and showed no interest in how I expected to do it after that. A spy might have tried to discourage me from working on the project, in the hope that her employers could complete it first. But a spy would surely have wanted to know all she could learn about what I was doing, and I would have been glad to teach it to her."

"That sounds convincing. I hope you are correct. But I am still left with several problems, beginning with what I am to do with you."

Coelus nodded. "Yes. I have been thinking about your problems a good deal of the night. So far as dealing with me is concerned, you could of course kill me. That would keep me from misusing the Cascade myself, a possibility that it finally occurred to me you must be concerned about. And it would keep me from telling anyone else about it. But if you wish to employ the Cascade yourself, you would then have to find someone else to finish the project. I can only think of two people in the kingdom who could do it, and I do not think either would be willing to."

"And who are they?"

Coelus shook his head. "Lying would, I expect, be pointless. But I choose to remain silent. There is no reliable way to extract information against a mage's will without injuring him. Until you have no further need of me, I do not think that is a risk you will want to take."

The Prince gave him an amused look. "I would certainly prefer to avoid such risks if I can. But you have not yet answered my question."

"Surely the answer is obvious. If your only objective is to suppress the invention, you should kill me and anyone else who knows anything about it, possibly including yourself—and somehow do it without calling attention to my work and so encouraging others to try to continue it.

"If, on the other hand, your objective is to complete the project and implement it, with yourself or someone else you trust as the focus, then the simplest way to avoid attracting more attention than you already have is to send me back to the college to continue my teaching and my research and trust me to keep my mouth shut. Unfortunately, if that is your intention, I am afraid another difficulty arises."

"That being?"

"Last night, I concluded that Ellen was right about the problems posed by the Cascade. Completing my work would make the world a worse place, not a better one. You and Maridon have shown me the danger of the Cascade being used for evil. She showed me that, even used for good purposes, the talent I wished to borrow to cure a plague or divert a flood was talent that already had uses in the hands of those it belonged to, perhaps, taken all together, uses at least as important.

"Ellen would not help me create the Cascade. Now that I am persuaded that she was right, I will not help you. I am sorry. I can see that the situation raises serious problems for you and perhaps for the kingdom. But it seems to me that the alternative raises still more serious problems for the kingdom and the world."

There was a long silence. At last Prince Kieron spoke. "I concede the strength of your argument. Nonetheless, I have my duty. Suppose that I do not develop the Cascade. How then can I fulfill my obligation of protecting my brother the King from enemies who will show no such restraint?"

"I have been thinking about that too. I do not think the situation is quite as hopeless as you suggested yesterday. The containment sphere blocks magic, including the magic by which the Cascade spreads. It should be possible, by containing his Majesty and the mages that protect him in something similar, to keep the Cascade from spreading to them. A mage controlling the pool from a Cascade would still have a very considerable advantage, but perhaps not an overwhelming one, especially if there were other places also so protected, such as the College."

The Prince gave him a skeptical look. "Maridon breached the sphere using only the power of the mages within the College."

Coelus nodded. "Yes. But he was standing next to the sphere, and as you know, magic weakens with distance. I expect His Majesty's guards could make it difficult for an enemy mage to tear open the sphere protecting them and His Majesty.

"And the containment sphere had no supporting mages. Its makers are long dead. I think it at least possible that such a sphere, actively supported by the mages it contains, could withstand a very great force.

"But I must concede that so far this is speculation. I have not built a containment sphere. So far as I know, only one has ever been constructed, its builder is dead, and I do not yet know how to duplicate his work. Ellen has done more research on the subject than I have but she, I gather, is gone. I have no idea how to find her and, if I did, I would not. I will, however, be happy to do what I can to devise defenses against the threat the Cascade poses."

"I thank you. I will consider your points and try to decide what to do with you. You have already missed your morning lecture, so I have at least a few more hours to make up my mind."

It was nearly noon by the time Gervase returned and was immediately brought in to the Prince.

"I was beginning to wonder what had happened to you."

"Under the circumstances, I thought your Highness would want as much information as possible. I used the guest room that Coelus had arranged for me for an evening of gossip with some of the magisters, and breakfast gave me a chance to listen to the students. Afterwards Magister Bertram was free, so I talked with him for a while."

"And you learned?"

"They all know something lethal happened to Maridon, of course, in an experiment Coelus was doing that other magisters were glad not to have volunteered to help with, and that it had to do with pooling more than two mages. They don't seem to know much more than that.

"Coelus had a morning lecture; someone else filled in for him after I passed on his note about being taken ill in town. Nobody seems to have noticed that one or two of their students are missing. Apparently it would not be the first time the boy stayed out all night. Some of his fellow students had at least a guess as to where he was."

"Not, I hope, a correct one."

"No. With the town whore, if I correctly took their meaning."

The Prince put another question. "What about the girl—Ellen? What could you learn about her?"

"She was not at breakfast—I asked. One of the other girls is a good friend of hers and seemed a bit concerned."

Alayn broke into the conversation.

"Did you find out what the missing girl looks like?"

Gervase nodded.

"Short, stocky but not fat, dark hair."

"Not a looker?"

Gervase shook his head.

"By what I could gather, brains not beauty. Her friend Mari, on the other hand..."

The Prince thought a moment.

"I will send someone to fetch the friend; I expect if he tells her it is about Ellen the girl will come."

* * *

"Send her in."

One of the guards opened the door. Mari walked through it, dropped a low curtsey to the Prince.

"Greetings, Your Highness. It has been some time."

The Prince stood regarding her silently for a long moment. Mari spoke again.

"It is a common name."

He replied with a visible effort. "Yes. I had not expected to find Duke Morgen's daughter as a student at the College."

"It is surely not that surprising, Highness. I am told that even princes can sometimes be found here."

"Sometimes, but rarely." He closed his eyes a moment. "It is true that you have talent. And yet... Just when did your father decide to enroll you?"

"This is my first year, Highness."

"And Nan died a little more than a year ago, leaving me... If I were inclined to suspicion, and if your father were not a man utterly without subtlety or intrigue, I might suspect some connection."

"Indeed, Your Highness. As might I, were I not an innocent and unsuspicious damsel."

Their eyes met, held.

"You were a clever child, and I see that you have become a clever lady. I do not think this is the time and place to discuss your father's plans. Still, it would at least not be boring."

"Even so. How then may I serve your Highness?"

"You may tell me everything you know concerning your friend Ellen, who seems to have vanished from the surface of the earth just when I wished her presence, and about Magister Coelus. It appears that their doings may touch nearly upon the kingdom's welfare and my duties to it. And ... I would advise you to speak the truth."

Mari nodded. "Advice you would not have to give to Ellen,

were she here. To judge from my experience, that is her fixed policy, even when there is no truthteller in the next room. A weakness, I suppose, but an endearing one. Is that the sort of information that is of use to your Highness?"

"It might be. I take it you are fond of the girl?"

Mari nodded. "Very. In some ways an innocent, in others the wisest person I have had the pleasure of knowing. And very generous with her time and knowledge. She has taught me and several of our friends more about magery these past months than all of the magisters together."

"And her connection with Magister Coelus?"

"Magister Coelus has been giving her a tutorial on the theory of magic, a field in which I understand, at least from her, that he has no masters and few equals."

"I thought she was your year. Have they started giving tutorials to students in the first year now?"

"To students, no. To Ellen, yes. She arrived, so far as I can tell, already knowing more than any student and half the magisters. It took a month or two for Coelus to realize that he had finally found a student fully able to learn what he had to teach. He offered her a special tutorial, she accepted. She attends the lectures and is very helpful in explaining them to the rest of us, but most of what she learns is from him."

"How much does she know of his work?"

"Whatever he has been willing to teach her; how much that is I do not know. He cannot have taught her all of it yet, since she has shown no sign of wanting to depart."

"Do you think that is all that is between them — teacher and student?"

Mari hesitated a moment. "Do I think so? No. Do they think so? Perhaps. I suspect Coelus is falling in love with her, but he may not have noticed it yet. As to her feelings for him … She regards him with great admiration, I think some fondness. Whether more I cannot tell.

"I have told you the truth so far as I know it, as your man in the next room will assure you. Now tell me why you need to know all this."

There was a long silence. At last the Prince broke it. "Your father and I have not always agreed, but I have never had any reason to doubt his loyalty nor have I any reason to doubt yours; I trust you can keep your mouth shut when necessary. The research that Magister Coelus was doing led him towards certain discoveries which would be of considerable value to the kingdom—or to its enemies. I wish to make sure that the results end up in our hands, not theirs, and to know who knows enough about his research to be dangerous. It sounds as though your friend may be one.

"If you could get a message to her, asking her to come here and assuring her of safety, would she believe you?"

"Perhaps. Would it be true?"

Another long silence, again ended by the Prince. "No. She sounds an admirable person, and one who might in time prove useful to the Kingdom; I would prefer to do her no harm. But I have obligations to my brother and to the kingdom he rules. If it turns out that the only way of keeping our enemies from learning magery that could be our ruin is to kill a charming young lady, or two, or three, I will do it. "

Mari smiled. "And you say so even though I have no truthteller to tell me if you lie. I am not sure your Highness is fit for politics."

"I do not think you need a truthteller, lady. And under the circumstances, lying to you might be unwise."

"There is that. If you have a truthful message for Ellen, I will take it. I cannot promise delivery; I am no more able than you to find her, probably less. But she may find me."

After Mari left, the Prince remained silent for some time, finally gave Alayn a quizzical look. Alayn was the first to speak. "So that is Duke Morgen's daughter. A formidable young lady."

"Yes. I wonder what terms her father is planning to offer me."

"You think he intends to propose a matrimonial alliance?"

Prince Kieron nodded. "Shortly after I become a widower, he sends his very beautiful and very clever daughter to be trained as a mage, providing her with the one qualification no rival can offer. I have no doubt that is his plan, and it is clear that she is of the same opinion. Not a lady to take lightly.

"Morgen is one of the most powerful men in the kingdom and one of the cleverest. I am my brother's closest adviser. We are not exactly enemies, but we clash sometimes on policy and, more often, on patronage. Our combined interest would be a faction loyal to His Majesty and more powerful than any likely rival combination.

"It is a tempting idea, even without the very tempting bait. And, since I am my brother's heir, marrying Morgen's daughter would tie Morgen more closely to the throne, which would be a very good thing. I have no doubt that that is what he intends. I am not at all sure that I will not let the plan succeed…but I will at least charge as high a price as I can manage."

* * *

Magister Bertram looked around the senior common room once more. All of the magisters were present and none of the tutors, as was, under the circumstances, proper. Coelus looked tired but not unwell. Interesting, even suggestive, but none of Bertram's affair. Bertram coughed twice to get the attention of the others, then spoke: "I asked you all here this evening to greet a distinguished visitor, one some of you already know." He nodded to Simon, standing by the door, who opened it and whispered to those outside. The Prince came to the doorway, looked curiously around and entered, accompanied by a second mage.

"His Highness Prince Kieron, His Majesty's Master of Mages and a most distinguished graduate of the College. Your Highness, may I introduce my colleagues?"

The Prince smiled and shook his head. "How could I forget Magister Simon, who very nearly despaired of my ever learning to construct a word of the true speech? Magister Hal, too. His lessons have proved useful to me in recent years. Magister Coelus of course was not here then, but I have met him since."

Simon was the first to respond: "I remember just what the word was that you succeeded in constructing but will refrain from sharing it. If I am ever charged with professional misdeeds and brought before you, it may prove useful."

The prince grinned. "Not if Magister Hal did his job properly. Having been well instructed in the ethics of magery, I am as immune to threats as to bribes. I hope. What violation of the bounds were you planning to commit?"

"I will have to consider the matter carefully."

After Bertram introduced the remaining magisters, Hal was the first to speak. "By your leave, Your Highness, I have a question I was not inclined to ask when you were a student but which may be permissible now."

"Ask away — I have answered enough of your questions in the past, or tried to. I hope this one will not prove even more difficult."

"It is quite simple, Highness. In all my lectures, you, as I recall, were never the first to answer any question. And yet your answers were correct at least as often as those of other students. At the time I formed a conjecture as to your reason and now I would like to know if it is true."

The prince thought for a moment. "A fair question, and one that deserves an honest answer. Before I came here as a student, I discussed how I ought to behave at some length with His Majesty my brother. He was concerned that the presence of a royal prince, heir presumptive to the throne, might disrupt the functioning of this valuable institution. I resolved never to be the first to answer a question, so as not to oblige others to agree with whatever I said, and held to that resolution."

Hal nodded. "Thank you, Your Highness, so I surmised. I am delighted at last to be able to thank you for your forbearance."

There was a brief silence. The Prince broke it. "I hope I may be able to give you further reasons to thank me. I confess that my purposes are not purely social. Among my responsibilities to His Majesty, I felt obligated to inquire as to the death of one of your colleagues, since it seemed clear that it was in some way due to magery. I spent some time with Magister Coelus yesterday and today and I believe now that I understand the unfortunate accident which cost the life of Magister Maridon. I do not expect that any further investigation will be required.

"His death has left you short a magister. Since he was the only earth mage on your faculty, his absence creates a problem for those students whose talents lie in that direction. Fieras here, an accomplished earth mage, has volunteered to take over Maridon's tutorials until you find a suitable replacement. While not a graduate of the College, he is a mage who has worked with me for some years and I have given him, I believe, a sense of what is required. Since he is already being compensated by the Crown for his services to me, there will be no additional expense for the College. I hope you gentleman will find that arrangement satisfactory. I insist only that you make no effort to lure him away on a permanent basis; I need his services."

Bertram was the first to respond. "I cannot speak for my colleagues, but the arrangement seems to me entirely proper, and it is one that leaves us even further in Your Highness's debt."

"Indeed it does." Simon looked around the room a moment. "If there is no objection, allow me to offer a toast to our new colleague." He nodded to a servant standing in the open door. A moment later a second servant appeared, bearing a tray with a bottle and glasses.

* * *

Fieras looked up at the knock on his door. "Come in."

The visitor was a girl, by her dress a student.

"I am Ellen. You sent a message that you wished to see me."

He looked her over carefully. Short, broad, dark hair. An amulet on a cord around her neck. Some talent, but not a great deal. Probably a waste of time—she did not look likely to conceal dangerous secrets—but if the Prince wanted to talk with her, talk with her he would, whether she wished it or not. "Yes, have a seat, this may take some time. His Highness wanted me to ask you some questions concerning your work with Magister Coelus." He motioned to the chair in front of his desk.

Ellen sat down, froze. Fieras got up and walked around the desk to her.

"Now what is this, I wonder." He lifted the amulet, twisted off the cap, teased out the scroll with the tip of his pen knife, read it. "Very useful, I'm sure." He dropped the scroll on the desk, stepped back.

"I do not expect you have studied quick-trigger static spells yet. As you can see, they have their uses. The last time His Highness wished to speak with you, you arranged to be elsewhere. This time you will not. Get up."

She stood.

"Follow me." He opened the door, went through it. She followed.

A few minutes brought them to gatehouse and gatemaster. The old man rose and grasped the iron ring to the massive front door of the college. Beyond the door the stone walk, bordered on each side by high hedges, crossed the front lawn, vanished at the brink of the containment sphere. The old man spoke a Word; Fieras watched curiously as the sphere dilated, opening a half circle hole, and turned back to the gatemaster. "Half the circle is below the ground?" The man nodded. Ellen was silent.

Fieras turned and strode through the gate, through the sphere, and up the hill slope beyond towards the village, then turned to look back. The road behind him was empty.

The gatemaster, summoned by the entering bell, responded to the mage's questions with a shrug of his shoulders. The magister had gone through the gate, the student had turned back. He had no idea where she had gone or why.

After a half hour search through the College, it occurred to Fieras to ask someone where the girl's room was. As he came through the door, Ellen looked up from her desk and the sheet of paper she was studying. "The custom is to knock before entering," she said, mildly.

"The custom is for students to obey magisters. Enough of this nonsense; get up and follow me."

Ellen looked at him curiously. "What makes you expect people to obey you when you give them orders?"

"I am a magister and a mage—you are a student and a girl at that. You are under my authority and will do what I tell you, willingly or not. I thought I had already demonstrated that. And you will not discuss the matter with others."

Ellen shook her head. "Even if I were willing to obey your orders, it is too late for that one."

"What do you mean? Have you been gossiping with the other students?"

"Not with the students. As soon as I was free of your compulsion spell I went to the senior common room and informed the magisters present that I was charging you with violation of the bounds and the criminal use of magic. I expect they will want to speak with you."

Fieras was speechless for a moment. "You charged me? And what authority do you think you have?"

"What authority do I need? The use of compulsion spells is a violation of the bounds of magery, whomever they are used against. If you know that, you know you are guilty of the offense. If you do not know it, then you have no business practicing magic in this kingdom."

The final words were spoken to the empty air. Ellen got up from her chair and set off after him for the senior common room.

Approaching, she heard raised voices. Peering through the door, she saw Fieras on one side of the room, Simon and Bertram on the other. Fieras spluttering, "And I say it is outrageous! Why should you believe a student, a girl student, over a mage recommended to you by His Highness?"

Simon responded calmly. "The accusation is indeed surprising, but we must determine its truth before deciding which of you has committed an outrage. The girl told us her story and offered to repeat it in the presence of a truthteller. If you are willing to give your account under the same conditions, we should be able to determine what happened easily enough."

"No! Even if I were willing to go through with such a thing, it would be useless. I am shielded against any magic that deals in any way with the contents of my mind."

"If the accusation is false, drop the shielding for long enough to prove it."

"I cannot. The spells are keyed to the Prince. Only he can cancel them. What would be the use of shielding my mind if any thug willing to apply sufficient force, or sufficiently persuasive threats, could force me to drop the shield?"

Bertram nodded. "It is a common enough precaution among servants of His Majesty, at least those entrusted with information of importance."

"And since that is settled," Fieras spoke in a tone to override dissent, "you may dismiss the charges and let me deal with the girl. Unless you wish to provoke not only my annoyance but that of my master."

Another voice broke in. Magister Hal was standing in the doorway. "Tell us what happened. Truthtellers are not the only means of determining truth."

Fieras shook his head. "I asked the girl to follow me to the village to speak with the Prince about matters I will not discuss here. When I saw she was not following me, I came back for her."

Hal came into the room, joined the other two magisters. "She charges you with the use of a compulsion spell. Is it true?"

"She is a student, not a mage. How could she judge?"

"You can judge. Is it true?"

Fieras hesitated.

Hal continued. "She also charges that, while she was held by the spell, you opened the protective amulet she was wearing and removed the scroll, in order to make sure it did not interfere with your spell. Is that not correct, Ellen?"

Fieras spun around and glared at Ellen, who came into view behind Hal in the doorway.

"It is." She spoke quietly but clearly.

"Nonsense. You are still wearing your amulet."

"Yes. But the case is now empty."

"And for all I know it always was. I have no idea where your scroll is, if it ever existed."

Hal broke into the exchange. "I, however, do." He held out his hand. "I found it on your desk a few minutes ago."

"You found a scroll on my desk? Aside from the discourtesy of searching my room, what does that show? Are you surprised to find scrolls on the desk of a mage?"

"This scroll, as it happens, has Ellen's name in the inscription. Also, I spoke to the Magister gatekeeper. His account accords with hers."

Ellen carefully drew the amulet's cord up and over her head, turned to Hal. "You may want to examine this also; it retains the spell cast on me. But be careful ..."

Fieras took two long steps towards Ellen, reached out and snatched the amulet and cord from her hand. Froze. Ellen went on, calmly. "The spell on the scroll was a protection against mosquitoes and bedbugs, which seemed to amuse Magister Fieras. The spell woven into the cord was a protection against magery, including compulsion spells. By the time we reached the outer gate it had absorbed enough of his spell to free me. Since it was a protection for me alone, it released the spell as soon as anyone else touched it." She gestured towards Fieras, still frozen. "As you can see. He is bound by his own spell."

Hal stepped over to the motionless mage. "Can you hear me?"

"Yes." Fieras's voice was a monotone.

"What is the release for the spell you are under?"

"The word 'unbind' in the true speech releases the spell."

Hal turned to Simon, who spoke the Word. Fieras looked around the room, blinking and speechless. For a moment there was silence. Hal broke it.

"Fellow mages. Gentlemen. I believe we have seen enough and more than enough support for these charges to put our fellow mage under ban, as law and custom require, until the matter can be fully judged. Do any here disagree?"

Nobody spoke. In a moment Hal continued, speaking directly to Fieras.

"By judgment of myself, Magister Henryk, and by judgment of all mages here present, you are held to be under suspicion of violation of the bounds of magery and accordingly banned from all use of the art until the matter is finally judged. You have the right, if you wish, to demand that we summon any additional mages nearby, put the facts to them, and ask if they will join in our judgment."

Fieras said nothing; Hal waited a moment, then continued. "You shall be taken to His Highness that he may arrange for trial according to law and custom. That will require at least two mages to accompany you. A damned nuisance, but I see no help for it."

Fieras finally spoke. "As it happens, they will not have to accompany me far. His Highness was not planning to leave the village until tomorrow morning. You—we—will find him at the inn, where I expect he will dispose of this nonsense, although with what consequences for you and the College I cannot say."

Chapter 13

After Ellen and the three magisters left the room, the Prince turned to Fieras. "You made this mess. Tell me how I am to get out of it and what I am to do with you."

The mage looked surprised. "It seems simple enough. Make it clear that they have no business interfering in the work of your servants and send them off. Then find another earth mage, one more willing to tolerate fools than I am, and send him to them in my place. As for the girl, she is just on the other side of that door. If her companions object to whatever you intend to do with her, there are more than enough of us to deal with them."

The Prince shook his head. "Replacing you is no longer possible. Most of the magisters feel strongly about violations of the bounds, as you have just seen, and about the independence of the College. Even Bertram, who hopes for a royal pension when he retires, is willing to risk offending me. Were I to be tactless enough to suggest any such thing, they would find one reason or another to politely decline it.

"I will admit, though not to them, that I have from time to time turned a blind eye to illegal uses of magery by mages working for me. As the present situation demonstrates, that may have been a mistake. You have acted in a manner that left none of the three mages who charged you with any doubt of your guilt. They are all distinguished men; many of the leading mages in the kingdom have been their students or colleagues at one time or another.

"To follow your suggestion would amount to a public declaration that I consider myself and my servants free of the restrictions that, by very ancient custom, bind all mages. I am not sure that it is in the interest of the kingdom for us to act in that way and I am quite certain it is not in the interest of the kingdom for us to say that we do. I do not know how the kingdom's mages would respond to such an announcement. And I do not intend to find out."

He paused a moment. "I do know what the response of one mage would be—he told me almost twenty years ago. In his final lecture Magister Hal explained that the present system of dealing with violations of the bounds supplemented, but did not replace, the traditional system. He then asked what should occur if the royal authorities became corrupt and refused to convict mages clearly guilty of violations. His answer was that the mages ought to act outside of the royal authority in the traditional manner.

"So, if a jury of local mages found you guilty, you would be banned forever from all use of magery. You would be subject to be killed, by any mage, for first violation of that ban. Not an attractive outcome."

"Would anyone outside the college take such a procedure seriously? So far as I know, nothing of the sort has occurred in my lifetime."

"That is because the mages have, on the whole, trusted the verdicts of the courts that I and my predecessors have established. The longer this is true, the less likely it is that anyone will revive the older procedure. But considering that Magister Hal is the leading authority in the kingdom on the law and custom of magery and that quite a large fraction of the more important mages have, like me, sat in his classroom, I think that if it did happen it would be taken seriously. That is why I intend to make sure that it does not.

"You will be tried as charged, I expect convicted and banned from any future use of magic within the bounds of the kingdom. If you wish to remain in the royal service, His Majesty should be able find a use for a mage outside the kingdom. Now go pack. The trial will be held back at the capital, as quietly as I can manage it. We already have the testimony of the complainant and the witnesses."

Fieras, for once speechless, left the room. The Prince turned to Alayn at his side: "Playing loose with the rules was a mistake. I cannot trust my servants either to refrain from breaking the bounds when it is not necessary nor to take reasonable care not to be caught when it is. My fault. I should have known Fieras better."

Alayn nodded. "Fieras was the only earth mage available, your Highness, and it seemed a good way of keeping an eye on things. I should have warned your Highness that he was inclined to arrogance. I have heard complaints before about his treatment of anyone not a mage, but I hardly thought it a problem in a college of mages."

The Prince shook his head. "My fault. Arrogance would not have been so bad had he not also been a fool.

"At least we now have the young lady in the next room, although the circumstances considerably limit what I can do. Carrying her off to the capital by force or magery would make a bad situation a great deal worse."

The Prince paused, struck by an idea. "I wonder..."

"If she planned this result? It hardly seems likely, Highness. She's only a girl."

"One who has just succeeded in twice outwitting a trained mage twice her age. And she seems to have made a considerable impression on Lady Mari, whose judgment I am inclined to trust. I look forward to meeting her."

"Shall I bring her in, Highness?"

The Prince nodded. There was a brief conversation at the door before Alayn escorted Ellen in.

"As the complainant in this case," the Prince began, "you are entitled to know how I intend to treat it. I am convinced by the evidence you have offered that Fieras should be tried on both of your charges, the former by a jury of mages, the latter in an ordinary court; if you are willing to put your testimony in writing with the usual safeguards, your presence in court should not be necessary. While I cannot, of course, guarantee a verdict, I will be very much surprised if the former procedure does not find him guilty, making the temporary ban on him permanent, or at least of a decade or more. As to the criminal procedure, if convicted, as seems likely, I intend to recommend limiting his punishment to a fine on the grounds that his acts, while illegal, did no actual harm.

"As the complainant and the intended victim, would you find that outcome satisfactory?"

Ellen thought a moment. "So far as Fieras is concerned, I would. But I would be better satisfied if I had reason to believe that your servants would not continue to act as if the bounds did not apply to them."

"I apologize. Do you have any reason, beyond this incident, to believe that they do?"

She nodded. "Joshua was brought here by a compulsion spell

applied by three of your mages. If you doubt my account, you may ask Magister Coelus. He was a witness. So was the guard who accompanied them." She nodded in the direction of Alayn.

"And yet no charges were brought in that case?"

"I had no proof. Neither Coelus nor Joshua chose to act. Perhaps they had not so recently heard Magister Henryk lecture on the limits of royal authority."

The Prince remained silent for a moment, thoughtful.

"I remember the lecture and I concede the justice of your point. The King is not above the law. Nonetheless, I will not promise never to violate bounds or law myself, nor will I promise to instruct my servants never to do so. Law-breaking is a bad thing, whether by the King's servants or anyone else, but there are worse things, some of which it is my responsibility to deal with. I will promise not to violate bounds or law save in the most extreme circumstances, and to do my best to see that my servants will not, so that incidents such as the two you have described do not occur again. If my people are charged, as Fieras was, I will do my best to see that they get an honest trial.

"I am sorry, but that is the most I can offer. As to the worth of my promises you may consult with your friend Lady Mari. Her father and I move in the same circles and she has known me, off and on, since she was seven or eight."

Ellen considered the matter for a while before responding. "Does Your Highness accept the same principle applied to others? If I, or some other mage, concludes that your Highness has become a peril to the kingdom or to the world, do you agree that it would then be proper to use magic to compel you to act as we believe you should, or to destroy you?"

"I see no flaw in the argument. Yes. Of course, should such a situation arise, I would no doubt think myself entitled to defend myself."

He paused and said, "Will you do me a favor?"

"That depends what it is."

"Drop your veiling spell. I want to know what I am dealing with."

A long silence before he spoke again. "I see. Fieras was indeed fighting out of his class. I am only surprised that he survived the experience."

Ellen looked puzzled. "Before I freed myself, I could not have killed him. After I freed myself, I had no right to."

* * *

"He let you go?" There was both surprise and relief in Coelus's voice.

She nodded. "Yes. He asked me to tell no one about your Cascade project, I gave my word and he accepted it. You expected him to try to hold me prisoner?"

"I was afraid he might, and worse, ever since I heard you had gone to him. That was why I sent you that message, to warn you."

"Why would the Prince want to do anything to me?"

"To assure your silence. If word of the Cascade gets out, someone else might work out how to do it and use it against the Kingdom or the King. His Highness thinks that was what Maridon intended, to make himself into a second mage king using the power of the Cascade."

"Very likely. Do you think the Prince will be able to keep the Cascade a secret?"

Coelus nodded. "The only people who know about it are the two of us, the Prince, and the three mages who helped with the experiment that killed Maridon. I believe the Prince intends to destroy or at least lock up the memories of those mages. It is not that hard a spell to do, with competent people and the consent of the targets."

"Would they consent? Having part of your memory missing is, must be, very odd."

"They will if the alternative is being killed — which it probably is. The Prince will do whatever he thinks necessary to keep the secret from getting out. He wants the Cascade to use on behalf of the Kingdom, but he wants even more to make sure it doesn't get used by anyone else against the kingdom. That's why …"

"…why you thought I would be at risk when he sent mages to fetch me. Because I know about it. I might have been, then. But this time I went to him as a complainant, accusing one of his people of criminal use of magery, backed by three magisters of the college. Everyone in the college knew I was studying with you. All the magisters knew you were the first person he spoke to when he arrived. If he had done anything to me, he could not have done it quietly. He might as well have made a public announcement that Magister Coelus was engaged in work the Royal Master of Mages wanted to keep secret."

She paused a moment. "That explains why he didn't kill me. But he could have asked me to testify against Fieras at the capital. Once gone from the college ... I might never have come back. Yet he didn't. I wonder why."

Coelus looked at her carefully before he answered. "Because he believed you. Because you are you. Also, perhaps, for the same reason he let me come back to the College."

"He let you come back to continue your work on the Cascade."

Coelus shook his head. "No. I told him I wouldn't."

She looked up at him in surprise. "Why not? It is what you want."

He shook his head again. "What I did want. I was wrong. You were right. Between you and His Highness I am now persuaded of that."

She was silent, waiting.

"You showed me that even if I used the Cascade as I intended, to do good things, there was still a cost—everything the people I drew power from could no longer do.

"The Prince showed me my other mistake. Forced me to face what Maridon had done—encouraged me to develop the Cascade in order to gain control of my magery, and yours and everyone's, for his own power. Maridon is dead. But once the Cascade schema is known, once it is known that such a thing can be done, someone else will see the same opportunity and try to take it. All the power of mages and common folk will be drained away. Not to stop a flood or cure a plague, like that which killed my parents, but only for power.

"I was wrong; you were right. I told the Prince I would give him no aid in developing the Cascade. When I got back to my office I burned everything I had written that might contain a clue to how to do it."

There was a long silence. At last Ellen broke it. "Why did the Prince let you come back if you were no longer of use to him? Just to avoid calling attention to what you had been doing?"

"Perhaps, but there was another reason as well. He was afraid that the Cascade might be used against the king by traitors or foreign enemies. It had occurred to him, as it had not to me, that the royal mages could not defend against it, since their power would be drawn into the Cascade to be used against them.

"I offered to try to design a defense, like the containment sphere, to be formed around His Majesty and a group of his mages. I have been working on it for the past several days. I hoped that this project was one you would be willing to help me with."

She considered the matter for a while before responding. "I am willing to help you design defenses against the Cascade, but there is one condition. The Cascade is a secret of yours I agree to keep. I have other secrets. I will not lie to you, but there are things I cannot tell you. I am sorry, but if you wish me to work with you, you will have to trust me."

Coelus looked back at her, spoke slowly. "There is nobody I would more willingly trust. I accept your terms."

* * *

Coelus spoke carefully. "The first step is to figure out the containment sphere, how it works and how to create something similar. You were working on that problem. Perhaps together we can solve it."

"That will not be necessary. I already know the equations of the sphere and the schema for creating it."

He gave her an astonished look.

"You figured all of that out in the month since we last discussed it?"

Ellen shook her head. "I did not figure it out. I was able to obtain an account by one of the mages who created the sphere."

"In the library? I would have sworn I had searched it."

She shook her head. "Not in the library."

"Where then?"

She said nothing. He gave her a puzzled look, paused, spoke. "This is one of your secrets?"

"Part of one, yes. I did warn you."

"Was I right? Was it done by pooling fire and weaving, by two mages?"

She nodded. "Yes. The schema was mostly designed by Olver, but it was implemented by a fire mage and a weaving mage working together."

"So in order to do it we must find a weaving mage. Perhaps someone here knows of a healer who will do. When Dag comes back I can ask him if he came across any—it won't be easy. Weavers are mostly women, so of course there isn't one on the faculty, not even one of the tutors. We've never had a woman on the faculty. I was hoping you would be the first."

"I did not realize you were planning my future for me."

Coelus looked embarrassed. "I don't want to lose you; you are the first person I have found who I can work with. I can't ask you to stay as a student for three years. We don't have three years worth of knowledge here to teach you. After your second year you will surely have accomplished enough to make it clear, even to my colleagues, that you should be on the faculty."

"I do not know what I will want then. What I want now is to devise a defense against the Cascade. And you will not have to search for a weaving mage."

"I won't? I thought you said …"

She looked at him bemusedly. "Have I ever commented that you are not very observant?"

"Not that I can remember. You did describe me as very stupid on one notable occasion. What have I failed to observe?"

"For the past several months I have been creating, and several times told you I was creating, spells of woven fire. You were so confident in your first guess about me…"

"Of course; I should have seen it the first day."

"The first day?"

"The first day I saw you, when you had let down the veil. Fire, a lot of fire, but you did not look like other fire mages. I had never observed a weaving mage before. So you pool both fire and weaving. Meaning you can build the thing by yourself?"

"I can build a sphere. I have built one. But it was only about a foot across so I do not think you can fit His Majesty and a troop of mages into it."

"What limits the size?"

"Weaving provides structure, fire provides power. It is the power that determines the size. I might manage two feet across if I was not planning to do anything else for the next day or two, but that is about the limit."

Coelus' voice was puzzled. "Then how was the containment

sphere built? Durilil was stronger than you are, but not a hundred times stronger. How did he manage a sphere almost three hundred feet across?"

"You can expand it over time, especially with several fire mages. You just keep pumping in fire. It does not all have to come from the mages so long as there are fire mages to control it. When you have the sphere as bright as it can be without bursting, you expand it. Keep repeating the process and you can get it as big as you want—if you have enough time and enough fire. Big enough to hold the royal palace won't be easy, though. And at that size it will take quite a lot of fire to maintain it."

Coelus nodded agreement. "That was the problem we started with: how the containment sphere maintained itself all these years. You thought it might be drawing power from the mages inside of it."

"I was wrong. The answer is much simpler. The creators of the sphere made arrangements for additional fire to be added from the outside from time to time to make up for the losses."

"And kept doing it for forty years. How in the world did they manage it?"

Ellen said nothing.

"I see. And you cannot tell me more."

"I cannot tell you more. But it did occur to me ..."

Coelus broke in. "That the containment sphere is more than we actually need."

She nodded. "The sphere blocks physical force, sight, and a wide range of magic. All we need is something the Cascade won't penetrate. I thought, since you devised the Cascade, that you should be able to work out the least protection that would block it."

Coelus thought a moment, then shook his head.

"It is not that simple, I'm afraid. We have to defend against any cascade that might be invented. Mine was based on the elemental star. Someone else's might not be.

"Still you are correct that it should not take something as powerful as the sphere. How much less..."

He closed his eyes, thought a minute, opened them and his wax tablet, and began to scribble.

* * *

100

Coelus stopped pacing, turned to Ellen. "His Majesty can be protected, but …"

She finished the sentence: "Not very well."

He nodded agreement. "We have a schema that will enclose a building of significant size in a sphere sufficient to block expansion of a cascade. But defending it from the power of a cascade in the hands of an outside enemy won't be easy. It might defend against another Maridon, with magery and nothing else. But it won't slow down an invading army with both the Cascade and a substantial team of battle mages very much." Coelus' face, usually bright with enthusiasm, grew grim.

"We have exhausted that line, we need to try another tack," said Ellen. "You know more about the Cascade than anyone else. What were the hardest problems in making it work? Is there any way we could make them harder?"

"Telling you more about the Cascade makes you more of a risk for the Prince. It might be dangerous."

"Not as dangerous as leaving the problem unsolved. What we have so far is a paper solution—we have to do better. Tell me."

He hesitated, thinking. "There were about half a dozen hard problems, ones that looked as though they would make it impossible. I do not see how any of them will help us, but I suppose the most likely is the efficiency ratio."

Ellen looked curious and uncomprehending; he again thought a moment before explaining. "I am going to have to oversimplify, ignore the differences among mages, the effects of distance and geography, and a lot more. Imagine you are starting with a pool of four mages plus one focus. The focus needs his power to control the process.

"Pulling someone into the Cascade costs you power, but doing it gains you power—both the new member's current pool and his ability to slowly refill it. Suppose each mage added to the Cascade costs you twice as much power as he brings. You start with four mages, use up their pooled power bringing in two, use up their pooled power bringing in one. You now have seven mages in the Cascade and not enough power to bring in another—the series converges. If you are patient enough, and if you can hold the present group together without spending power, you could wait a day or two for the pools to refill and get about five more, but it would be a slow process.

"Suppose instead that each mage added costs you half as much power as he brings. Four bring in eight, eight bring in sixteen, sixteen bring in thirty-two. The series diverges. In almost no time you pull everyone in the region into the pool.

"Generalizing, if the efficiency is below one, the series converges and the Cascade breaks down. If it is above one the Cascade works. When I wrote my first schema for the Cascade, its efficiency was at about eight parts out of ten; ten mages had enough power to pull in eight. By the time I did the full scale experiment, it was up to nearly eleven. I might be able to get it a little higher, but not much."

"So the series diverges, the Cascade works, but barely, and you end up with most of your mages depleted?"

"For a while. But remember you still have their inflow. You end up with pooled power from the final layer of additions, the inflow from everyone. As I said, I am leaving out a lot, but that is the basic logic of it."

Ellen thought a moment, spoke slowly: "So if you could somehow push the efficiency down a little, by making the cost of pulling someone in a little higher, the Cascade breaks down?"

Coelus nodded. "But I do not see how. It is hard enough to put a protective sphere around the King with a whole team of mages. Now you want to put one around every mage in the kingdom."

Ellen nodded. "Smaller bubbles are a lot easier. And weak bubbles; they do not have to stop the Cascade, just make it a little harder. I am not sure we can do it, but I'm not sure we can't."

"It still sounds impossible, but I agree that it is worth trying to follow out that line to be sure. Most ideas don't work; you just have to keep trying until you find one that does."

Ellen looked again at his face, gave a relieved smile. "I have an idea that will work."

"And what is that, most original of students?"

"Sleep. Both of us need it; it's past matins. Good night; I'm for my room."

She went out of the room. Coelus looked after her for a moment, then turned back to his wax tablet, stared at it blindly for several minutes before getting up from his chair.

Chapter 14

"You asked for an audience. What can one of my uncle's mages want from me?"

The room was bare of ornament save for a richly woven rug whose blue and silver echoed the silk robes of its owner. Fieras paused a moment to be sure he had his carefully rehearsed speech clearly in mind. "I am no longer in His Highness's service, my lord. For causes that are closely linked to my reasons for coming to you."

Lord Iolen said nothing, waited.

"I discovered His Highness engaged in a project about which I had serious suspicions. When I raised them he arranged to have me accused of misuse of magic, convicted me, and on that excuse released me from his service."

"It must have been a serious matter to lead to such consequences. Tell me about this project."

Fieras paused a moment, did his best to look undecided. "His Highness is a powerful man and I will be telling things he does not wish known. Can your lordship promise me your protection?"

"I am not without resources. If what you tell me can be used against my uncle, I will protect you so far as I am able. If I cannot, I will at least do my best to get you safely out of the kingdom."

"I rely upon it, my Lord."

Fieras paused. "What does your Lordship know of the mage's college at Southdale and of a mage there named Coelus?"

"It has the patronage of His Highness and His Majesty. Some of its graduates are in my service, more in my uncle's. I am familiar with none of the mages who teach there. What more should I know?"

Fieras spoke carefully. "Magister Coelus is, at least in His Highness's view, talented not so much in the use of magery as in its invention. He has created spells, some in common use. He is now creating a spell so powerful that His Highness, on learning of it, dropped everything he was doing and set off for Southdale. I accompanied him. He has made arrangements with all who knew of the spell intended to prevent anyone else from learning of it."

"Secrecy has been so high that its nature has been kept even from those in his service. His excuse was that a group of mages wielding the spell would constitute a threat to His Majesty; he feared enemies outside the kingdom, if they learned of it, might work out the necessary schema for themselves. It is most disturbing that His Highness wishes to restrict knowledge of so potent a weapon to himself and a handful of mages under his control, especially since he is both a mage and heir presumptive."

Fieras fell silent. Iolen thought a moment before speaking: "I understand your concern. What do you propose that I do?"

"Your Lordship has contacts within the military. If some high ranking officer friendly to your Lordship was willing to detach a suitable force, on the understanding that the secret you searched for would be of great use in war. His Highness is now considering how to deal with the Forstings at the far northern reaches of the Kingdom, or so it is said. The College will soon be empty of students and half empty of magisters. Coelus might well be persuaded, threatened or spelled to yield up his secrets, to serve the kingdom."

"An interesting plan, and a token of your loyalty. I will consider it. Meanwhile I suggest that you move your possessions here. I shall instruct my people to provide you with suitable accommodations. The fewer who know of these matters the better, I think — though not quite so few as my uncle would prefer."

"I thank your Lordship. There is one more thing I ought to mention."

Iolen said nothing, waited.

"Three mages who took part in an early trial of the spell are in His Highness's custody. I believe I know where. He intends to block their memories, which will take time. If your lordship could find a way of getting to them and the knowledge they hold, you would have as much information as His Highness does. If we are unable to obtain the services of the mage who invented the spell, we might obtain clues from them."

Lord Iolen thought a moment, nodded. "Access should not be difficult; the golden key opens all doors. We cannot seize them, but there may be another solution."

* * *

The two girls watched the coach rumble out of sight bearing

their friends home for the summer break. "Edwin wasn't with them," Ellen remarked to Mari. "Isn't he going home?"

"He took the coach yesterday and skipped the dinner last night."

"That's odd. Did he say why? Something wrong at home?"

"He didn't say, but it was obvious enough," Mari said. "He didn't want to spend two days in the same coach with Alys."

"He spent a lot of time with her last break," Ellen said, puzzled. "I thought they were friends."

"They were friends. The problem is that that was all Alys wanted to be."

"And Edwin?"

"Last week Edwin asked her to marry him. He's in love. He wanted her permission to request his parents over break to speak to hers."

"And Alys doesn't want to?" Ellen asked.

"Alys is happy to have men in love with her, three or four at a time by preference. College would be perfect for her if only she didn't have to actually learn something here. She keeps them all interested by not favoring any one too much. When she drew the line with Edwin, he, being a nice boy, proposed. Having no desire for a big belly with or without a wedding ring to accompany it, she turned him down."

"He has been quieter than usual the last few days. I thought it was just the end of term, with everyone about to go off. How did you…?"

"How do you see things with your eyes closed? It's been obvious for the past month. And I have had the story from both of them separately. Poor Edwin. Two days in a coach with Alys would amuse her, but he'd be a wreck. Besides, a girl who likes lots of men in love with her is a bad prospect for a wife. I just hope he can get over it. He needs someone else. There are many more girls in the capital than here, so with luck…"

The two fell silent, Mari watching Ellen. After a minute she spoke again: "Edwin isn't the only man in the college who is in love."

Ellen said nothing.

"Alys is right, you know; anyone with eyes can see it. When you and Coelus are in the same room, he is almost always looking at you. The tone of his voice when he speaks to you is different. It's as if, for him, the rest of us are only half real. One of these days, or months, or years, he is going to ask you if he can speak to your mother. If you don't want that to happen, you should be thinking now of what to do. If you do want it… "

"And what about me?" Ellen's tone was light, almost careless, if the listener had not known her. "What can anyone with eyes see?"

"You have more practice hiding things than he does. Seeing you together it might be only a partnership of minds. But the tone of your voice when you mention him is different, just a little, from when you talk about anyone else."

Ellen looked down a moment, then back at Mari. "Suppose you had been living in a foreign country for a long time, doing your best to speak their language, dress the way they do, fit in, and then you met someone from your own country who spoke your language and understood you when you spoke it. That is what it is like. I am not sure if I'm in love with him — but I know that the College would feel cold and empty if he left."

Mari nodded her understanding, gave her friend a quick hug. It was some time before Ellen spoke again, this time in a deliberately casual tone.

"How are you getting home?"

"Riding, thanks be. Father wanted to send a coach, but since you weren't willing to accompany me to Northpass, I persuaded him to send two men and my favorite mare instead — they're at the inn waiting for me. It's beautiful weather, nice countryside, good roads. What about you?"

"I'm staying for another couple of weeks to finish a project with Magister Coelus. After that I plan to go home for a while. I have quite a lot to tell Mother and I hope she will have ideas that will help me with my work. Will you be at Northpass all summer?"

Mari shrugged. "I expect to be with the family all summer. Father thinks the Forstings on the other side of the pass are up to something. After he and Prince Kieron deal with it or prove Father wrong, I expect to be back at our townhouse in the capital. If you have time free later in the summer, you might visit. If I am still up north I can leave word to lend you a horse. You can ride up — it's only about four days travel, the last through pretty empty country, but I expect you can protect yourself well enough."

Ellen nodded. "Yes. And thank you for not saying so last time, when Alys was being silly about my riding home alone. I expect I am less at risk than anyone else in the College, but it does not do to say so."

The two girls were quiet for a while, absorbed in their own thoughts, until a familiar voice interrupted.

"Did everyone get off all right? Would've said goodbye, but something came up." Jon stopped for a moment. Ellen, correctly reading his glowing face, put the question. "What sort of something? Did your plan to get a free ride work out?"

"Not yet. Not sure if they needed an extra groom or not. Expect will manage one way or another, but not this week."

Mari interrupted him. "Because? You look like my younger brother, opening gifts on midwinter day. Tell us what happened."

"It's the library. Magister Jerik offered me room and board the next two weeks, exchange for helping with the manuscripts in the back room. There are all sorts of things there," he turned to Ellen, "including a draft of Olver's first treatise in his own handwriting! Thought you would find that interesting."

"Very. So will Coelus. It might clear up some of the things we were not sure about when we read through the treatise. Could you tell how close it was to the published text?"

Jon shook his head. "No. After the first few pages, I get lost. It's for you and Magister Coelus, not me. But a lot of other interesting things there and I get to read all of them! Need to go home eventually—mother and father and all the younger ones will want to see me. But I can wait till the coach people willing to trade a free ride for help with the horses. The longer it takes ..."

"... the more of the library you get to absorb. Mari is leaving, but I'll be here a bit longer, so if you want my help, just ask."

* * *

Fieras entered the room, a thick sheaf of papers in one hand, bowed to Lord Iolen.

"You have read it all?"

"I have. I am impressed. I am not sure I want to know how your Lordship managed it, but I am curious to know what the condition of the three mages is and how soon His Highness will discover that someone else has gotten at them."

Iolen responded with a cold smile:

"Sometimes a little thought does more than either force or magery. The three mages are in the same condition my man found them in. With reasonable luck, my uncle will never know."

Fieras said nothing, but his face spoke for him.

"How did I do it? My man, a mage skilled in the art of improving recollection, visited each of the three. He explained that, to implement the process for memory elimination, a complete account was required. He wrote it down. We now have a better description of the Cascade experiment than His Highness does."

Fieras looked down at the papers. "What each did, where he stood, what the symbols were, what the other mages did. All here. Have you further stratagems for possessing the Cascade, now that we know what we are looking for?"

"I have. I considered simply reporting to His Majesty his brother's plot against him. But that might only rouse his ire. His Majesty is unfortunately only too willing to trust His Highness.

"Better, perhaps, to seize possession of the spell ourselves. For His Majesty's use in the defense of the kingdom, of course." Lord Iolen nodded towards the papers in Fieras's hands. "It seems that His Highness knows of the Cascade but does not yet possess the spell in a safely usable form. Performed only once, it killed the mage casting it. The mage who devised it, with further efforts, should be able to perfect it. I do not know why my uncle has not yet arranged for him to do so, but his failure is our opportunity."

Fieras paused, then spoke. "I believe that Magister Coelus was reluctant to cooperate; I am not sure why. Perhaps he no longer cared to see his creation put to use. There was also a girl, his leman, I presume; her role is uncertain. His Highness would no doubt have finished dealing with the matter, but the recent difficulties in the north ..."

"Interrupted him, giving us our opportunity. I intend to take it.

"I have sent a message to Captain Geffron, commander of the nearest garrison to Southdale. He owes his present position to my patronage and is a patriot. For a spell useful in the defense of the kingdom, he would not scruple to provide us any aid within his power.

"Reveal nothing of the precise nature of the spell to anyone. I have means of assuring the silence of the memory mage who obtained it for me. Consult with the learned Rikard about what resources we will require and which mages we will want to employ. I have instructed him to put a protective spell on the papers I have given you. You will take care to reveal nothing, to anyone."

Lord Iolen cast Fieras a stern look. The mage nodded. "I understand, your Lordship, and I will obey."

"See that you do. I am able to properly reward obedience. Also disobedience. I will send Rikard to your room in a little while; be there."

Once back in his room, Fieras considered his situation. It would be prudent, for the moment, to seem to be entirely obedient to his lord's commands. But something in the conversation ... Once Iolen had the schema for the Cascade, there was one reliable way of ensuring the silence of others who knew of it. A pity he hadn't the name of the memory mage.

Chapter 15

Coelus looked up from the pile of old letters on his desk, face alight, as Ellen came through the open door. "I've found her."

Ellen looked puzzled. "Found who? What are those?"

"Letters; your friend Jon found them, going through stacks of documents in the back room of the library. When I searched the library three years ago I was looking for records and treatises. I must have skipped right over these."

"What sort of letters?"

"Letters from a mage named Ascun, one of the magisters here, to another mage named Ger. Ger must have become a magister later; that would explain how the letters ended up here." He paused a moment. "They were written forty-eight years ago. "

There was an expectant silence.

"Just before the sphere was created?"

"Yes. Less than a year before if I have worked the dates out correctly."

"And what did you find in the letters?"

"A name. Melia."

Ellen gave him a surprised look, said nothing, waited.

"Melia was a weaving mage close to Durilil. Ascun calls her a witch, of course. A very accomplished weaving mage. Lovers or friends, nobody seems to know."

He paused, then looked at Ellen. "But everyone knew that they were working together. Weaving mages are not that common. Odds are a hundred to one that she is the other mage, the weaver who helped him build the sphere."

Ellen said nothing, so he went on. "Durilil was in his sixties, but she was younger. If she was thirty then, she could easily be still alive now. The schema for the sphere that we have is only the final step of their work; she must know a lot more. Someone must have heard of her around the College, or perhaps the Prince…"

Ellen finally spoke. "You wish to find Melia and speak with her about her work on the sphere?"

Coelus gave her a puzzled look. "Yes. Of course. The problem is how to find her."

Ellen shook her head. "That will not be a problem."

For a moment Coelus was silent with surprise. "You know where she is? You have met her? You know her?"

Ellen nodded. "I've known her all my life. She's my mother."

* * *

"Is your end ready?"

Coelus looked up from the crowded work bench. "Almost."

Ellen leaned over his shoulder to see. The miniature star was complete — at one corner a lighted candle, at the next a goblet of water, then a saucer full of soil, and finally a tiny bladder blown tight and tied. Each token sat on a small square of paper, each paper had its glyph. Coelus finished the glyph on a final square, added his name, placed it carefully in the center, stood up. "Your turn."

Ellen moved back to the other end of the table, where a small lamp was burning, next to it an unlit candle. She reached into the flame. With quick movements and a few murmured words, she wove a tiny sphere of flame, a soap bubble some four inches across around the candle. A final gesture and the candle sprang alight. "Ready."

Coelus picked up from the bench a thin rod of polished wood, touched one of the two glyphs on the central square and then, one after another, the glyphs sitting under the elemental tokens. Ellen watched fascinated as the faint star of elemental lines appeared, so thin as to be barely visible even to her. Coelus looked down at his work, shook his head. "Is it there?"

"Yes. I can see it."

He stood back as far from the table as he could and stretched out the wand to touch his name on the central square and then the glyph next to it. He closed his eyes. From the center of the star, where the four lines joined, the shadow of a line leapt towards the bubble at the other end of the table. For a few seconds it wavered, as if looking for a way through to the candle. The two mages watched, fascinated. Then the shadow line vanished. Ellen looked up from the table. "The star is gone. I think it worked."

"That is at least some evidence. I do not see what else we can do to test the schema, short of building the thing to full scale and running a cascade outside it. Which ..."

Ellen finished the sentence. "Does not seem like a good idea. I do not see what more we can do along this line either. But at least it works in miniature; there was not a trace of fire coming back from the candle to the pool, so the Cascade was not getting through. And I built the sphere using our most recent schema, so it would not take enormous amounts of power to do the full sized version."

Coelus nodded agreement. "Yes. That line is done and tested, as far as we can test it. I think we both deserve a small celebration."

He opened the door of the cabinet next to the work bench. Inside was a tray, on it two glass goblets, a small pitcher. He took the tray out, set it on the empty middle of the workbench, poured wine into both goblets and handed one to Ellen.

The two sat for a few minutes after their silent toast. Coelus started to say something, stopped, finally spoke. "I think I understand your secret now. Your mother did not want..."

"...Mother likes a quiet life. Where we live, people know her as a healer, respect her. Mari said something once about daydreams of being a famous mage. That isn't what mother wanted."

"And Durilil. Do you know?"

Ellen hesitated a moment. "She was twenty-two when they built the sphere. Like me she came early to power. Beyond that—it is not the sort of question one asks a mother."

"I suppose not." He hesitated a moment. "My mother died when I was nine. My father was one of the first plague victims that year. She nursed him and died a week after he did."

"I'm sorry. I had a much easier time of it." Her hand on the work bench moved and, almost without her willing it, touched his. For a while neither spoke. Coelus closed his eyes, remembering how he had first seen her, in woven fire. Fire and weaving. Durilil and Melia. If Durilil had not vanished, it would make perfect sense—if a man past ninety could father a child. Finally he broke the silence. "If you were thirty years older, I would not have to ask. You would be the answer."

Chapter 16

Magister Bertram looked up as the porter entered. "Visitors at the front gate, Sir. They asked to see someone in charge here. Magister Gatekeeper sent me for you."

Bertram stood up, pulled out the wrinkles in his robe, brushed off a bit of dust and followed the porter out. A few minutes brought him to the gatehouse into which the magister gatekeeper and half a dozen visitors had crowded. One stepped forward, tall and elegantly attired: "I am Lord Iolen, nephew to His Highness Prince Kieron, who, as you may know, has been working with one of your colleagues on a project of importance. He was called away on a matter of some urgency, so I have come on his behalf. This is Captain Geffron, whom I believe you know."

The captain stepped forward, nodded. Bertram bowed to both men. "It remains only for you to say what I, and the College, can do to serve you gentlemen."

An hour later, Bertram and Lord Iolen met with Coelus in the senior common room. Bertram introduced the other two to each other.

"Lord Iolen is here from His Highness; I expect you know better than I the work he has come to assist you with."

Coelus looked a moment puzzled. "I did assure His Highness of my cooperation in one of the projects we discussed, and Ellen and I have made substantial progress, though not as much as I would have wished. I do not think any assistance is needed. When His Highness comes back, I will be glad to explain our work to him so far."

Iolen paused a moment before replying. "I have a number of skilled mages with me, whom I was given to understand might be needed for your work. His Highness is concerned about the secrecy of the project. I am prepared to take precautions to prevent word from getting out."

"Wouldn't making a fuss be more likely to draw attention than avoid it? I confess that I know little about such matters. I welcome your cooperation, as long as you do not interfere with our work."

* * *

Jon looked up from the scroll. The hand tugging at his sleeve was Ellen's. "What is it?"

"I need your help," she whispered.

"What for?"

"You remember what Mari told us about Lord Iolen, the Prince's nephew?"

"Son of the prince lost out when King Thoma died? One who hates Prince Kieron with a passion?"

Ellen nodded. "He's here with a bunch of mages and soldiers. He claims he has come from the Prince to help with work Magister Coelus is doing for His Highness. He's obviously lying. I think I know why, and someone must get a message to the Prince. The easiest way is through Mari. She is either at her father's town house in the capital or in Northpass Keep. I can give you money to rent a horse and pay for food and lodging. If you can get out of the college without raising any suspicion and ride as fast as you can to the capital, you can get my message to Mari and she can pass it on. You must be careful; Iolen may have guards watching the entrance."

Jon nodded. "Yes. Do you have the message?"

Ellen passed him a folded piece of paper, sealed.

"It's for the Prince. Mari can look at it if she wants. And you will need this."

She handed him a small, heavy leather bag. He glanced in it.

"That's gold. It's more than I'll need."

"Better too much than too little. I have more. If I were you I would stop dressing as a student once out of sight of the gate. I don't know what precautions Iolen is taking. Good luck." She squeezed his hand, turned, left the library.

Another few minutes brought her to her room. She had the trunk open, both layers of her usual clothing off and the tunic her mother had woven for her part of the way on when there was a knock on the door. She finished drawing it on before speaking.

"Yes?"

"You are wanted by Magister Coelus. I'll take you to him." The voice was a strange one.

"Just a minute. I was changing."

She pulled on her over tunic, checked that the amulet with its

114

cord was around her neck and quietly closed the chest. Standing on her bed she unlatched the window shutters, pulled herself up to sit on the sill and slid feet first through the window.

"Very fetching. Stand still."

The speaker was a mage, standing by the wall ten or fifteen feet from the window. He gestured towards a soldier at his side, who lifted the bent crossbow he was holding.

"You probably know a little magic, but if you try anything tricky, you will very much regret it. Take the amulet and cord off and toss them in this direction." Ellen obeyed.

"Very good; glad to see that you are a sensible girl."

The mage raised both hands, moved them in a complicated gesture, said a Word. For a moment Ellen felt a flush of warmth, from neck to upper thigh, where the protective garment lay against her skin.

The mage stopped moving, hands still raised. There was a loud snapping sound. The soldier looked down at his bow, now unbent, the string broken, the quarrel still sitting in its channel. He dropped the weapon, reached for his short sword and snatched his hand away with a curse.

Ellen spoke calmly. "I am a fire mage. I burned your bowstring and the handle of your sword. If necessary I will burn out your eyes. You are going to escort me to the front gate and out. If anyone asks, Lord Iolen commanded you to take me to the inn. If you do anything to raise suspicion, you will never see again. Do you understand me?"

The archer looked at her, nodded.

She turned back to the mage. "On my command you will lie down, close your eyes and fall asleep. When you wake you will remember nothing that has happened in the past ten minutes. Do you understand?"

"I understand." The voice was flat, toneless.

"Make it so."

* * *

"His Highness made it clear that I was not to discuss my work with anyone. I think that includes you. It certainly includes them." Coelus gestured to the two mages standing behind Iolen.

"An admirable precaution. These, however, are two of the mages who are to assist you with the Cascade."

Coelus gave him a puzzled look. "The Cascade? I have told His Highness that I would not work on that. I thought you were here about my work on precautions to protect His Majesty."

"That is important too. But our first priority is developing the Cascade itself. You cast the spell once already. By now you surely should have contrived a second and better version. It is that which I have come to help you with."

"Then you can go again; I made the situation clear enough to His Highness." Coelus turned back to the papers on his desk.

"And I am making it clear to you. Your orders are to provide a detailed description of how best to implement the Cascade. My men will act on that description and I expect the spell to work. If it does not, you will find what is wrong and fix it. Do you understand?"

"I understand your commands. What I do not understand is why I should obey them."

"Because if you do not, both you and your leman will suffer for it."

It took Coelus a moment to understand. "The lady in question is my student and nothing more. The last mage who tried to force her to do something ended up convicted of violation of the bounds and banned from the use of magery. You are not a mage, but your servants are. If they intend to impose compulsions upon either of us, they might consider the consequences."

For a moment there was silence; Iolen broke it. He stepped to the door; in a moment two men came in, armed with crossbows.

"I suggest that you not move," Iolen said. "Unless your spells can disable all five of us, it would be wiser not to cast them."

Coelus said nothing. In a few moments he found himself gagged, his feet tied to the legs of the chair he was sitting in, his hands free. Iolen spoke again. "I am leaving you with a pen and a stack of paper; you are to use them to write the information I require of you."

He turned to the two guards. "In a little while he should start writing. Let him do so; if he tries to destroy what he has written, prevent him. Is that clear?"

The guards nodded assent; Iolen and his accompanying mages left the room.

* * *

Ellen burst through the door of Master Dur's shop, fortunately empty of customers. "Lord Iolen, the King's nephew, is here with men, soldiers and mages. They have the College, they have Magister Coelus. They must know about the Cascade; it's the only reason they would be doing this. What can we do?"

Dur nodded. "Coelus is in his office, guarded; I've been watching. Iolen's people are probably setting up the Cascade; we had better get there to stop them. I'll tell you the rest as we go."

The two hurried out of the shop and down the path to the College. "Your friend Fieras is with them. The Prince must have let something slip to him. Fieras has four mages with him, one for each element, which probably means he's going to be the focus. I spent the past half hour pumping fire into the containment sphere, in case I need it. If nothing better occurs to me I will wait till the last moment and burn him to a crisp; we should be able to get your young man out of the place in the confusion. And since Fieras is under ban, killing him when he is using magic is not only well deserved but entirely legal. With luck, Iolen will assume that Fieras went the way of Maridon. Cut left here; there may be men at the gate."

They angled off the grass towards the edge of the containment sphere. In a few minutes, Ellen stopped. "Father, look."

She was pointing at a group of men, three of them in armor, clustered around a tree a little distance outside the dome. Dur stopped, stood still a moment with his eyes closed before speaking. "Lord Iolen is being careful; sensible man."

Ellen gave him a puzzled look. "What do you mean?"

"The Cascade is being created in the same location that Coelus created it, the magisters' lawn. Iolen has crossbow men stationed on the other side of the barrier. I'll give you high odds their instructions are to watch the barrier and, if a hole appears, put a crossbow bolt through it into any mage in sight. That doesn't protect the people inside the sphere, but it means that if whoever is the focus wants to imitate Maridon and try to expand across the countryside, the odds are good that he will fail. If they don't get the mage responsible—and he's the one who would be closest to the barrier—I expect that killing one of the others would still break the pool and stop the Cascade."

Ellen nodded. "The focus could still take control over everyone inside, then work from there. What is to keep Fieras from putting a compulsion on Iolen himself?"

"I don't know, but I expect the problem has occurred to Iolen. Whatever else he is, he isn't a fool."

Ellen touched his arm, pointed. "They've seen us; one of them is coming this way."

Durilil again closed his eyes for a moment, turned towards the barrier. "Get us through." He turned back towards the approaching soldier, gestured. Ellen lifted her hand, spoke a Word; the barrier rippled, dilated. The two mages passed through it, stepped over a low wall onto a path through the college herb garden.

Dur stood still a moment, eyes closed, as the hole in the barrier shrank to a point and vanished. "We are in time; the mages are arranged at the points but he hasn't started the schema yet. It is indeed Fieras at focus; surely Iolen has more sense than to trust him."

Ellen nodded agreement. "I don't know what Iolen has planned, but I have an idea. If it does not work, use yours."

* * *

On the magisters' lawn the four mages had arrayed themselves on the marks Fieras had drawn. Fieras stepped to the center but was stopped by Lord Iolen's voice.

"One moment, please." He motioned to the mage beside him. Two men with crossbows at the edge of the lawn, their backs to the wall of the magister's wing, raised their weapons.

"Before you start, there is one small precaution to be taken. Rikard is about to cast a spell on you. You will not resist it." He glanced at the archers to make his meaning clear.

Fieras stood frozen, his face a mask of surprise. "What sort of spell, My Lord?" he asked.

"A loyalty spell. Such spells do not last long on mages, but it should suffice. Rikard has written out a scroll with a second loyalty spell. As soon as the Cascade is active and you have the necessary power, cast it on Magister Coelus. You will tell us if it is necessary to fetch him or if it can be done from here. When you have cast both spells, release the pool and the Cascade. If you cannot see how to do so, you will use the athame on the table next

118

to you to cut one of the lines."

He nodded to Rikard, who began the invocation. Fieras, after one desperate glance around, did nothing. Finished, Rikard approached Fieras and handed him a scroll; Fieras took it. Iolen spoke; "You may now begin the schema."

Everyone fell silent as Fieras began the first invocation of the schema. Rikard saw the first line of the star spring up, red as fire, as the first of the four mages spoke his Word. A second line, a third, a fourth. Fieras, at the center of the star, raised his hand, opened his mouth.

Ellen, watching with her eyes closed, separated from lawn and mages by brick and stone, spoke a Word. In front of Fieras the surface of the containment sphere rippled and began to dilate. Through the hole Iolen saw grass, a tree, men; he opened his mouth to yell. From the far side of the barrier the twang of a plucked string, then another. Fieras looked down, astonished to see the feathered end of a crossbow bolt protruding from his chest, dropped to one knee then to both, collapsed. A third twang; the mage on the fire point of the schema, in front of Fieras at his right, clutched at his stomach, doubled up and fell.

* * *

As soon as Coelus heard through the open window of his room the first word of the invocation he picked up the pen and began to write. A moment later he beckoned one of the two guards over. The man looked down at the paper. It was covered with symbols, each a cluster of what looked like stylized pictures. He leaned over, looked more closely. Something about them...

As the guard slowly raised his head, Coelus nodded in the direction of the other. The first guard motioned the other over. "Take a look at this."

The other guard bent down to look. The first guard untied the cord holding the gag in Coelus' mouth as the other bent to free his legs. Coelus stood unsteadily, picked up the sheet of paper, folded it, and slid it into his pouch.

"You were instructed to remain here until I returned," he said, softly. "Do so. Remember nothing more."

His cloak was hanging by the door; he put it on and left the room.

* * *

Dur turned to his daughter. "Good work. With luck, Iolen will think Fieras opened the hole. We have to find Coelus and get him out of here. I don't want to look like this when we find him, so we only have half an hour or so. There is a limit to how much fire the sphere can hold for me."

Ellen nodded, closed her eyes, in a moment spoke.

"He got himself out; I don't know how. He's on his way to the front gate."

"Can you get us to him before he reaches it? There are guards at the gate."

Ellen nodded, led her father into the north wing, out a door opening on the paved courtyard that separated the kitchen from the magister's wing. At its south edge another door gave access to the main corridor.

Coelus saw the door open. Through it, to his surprise and relief, came Ellen followed by a stranger, a man of about forty with a vaguely familiar face. Coelus was the first to speak. "You are all right? They didn't do anything to you?"

"I'm fine but we have to get out of here; follow me." She turned back through the door.

"You can't; that doesn't lead to the gate."

The stranger spoke: "Just follow her; you'll see."

Chapter 17

Iolen looked around the lawn, turned to Rikard. "You're the mage; you tell me. How did Fieras overcome your loyalty spell? Did he somehow use the spell he was casting?"

Rikard considered his lord's question for a moment before answering. "I am not sure he did overcome it, my Lord. I saw him do nothing related to the containment sphere in the seconds before it opened."

"The mage who died before had made a hole in the sphere, trying to spread the Cascade across the kingdom. So did Fieras."

"What mage who died?"

Lord Iolen's puzzled look vanished. "Of course. You haven't read the report on the Cascade—I was trying to keep it to as few people as possible. Take Fieras's copy; it's over there on the table, underneath his athame. Take your spell off it first; a stack of blank pages won't be of much use to us.

"We just tried to replicate Coelus's experiment of months ago, a spell to permit one mage, with the help of four others, to drain power from all the mages he can reach. One of Coelus's colleagues was the focus. He took control, breached the containment sphere, and was about to spread the Cascade outside the sphere when something burned him up. I had men stationed on the other side of the boundary in case it happened again."

Rikard began to speak but changed his mind. Bowing to Iolen, he crossed the lawn to gather Fieras's papers and returned. "I will read these. Maybe they will help me understand what happened. Who else here knows about the containment sphere and how one opens it, your Lordship?"

"Magister Bertram is the most senior of the magisters still here," Iolen replied. "If he does not know he probably can tell us who does; report to me at the inn after you have spoken with him. Bring all that you can find in Magister Coelus's office that might be of use, anything in his writing."

An hour and a half later Rikard, on his way up to Iolen, passed a worried Captain Geffron coming down the inn stairs. A servant brought in goblets of wine, then withdrew. "I saw the

Captain coming out, my Lord," said Rikard.

Iolen nodded. "I told him Magister Coelus had vanished, kidnapped, perhaps, by Forsting agents using a compulsion spell. I offered two of my men who know what Coelus looks like, one for the forces watching the road and one for those searching the village. I also offered your help; a truth teller should be useful in the search. If anyone asks, you are looking for a missing magister who had a spell go wrong and might be a bit off his head as a result. With luck, if Coelus starts talking, nobody will believe him. What have you learned about how Fieras got through the containment sphere?"

Rikard had spent some time thinking about what to say. His lord was, on the whole, a fair as well as a generous master, but pushing the argument too far might be risky.

"As far as Magister Bertram knows, the entrance gate is the only way through the sphere and only the gatekeeper, a retired magister who knows the spell, can open it. I don't know what they would do if the gatekeeper happened to drop dead. But I learned two other things. The papers you gave me say that Maridon didn't breach the sphere until after the spell was complete and the power of everyone inside the sphere had been gathered. And he did it by walking up to the surface of the sphere and literally ripping it open with his hands. That doesn't accord with what we saw Fieras do."

Iolen thought a moment before answering. "Fieras had read the account, had plenty of time to make his own plans. Even if we don't know how he managed it, we did see him do it."

Rikard hesitated a moment, then made up his mind. "We saw the hole, my Lord. We do not know if Fieras was the one who made it. I learned something else."

Iolen waited, said nothing, his face unreadable.

"Magister Coelus knew more about magic than anyone else in the College. He was interested in the sphere and had one of his students studying it for him. His office overlooks the magisters' lawn; when the sphere opened, he was not fifty feet from it."

"You think he somehow opened the sphere. How and why? He was bound and gagged."

"And got free just as Fieras was casting the spell, slipped two guards and left them with no memory of what happened or where he had gone. Perhaps he was planning to make a hole and leave through it and somehow got the placement wrong."

Iolen shook his head. "Speak up. If I made a mistake I want you to tell me, not polite lies."

Rikard relaxed; he was over the tricky bit. "As your Lordship commands. I think he somehow knew, or guessed, the precaution your Lordship had taken. How I do not know, any more than I know how his leman managed to get away from two mages and a guard. There's much going on here I don't understand."

"You think Coelus opened the hole as Fieras was finishing the spell so he would be shot down by our own people?" Iolen said, evenly.

Rikard nodded. "Yes, My Lord. I don't know how he did it, but it makes the most sense. The only other mage who could have done it is the gatekeeper. And that makes no sense at all."

"And he sent us—me—haring off on a false trail, Fieras's. If so, our Magister Coelus is a very clever and very dangerous man."

"Yes, My Lord. I am afraid he is."

Iolen closed his eyes for a minute, sat thinking. Finally he opened them again. "If you were Coelus, what would you be doing now, other than laughing at us as fools?"

Rikard pondered. "If Magister Coelus is loyal to His Highness, he may be headed there. If in service to the Forsting or another faction, he may be playing for time until he has something to sell to them or he may be on his way out of the kingdom along with his leman. If he is loyal to His Majesty and falsely suspects your Lordship is not …"

Rikard faltered. Should Lord Iolen ever be arrested for treason, it would be useful to be able truthfully to say he knew nothing. Iolen finished his sentence for him.

"…then he is off to His Majesty. I have taken precautions to avoid any misunderstandings along those lines—His Majesty is not all that easy to get to, and I have friends at Court—but there is always some risk. The road to the capital goes past the garrison, and they will stop anyone suspicious. I only hope it isn't too late. Have you a fourth alternative?"

Rikard nodded. "Coelus said he told His Highness he would no longer work on the Cascade. He did not say why. Perhaps he believes that you are in truth working with his Highness and is hiding from both of you.

"We have half a dozen competent mages available, and Gyrgas may survive. There must be many things associated with Magister Coelus in his rooms. If he is still nearby, I expect we can find him."

* * *

Coelus looked around the room curiously — a chair, a desk and a shelf containing several codices, a clay bowl with a spoon in it, and a mug. A single bed. He turned to the stranger. "I wasn't paying attention; where are we?"

"A room over one of the shops — we came in by the back door." He gestured to the ladder in the corner, "That goes to a trap door to the roof. If Iolen's people come looking for you, go to the roof and hide behind the low wall there. Ellen and I will dispose of the ladder."

"Don't they know about Ellen? The Prince did. She needs to hide too."

The other nodded: "She will. But hiding you from eyes and ears won't be enough; if Iolen decides to search for you he will have mages out as well. Ellen needs to make both of you invisible to them."

Ellen turned to Coelus. "I am going to weave you the same protection I used, making you invisible to a mage's perception. Unless one is familiar with it, it blocks in both directions, so you will have to depend on your eyes for a while. And you have to stand still while I do it."

Coelus, standing still, closed his eyes and took a last opportunity to examine the other man. Either not a mage or a very tight veil, tight enough to hold even at a range of a few feet. What else he was...

Ellen gestured toward the lamp on the table; it flamed alight. From it she drew a thin thread of flame. Coelus watched, rapt, as her flickering fingers wove it into a fabric, formed the fabric about his body. He closed his eyes again; for a moment his world was flame, entirely surrounding him. The flame faded, but the world beyond him remained invisible. He opened his eyes. The other man was speaking.

"Don't forget yourself, love."

For a moment Coelus stopped breathing as he watched Ellen,

with a gesture he had seen before, pull a final thread of flame from the lamp, stroke it down her body, and sit down on the bed. The stranger closed his eyes, turned from one to the other.

"That should be sufficient; I can barely see you and I'm a lot closer than Iolen's mages will be." Which meant that, whatever else he was, he was a mage.

"Since Iolen won't be looking for me, I'll fetch dinner in a little from the cook shop. Before I do, it might be prudent to put together what we know to try to figure out what Iolen is doing and what he is going to do. Why don't you start." He nodded to Coelus.

"Before I tell you what I know," Coelus said, deliberately, "I need to know a little more. In particular, who you are."

The other smiled. "Very prudent; you would not want to be telling a random stranger all about the Cascade. His Highness' warning seems to have done some good."

"You are from the Prince?"

"No; I have been watching both you and him for my own purposes. I think Ellen should make the introductions."

"I'm sorry; I should have. But everything was happening so fast." She stood up. "Father, this is Magister Coelus. Magister Coelus, this is my father."

A long silence. Coelus' expression was a mixture of surprise and relief; Dur, who looked quietly amused, was the first to speak.

"So that, at least, is one thing you do not need to worry about. As far as keeping secrets is concerned, I think I know at least as much about the Cascade as either Ellen or Iolen and his people. As I gather you already know, Ellen's mother helped create the containment sphere; one advantage of knowing how it was constructed is that it becomes possible, with practice, to see things happening inside it.

"We may not have a lot of time. What was Iolen up to with you, and how did you get away?"

"I don't know Iolen's purpose; he claimed to be coming from the Prince, but I doubt it. He wanted me to tell him how to do the Cascade. I refused. He had me gagged so I couldn't speak any spells, tied my feet to the chair but left my hands free. I was to write what he wanted and my guards were instructed to stop me if I tried to destroy anything I wrote.

"I think he planned to run the Cascade inside the containment sphere, using whatever he had gleaned from the mages who helped last time. The mage at the focus was to cast a loyalty spell on me while the Cascade was draining my power into his. I would be unable to resist, and with that much power behind it the spell should hold for a considerable time. I knew what he wanted. Once made loyal to him I would do it.

"I waited long enough so the guards would think the spell had been cast, then used paper and pen to perform a spell of my own, using glyphs instead of words. I got one of the guards to take a look at it. He drew the other one over, then both of them untied me. I did not know when or if Iolen's mages would manage to accomplish the Cascade. I was trying to get to the outside of the sphere before they did so when you met me."

Dur nodded approvingly. "Very sensible, and reasonably accurate. Iolen first had one of his mages cast a loyalty spell on the focus—Ellen's friend Fieras. The plan was to have the focus start the Cascade, use the power to cast a loyalty spell on you, then dissolve the Cascade and let you tell them how to do it better next time. Just in case something went wrong and Fieras managed to get control and break through the sphere as Maridon had, Iolen had crossbow men stationed on the other side with orders to watch for a hole in the barrier to open and, if it did, shoot the mage on the other side of it. A well thought out scheme, if a little on the elaborate side. I had my own plan for stopping him, but my clever daughter came up with a better one." He turned to Ellen, waited.

"All I did was to open a hole in the barrier, about where Maridon did, just before Fieras finished starting the Cascade. The later done, the more likely that Iolen would assume Fieras was responsible."

"And? Did Fieras finish the Cascade and start casting spells?"

Dur shook his head. "Not with two crossbow bolts in him he didn't. The third hit their fire mage; I don't know if he survived or not. I told you she was being clever. What we don't know is whether we fooled Iolen or what he plans to do next. He met with several of his people at the inn not long ago, but he has strong privacy spells and I haven't yet gotten through them."

Coelus interrupted. "Do you know what he is doing, what the

point of all of this is?"

Dur nodded, turned to his daughter. "Thanks to Mari, you know the politics better than I. During the six months that King Thoma was dying I was busy dealing with an infant fire mage; good thing your mother is a healer."

Ellen gave him a rueful smile, spoke to Coelus. "Don't believe him; I started early, but not that early. I think he has been saving that line up for the past seventeen years, waiting for someone to tell it to."

"Nonetheless, I paid little attention to kingdom politics back when the old king was dying; babies take up a lot of time and attention even if they aren't setting everything in sight ablaze. Tell Coelus what Mari said."

"The old king, Thoma, never got along with his eldest son; there were rumors, but nobody seems to really know why. On his deathbed he tried to get the great lords of the realm to support his second son for the succession. His third son, Prince Kieron, supported the eldest brother; they had always been close. Near the end Kieron hid Prince Petrus from their father's people until the old king died, then helped him put down their brother and his supporters.

"By the time it was over and Petrus was crowned, Josep, the second son, was dead. Josep's son Iolen inherited his lands and his surviving supporters. He has, of course, sworn allegiance to His Majesty but hates the Prince and does what he can to oppose him in court.

"So Iolen claiming to be acting on behalf of Prince Kieron was surely a lie. I couldn't get word to you safely then. He had to be here about the Cascade, meaning you would be the first they went after; I thought our best chance was to get word to the Prince. I asked Jon to take a message to Mari for His Highness. Then I fetched Father and we slipped back into the College, skipping the front gate, to see what we could do about stopping Iolen and getting you out."

She fell silent. Dur continued. "Clearly, Iolen found out about the Cascade and decided to stake all on getting it to work under his control and then using it to eliminate his uncles and seize the throne. The question now is how he will attempt to cover his tracks. All the possibilities that occur to me involve a lot of blood, some of it yours. If all else fails, he might run for the border and hope the Forstings have some use for a royal pretender... What's that?"

A voice below, and a hammering on a door. Dur pointed at the ladder; Coelus caught Ellen's eyes.

"I will be all right. Go."

He fled up the ladder, Dur down the stairs. Ellen slid the ladder under the bed then followed her father.

The hammering at Master Dur's closed front door proved to be his neighbor, the manager of the cookshop, with four other men, three of them armed, one a mage. Dur opened the door and stood back to let them come in. His neighbor turned to one of the armed men.

"This is Master Dur, the jeweler who lives here." He noticed the girl coming through from the back room. "Your granddaughter?"

Dur put his arm around her, gave her a hug. "My own flesh and blood. Her mother lives a few days east of here, but she's visiting. What's the problem?"

One of the armed men came forward. "We're looking for one of the magisters from the college, a man named Coelus; do you know him?"

Dur nodded. "Younger than the rest? I think I've sold things to him from time to time. What do you need him for?"

"Apparently he was trying out some spell or other and something went wrong. He's nowhere to be found and his colleagues are afraid he may be wandering around with his memory gone, or thinking he's a squirrel, or whatever happens to mages when they make a mistake. He might be with a student of his, a girl, maybe five or six years older than your granddaughter."

Dur shook his head. "Wherever he is, he isn't inside this house. And, aside from my little sweetheart here, I haven't seen any girls around this evening. I'll keep an eye out. If I see something I think you ought to know about, where do I send word?"

"Captain Geffron is in charge of the search; he's at the inn." The officer turned to look at the mage behind him. The mage nodded; the group of men left the shop. Dur closed the door, bolted it, turned back to Ellen.

"Before we fetch your young man down from the roof you might want to restore a few years and change back into what you were wearing. No need to confuse him — or give him ideas."

She nodded: "And you might want to take a few years back off."

Chapter 18

Lord Iolen looked around the inn room. Two of his own people — Rikard for the mages and Ivert, commander of his guards — and Captain Geffron. A second mage was standing in the doorway; he nodded to his lord, left the room. Iolen waited a moment to be sure he had the attention of the others before he spoke.

"We are as secure as magic can make us, so it is time to sum up our present situation and tell you my plans. We have no further need for the assistance of Captain Geffron, so he may take his men back to their garrison under strict orders of confidentiality, to await his call to the capital to confirm my report to His Majesty on this matter.

"Magister Coelus and the missing student have eluded us. Coelus, we must assume, is the Prince's creature and has gone to his master. When I report to His Majesty, I shall argue that His Highness has tried, treasonously, to obtain the secret of Coelus's work for himself, without informing His Majesty."

He stopped a moment, looked at the other two, continued.

"My coming here myself without informing His Majesty was of course justified by the need for my actions not to reach the ears of certain of His Highness's friends at court, since His Highness was then in a position to implement the spell with Coelus before he could be stopped.

"You are free to pass on as much of this to our people as you think prudent, save only that nothing should be said concerning the nature of the spell we were seeking. Make it clear that, in case of difficulties, I will continue to protect them. Are there any questions?"

Ivert got up. "None, my lord. With your leave I will make the arrangements for our departure in the morning."

Rikard waited until the guard commander had left before speaking.

"My lord. What if the Prince hears what we have been up to and attempts to seize power for himself immediately by implementing the spell? Should we not forestall him by doing so ourselves? There is some risk to whatever mage serves as the focus, but since Your lordship and I are now the only members of our party who have read the complete report on the previous attempt..."

He fell silent; Iolen responded with a cold smile. "If we do, and it works, how are you proposing that the spell should be used?"

"His Highness depends for protection chiefly on his own mages. The mage at the focus will have an enormous amount of magery at his command — including the power of the mages protecting His Highness and of His Highness himself. That should make it possible to breach any protections His Highness may have established, determine if he is in fact engaged in treason, and if so take suitable actions against him."

Iolen's face did not change.

"I presume that would require skill as well as power?"

"It would, my lord. I propose that we attempt the Cascade once, here, using Albin as the focus. I will first cast a loyalty spell on him; your lordship will instruct him to terminate the Cascade as soon as it is clearly established. If that succeeds, I propose that for the second attempt, somewhere closer to his Highness, I should be the focus."

There was a long silence before Iolen spoke.

"Yes. Write out the instructions for Albin; the other four should still have their copies. As before, each only needs to know his own part."

* * *

Dur lifted his hand from the lid of the small furnace, exposing the fire rune inlaid into its center, turned to his daughter, spoke softly.

"Your young man is asleep?"

"Magister Coelus was asleep a minute ago. Did you get through them?"

Dur nodded. "If you two ever create an adequate privacy shield, Iolen should be your first customer. They're going to try again tomorrow morning — outside the College. In the inn, in fact; the main dining room is big enough."

"How do we stop them from doing it?"

He shook his head. "We don't stop them from doing it, we

stop it from working. You haven't figured out yet how to push the Cascade's efficiency below its critical value, so we need to try something simpler. Can you weave your mother's shadow cloak?"

An hour later, Ellen was moving furtively through the village, stepping off the path into a dark passage between the inn and a neighboring house as a handful of travelers passed out through the inn's brightly lit door. Once through the doorway herself she moved quickly into a corner where nobody was likely to run into her, stood still watching the stairway and the area at its foot.

Her first attempt got only as far as the landing. A man appeared at the head of the stairs heading down; she considered briefly the size of the landing, chose the more prudent alternative. The second attempt succeeded, bringing her to the top of the empty stairway, from there to the corner farthest from the doors to the second floor rooms.

Two men emerged from the upstairs dining room. One went down the stairs, the other, the mage who had tried to capture her outside her own window three days before, turned right and went into one of the bedrooms. He put the papers he was carrying down on the small table between the beds, one already occupied, turned, closed the door.

Ellen waited as the inn gradually grew quiet, with guests straggling out the front door, the thud of doors closing on rooms. The upper hallway, lit faintly by the light of a lamp at each end, was empty. Closing her eyes, Ellen let her mind pass through the door in front of her. Inside both men slept. The guards at the hall's far end were awake, absorbed in a game of dice; a fourth guard stood at the front door of the inn, now shut. Iolen and one of his mages occupied a second bedroom, on the other side of the large upstairs room where Mari had entertained her friends. The lord seemed to be asleep; the mage riffled studiously through a stack of papers.

The lamp at her end of the hall went out. Ellen waited a few moments to be sure no inn servant was coming to relight it, then went quietly to the door of the room and eased it open. Its occupants were still asleep, one with his face towards the wall, the other on his back, snoring peacefully. She moved to put her body between him and the papers on the table before calling a tiny flame from her fingertip to read by its light the top sheet of paper.

The writing was in a clear hand, a set of instructions interspersed with single words written in the true speech, once a whole phrase. In some places words, in one a whole line, had been crossed out and replaced. From the wallet at her side she drew out a quill, a tightly stoppered bottle of ink.

In a few minutes she was done, quill and ink back in her wallet, and had slipped back out the door. She stopped at the head of the stairs, looking down to be sure there was nobody between her and the front door; the space was lighted by several lamps and the dull glow from the fireplace. The door was closed, the guard seated in a chair blocking it.

Ellen closed her eyes, pulled shadow out of the corners of the room and wove it about the man's head. Gradually his neck bent his head forward onto his chest; there was the faintest sound of a snore. She drew a long breath and started down the stairs.

A blow from behind. Ellen stumbled down, caught herself on the landing and turned.

"What the…"

It was one of the guards, looking straight at her. For a moment neither moved.

Suddenly, all the lamps and torchlights went out. The guard grabbed for her arm. She twisted free and fled down the stairs through the dark, the guard blundering down after her, calling out for help. The guard at the door, still half asleep, took a few steps towards the stair. She dodged around him, pushed the door open—the bar was off—and a moment later was running down the street through the night.

* * *

"My Lord."

Iolen finished pulling on his over tunic, turned to Rikard. "Something wrong?"

"Perhaps, My Lord. Last night, after we went to bed, one of the guards, coming down the staircase, ran into someone."

"And? Had he been drinking?"

"I don't think so, My Lord. It was a woman. Everything went dark; she pulled away and went running down the stairs. By the time they got the lamps lit again, she was gone."

Iolen said nothing, waited for the mage to continue.

"All the lamps and the fire on the hearth went out at the same time, just after the guard ran into the woman on the staircase. The guards couldn't see in the dark; the woman had no trouble getting down the stairs, around the guard at the door, and out."

"You believe it was magery?'

"Yes, My Lord."

Iolen thought for a moment. "Can a mage make himself invisible?"

"I can't, My Lord. I wouldn't be astonished if someone else could; I've heard of things at least close. Coelus, by all accounts, is a mage who invents new spells."

"And his missing student is a woman. So, you think it was she?"

"Something like that, My Lord. Coelus is air, not fire, so I'm not sure he could put out the hearth fire that fast."

"Did she get anything?"

"Not as far as I can tell, My Lord. I checked the chest with the papers in it; the spells hadn't been touched. Getting through them would not have been easy for a trained mage, let alone a girl and a student. We don't know what she might have heard."

"There has been no time for a message to the Prince to bring anyone from his camp here yet. Either Coelus had people in the village or someone else is taking a hand. Who?"

Rikard shook his head. "This time of year there are hardly any mages at the College. Perhaps someone else at court got word of where you were going, or why?"

"You think one of our people ..."

"Isn't. We can question them all."

"While you do that I will secure the main dining room of the inn to reinvoke the spell in; I'll tell the innkeeper we are having a conference and want none of his people within earshot. Have Ivert station one guard outside the door, another outside the windows. What am I forgetting?"

Rikard thought a moment.

"We will need to clear the floor; I'll borrow one of the guards to help move furniture. Easiest if you have everyone meet in the upstairs room for morning meal, keep them out of the way until needed. I'll let you know when we're ready."

An hour later, Rikard, Iolen and the five mages filed into the big downstairs room, which had been cleared. Positions for the mages were marked in chalk on the floor, each with its proper symbol. The mages assumed their places, written instructions in hand. Albin took the central position, gave Rikard an enquiring look; Rikard turned to Iolen.

"We are ready, My Lord."

"Albin understands his instructions?"

Albin turned his head. "First, Rikard will enspell me. As soon as I feel power flowing into me beyond our five, I will dismiss the spell I have just cast. If I cannot, I am to cut the nearest line with my athame."

Albin nodded. Rikard raised his hand, spoke a long sentence in the true speech, let his hand fall. Albin began the first invocation, the other mages joining in in turn, each answered by Albin. Rikard, watching with his eyes closed, saw the first line appear, the second, the third. Albin spoke the final word.

"It isn't working." Rikard turned to Albin. "What did you feel?"

"A trickle from Gilbert, Vyncent and Gregor, nothing from Steffan. The last word, that was supposed to start the Cascade, didn't do anything."

"Are you sure you got everything right? I didn't see anything happen when Stef was supposed to come in. And something sounded off—not quite as I remembered it."

"I said it just as you wrote it. See for yourself."

Rikard peered at the sheet of paper. "That's not my writing. Not all of it."

Iolen was the first to react. "Something got changed?"

"Yes, My Lord. In two places what I wrote has been crossed out, inked over so it can't be read, and different words written above to replace it."

Iolen turned to Albin. "When you went to sleep last night, where was the paper?"

"On the table by my bed, My Lord. I studied it before I went to sleep, went over it again in the morning to be sure I had it right."

Iolen smiled. "So that was what last night's visitor was up to. Clever, but not clever enough. Rikard, come with me; the rest of you stay here. We'll be back shortly."

On the way up the stairs, Iolen spoke again. "If you hadn't looked at the paper, their trick would have worked. Since you did… We can get one of the sets of notes out of the chest, redo the instructions from that. Then run the schema again.

"And it will work."

Rikard looked at his lord curiously. "Because?"

"Because if what we were doing wasn't going to work they wouldn't have risked getting one of their people caught trying to stop us."

* * *

Dur turned to Ellen and opened his eyes. "Rikard spotted your improvements to his instructions. That means I have to work quickly." Coelus was seated on the bed. "Stay here; we will be back shortly."

Ellen went downstairs and into the front of the shop to bolt the door, checked the back door as well, then joined her father by the small furnace. Taking a deep breath, he put his right hand down over the glyph on the cover and closed his eyes.

The fire poured into him, more and more fire, intoxication, pleasure verging closer and closer to the limit of what flesh could bear. With an effort he pulled back from the brink, found again the knife edge balance between the world of fire and the world of matter, between ecstasy and life. He let out the held breath, raised his left hand, pointing, held the pose for a long minute as he brushed past the privacy spells about the inn to explore one room and its contents.

"I think that should do."

"Father."

He looked up into Ellen's worried face, raised his hand to feel his hair. A strand came off, dead white. "That is the other risk." He leaned down, this time with both hands on the furnace. As she watched, fascinated, the wrinkles in the ancient face smoothed, the twisted veins in the hands shrunk away. When Dur stood up again, his white hair was the only visible change from his appearance an hour before.

Coelus spoke in a tone of astonished wonder. "You are all three of them." He paused at the head of the stairs before descending.

"Ellen's father, of course. And Master Dur, the old jeweler whose shop this must be; a minute ago you were even older than that. And the portrait of Durilil that used to hang in the lecture room. I thought you looked familiar the first time I saw you."

Durilil nodded. "I should have burned it up twenty years earlier, but it was a good painting and I hated to destroy another man's work. Once I decided to live here, there was no choice; I made Master Dur twenty years older than the picture, but someone with an eye for faces might still have recognized me from it."

Coelus was still thinking. "So the Salamander did not burn you up after all."

He stopped a moment, looked around the room. "You found it. You must have. That's why ..."

"King Theodrick had a team of mages. I have something better." He gestured to the furnace. It took Coelus only a moment to understand.

"I thought the glyph was a warning, wondered why it wasn't in some form ordinary people could read. I forgot that the fire symbol has another meaning. Is it part of the binding?"

Durilil shook his head. "You cannot bind an elemental, as you of all people should know; you got things mostly right in your thesis. The glyph is a road sign to help keep the Salamander where it wants to be. When your world is nothing but fire it is quite easy to get lost, at least what we would call lost.

Another thought occurred to Coelus. "It was the Salamander that killed Maridon?"

Durilil nodded. "Quite unintentionally. I assume you had the spell devised so that some fraction of the power absorbed from the Cascade went to channel the rest, otherwise no mage could survive being the focus."

"Yes. But it didn't work."

"How could it? When Maridon tapped the Salamander, all he had to protect him was the power of ten or twenty mages. He went up like a moth in a furnace."

* * *

Iolen and Rikard were at the top of the stairs when they smelled the smoke. Iolen stepped forward towards the door; Rikard caught his arm. "Just a moment, My Lord. It might be a trap."

He spoke a brief sentence, accompanied it with a gesture, stepped to the door, unlocked it and flung it wide, stepping back as he did so. The room was full of smoke. As it cleared, the two men could see that the pile of papers on the table had been mostly reduced to ash.

"Coelus' papers from his office?"

"Yes, My Lord. I was looking through some of them for clues to how the spell worked last night."

"Is the chest safe?"

Rikard said nothing, bent over the small chest sitting by the head of Iolen's bed, said something softly. "You can unlock it now, My Lord."

Iolen reached into his tunic and drew out a key hanging on a cord around his neck. In a moment the chest was unlocked. Rikard spoke more words over it before lifting the lid.

Smoke billowed out. The sheets at one end had been entirely consumed, reduced to a fine ash, but papers at the other end had fared better. Rikard lifted them out carefully. All were scorched, some destroyed, but many were at least partly legible.

Iolen was the first to speak. "I thought you had the chest protected."

Rikard looked up from the pages. "A skilled and very powerful mage standing next to the chest could perhaps have defeated its spells, although I doubt it. But the room was locked, the inn guarded. I don't believe any invisibility spell could be strong enough to have gotten a mage to the side of the chest undetected, after the precautions I took last night. No mage alive could have gotten a fire spell from outside the inn to inside that chest."

"And yet someone did."

Rikard shook his head. "I don't think so, My Lord. He didn't get the spell into the chest, we did."

He stopped a moment; Iolen looked at him blankly. Rikard thought a moment before continuing. "The first things we saw burning were Magister Coelus' papers on the table. His papers in the chest were what started the fire there. Ours, the two copies of the notes you obtained on the Cascade, weren't burned by a spell, but from lying next to burning paper. That's why some are left."

"Whether the spell set our papers alight or his, it still had to get through your protections to do so."

"No, My Lord. Magister Coelus must have put a spell on his

papers, with a trigger to ignite if they were away from him, or out of his room, or out of the College for more than a certain length of time. Like the spell I put on the notes you gave to Fieras which turned pages blank. So the spell was already inside the chest when the protective spells went on. Have you another copy somewhere?"

Iolen shook his head. "Too risky."

"Then I am afraid you will have to go back to whomever you got the information from and have him provide a fresh copy."

Iolen's smile was cold.

"I am afraid that will not be possible. Retrieve what you can from what we have; with luck one copy may provide some of what the other has lost. Tell the others that we will be on our way home as soon as possible. I expect His Majesty can find someone to recreate the spell from what we have."

Chapter 19

Ellen glanced around the familiar room, shelves over Coelus' desk now empty of their usual piles of paper. The reality of Ellen's parentage was just sinking in to Coelus.

"He has to be well over a hundred. He must have been in his eighties when you were conceived."

"Past ninety, actually. But he's a mage. And with enough power …"

"He can be any age he wants to be. I finally worked that out, when I saw him doing it. As Master Dur he was in his seventies, as your father he was forty or so, and as himself …"

"A hundred and twelve. And long dead if not for what he found."

"I should have guessed—Master Dur. Then again, Durilil is a common enough name. Because of that silly superstition."

Ellen smiled. "Remember what you told us in your first lecture, that a mage's skill can be judged by how little magic it takes him to achieve his aims. Father made himself invisible with no magic at all. A mage can't afford to change his name. If you want to hide a tree, you plant a forest and wait. Father started the rumor about naming children after mages the year after he found the Salamander."

"Why, after he found the Salamander, did he disappear? If he had come back he would have been the most famous mage in history."

"If you had kept on with the Cascade and done what Maridon wanted to do, used it to seize power, you would have been the most famous mage in history. Why didn't you?"

"I told you, a long time ago."

"You told me two reasons. There's one more you didn't think of.

"Suppose you developed the Cascade, and you used it to try to do good, and only you could do it, as only Father can do—what he does. And suppose His Majesty, or the next king—perhaps Lord Iolen, if the Prince happens to die before the King does—decided that we should end the Forsting wars once and for all by killing everyone in Forstmark. I expect you could do it."

It took him a moment before he could answer calmly.

"I expect I could. But I wouldn't; you know I wouldn't."

"Yes. And then the King appeals to your loyalty, or threatens the people you love—you might have a wife and children by then. Or tells you the Forstings have a magical weapon of their own and if you don't use the Cascade, they will conquer and kill us. At some point you either do what he asks—and I don't think you could, not really—or you use the Cascade against him. And then you are Maridon. I don't think you want to be Maridon."

It was a long minute, his eyes seeing nothing in the room, before he answered.

"No."

"Neither does Father. What he has doesn't drain other people's magic the way the Cascade does. But it's not as useful either. You can't cure a plague with fire, or turn a flood. But it's very good for killing people. That's why he decided, after he had found what he was looking for and made his terms with it, that he should just let everyone think the same thing had happened to him that had happened to his friend Feremund."

The two were quiet for some time, both thinking. Coelus was the first to speak. "So he has unlimited power, but he can't use it."

"He uses it to keep from getting old. And he can use it, if he's very careful, in other ways that aren't obvious. He used it to destroy Iolen's notes on the Cascade and set fire to your papers, so that they thought it was a spell you put on them and the damage to theirs just an accident. But he can't do that sort of thing very often or someone might figure it out. And even though he has an unlimited pool to draw on, there is still a limit to how much fire he can channel."

There was a knock on the door. A porter handed a message to the Magister and politely withdrew. Coelus read it. "His Highness is back. He wants to see me. Do you want to ..."

Ellen shook her head. "I'm a link to Father; the less he sees and thinks of me the better. I'll wait in your lab."

It took only a few minutes for the Prince to arrive; Coelus offered him a chair, sat down himself. "What can I do for your Highness?"

"Tell me what you know of Lord Iolen's doings and what

progress you have made on the project you were engaged in when last we spoke."

Coelus thought a moment before replying. "The second question first; it is easier to answer. We have a schema we believe will protect a building large enough to contain His Majesty and many mages, possibly large enough to cover the dimensions of the palace. If we are correct, the protective sphere could be maintained by the efforts of a single mage drawing on a fire sufficiently fueled. It would not block all magic or prevent people from coming in and out, unlike the protection around the College, but it would prevent any mage deploying the Cascade from spreading it into the sphere. I have written out a detailed account of that schema for you."

Coelus opened a drawer in his desk, drew out the papers, and handed them to the Prince, who looked through them briefly before putting them into the wallet at his side. "If someone in the kingdom duplicates your work, this will be of some use, but only some. A mage controlling the Cascade might not be able to defeat the mages who protect his Majesty, but he would be at an enormous advantage in any other conflict. I am grateful for this, but I must still require you to do all you can to keep the secret of the Cascade. And if someone else does duplicate it, I may have to ask more of you again."

"Your Highness may always ask. I do not promise what my answer will be."

The two men observed each other in silence. Finally the Prince spoke. "I had a second question."

"Iolen. He came here claiming to be acting on your behalf and asked me to tell him how to do the Cascade. He knew you had been here before him but did not seem to know that I had refused you. When I refused to do what he wanted, his people gagged me to keep me from speaking spells, bound me, and demanded I write out instructions for the Cascade. I think he tried to implement the Cascade and use it to put a loyalty spell on me, but if so something went wrong. While he was trying to make the Cascade work I was able to write out my own spell to counter the guards. I escaped to the village and have evaded them since."

"And your lady? Did Iolen go after her too?"

"Ellen? He tried, but with no better luck than your mage had.

Does Your Highness know what Iolen was doing and what has become of him?"

"I believe he was trying to obtain the Cascade and use it to murder His Majesty, myself and my son and claim the throne for himself. When he failed, he claimed to have been acting against a treasonous plot by me to command the Cascade. He intends to bring this claim to Court."

"Will His Majesty believe him?"

Prince Kieron shook his head. "No. The use of truthtellers will prove that he tried to implement the Cascade and I did not. His Majesty will be reluctant to use them on us, but if need be I will give consent. My brother trusts me and does not trust our nephew, both with good reason. Iolen might hope enough people would believe him to force His Majesty to accept a compromise, to leave Iolen unpunished. If that is his plan I do not think it will succeed."

"Could he be planning to threaten to make public what he knows about the Cascade if charges are pressed?"

"That would be to openly proclaim himself our enemy. I do not think he could make such a threat and live, despite His Majesty's reluctance to spill the blood of our kin. I may be mistaken, but I believe Iolen's threat is done, and Iolen with it. But I may need to call you to Court to testify to what you saw; remain here until I send word."

Almost as soon as the Prince had left Coelus' office, Ellen came back in from the workroom. "I heard what he said. If he is right …"

"If he is right about Iolen, the immediate threat is over. We still need to find some better defense against the Cascade, but we may have more time to do it in. Can you stay through the summer to work on it?"

Ellen shook her head. "I have a better idea. Father was planning to go back home to Mother as soon as it was safe to leave, which I expect means tomorrow. I'm planning to go too. Why don't you come along? You could work on the project there. The two of them know more about making barriers out of woven fire than anyone but Olver—and I know Mother would be interested in meeting you."

Coelus looked at her, struggled not to let too much show in

his face. Ellen looked back calmly. Finally he spoke.

"I would very willingly accept, but you heard the Prince. He wants me to stay until the matter with Iolen is settled. He will be displeased if he sends for me and I have disobeyed. And he is right; what I have to say in his support might settle the matter."

"You will come once the Prince is done with you?"

"Yes. I promise."

"Then I'll stay a few more days to help you work on the project and decide what we need to take with us. It will be easier for you to find Mother if I am with you."

Chapter 20

Coelus looked once more at the elegant writing on the scroll, then up at Ellen. "It's from the Prince; he's back."

"And?"

"He isn't sending me to the capital, so I suppose everything must have worked out. It's an invitation to a dinner he's having at the inn. I think it must be intended as a victory celebration."

Ellen looked unconvinced. "A long way to come just to have dinner with you. He'll try to persuade you to work on the Cascade, to have it ready just in case someone else develops it."

"He can try. He invited you too, so you can keep tabs on me if you think I'm weakening."

When they got to the inn they were directed to the main dining room, converted for the evening into a private feast hall. Coelus was seated at the Prince's right, Ellen next to him, a portly older man introduced as Wilham, one of the Prince's mages, on her right, a dozen more men, mostly strangers, around the long table.

The Prince stood to greet the two guests. "I am happy to see that you were able to come, Magister Coelus, and to bring your very accomplished lady. Tomorrow several of my people will want to discuss the work you have been doing and their experiments with the protective schema you provided. But I thought it would be pleasant to spend this evening celebrating what has been so far accomplished."

"Then Lord Iolen is no longer a threat?"

The Prince hesitated a moment before answering. "His Majesty is aware of Iolen's treason and remains satisfied with my loyalty. I have explained to him what I know of your work; he has asked me to continue to concern myself with it on his behalf."

As the Prince spoke, servants in his livery were bringing in the first course, pouring wine, serving platters—a roast, wedges of meat pie, sausages. One servant was passing behind the guests taking their cups, refilling them, replacing them. A second course was served. The Prince conversed with the guest on his left, a stranger to Ellen; she turned to speak to the mage on her right.

"Did you have a pleasant ride here from the capital?"

Wilham nodded, looked at her curiously.

"His Highness tells me you are a fire mage; is it true?"

She nodded.

"I have never encountered a woman with that talent before. I am fascinated; your existence would seem to support the Learned Olver's views on the nature of magic."

"You doubted them?"

The man shrugged. "I'm a practitioner, not a scholar. I've learned two spells created by your friend Magister Coelus, who I gather follows Olver's approach, and they work. But most of what I do is older than that. His Highness takes Olver's work seriously, but I would find a woman who is a fire mage more convincing than any number of arguments about basis stars and the like."

As he spoke the servants brought in the third course and the mage returned to the serious business of eating. He was a water mage and a strong one, unveiled but, like all of the Prince's mages, with protective spells of some sort on him. The servant pouring the wine too was a mage; she wondered if he was a specialist in potions, poisons, and similar difficulties.

Finally Wilham finished the serving of mortress on his plate, took a last sip from his goblet, reached over for one of the candlesticks on the table, pulled it closer, snuffed out the flame. He turned back to Ellen: "Show me."

She looked at the candle; nothing happened. After a few seconds she turned back to the water mage, the puzzled expression fading from her face. "You are damping it."

He gave no reply, turned to the Prince, who had been watching both intently. "It worked."

Prince Kieron stood up, spoke quietly to Coelus: "The situation is not as simple as I made it sound. The two of you had best come with me."

He led them out of the dining room. Wilham followed, still holding his wine cup. Outside the door two more mages joined them. The Prince climbed the stair, went through the middle door into the small dining room where he had spoken with Ellen a month earlier, gestured them to two of the seats around a small table. Wilham took a seat between the table and the door, still holding the cup; the other two mages remained near the door, standing. The Prince walked once around the table speaking words too softly for the others to hear, sat down. "We are now private."

He waited a moment; the other two said nothing.

"Iolen fooled me. He sent His Majesty a request for a hearing, knowing that I would insist on delaying it until I could learn what he had been up to here. He then instructed his servants that he was not seeing visitors. As soon as I left the capital to come here he left heading north, alone. His Majesty sent orders to Northpass Keep to stop him, but he has a two day start, a fast horse, a courier's pass for remounts and, I expect, a fair amount of gold. Once through the pass he's on Forsting soil, with a considerable army between him and us. If he wants he can even pick up his wife and son on the way; they're with Earl Eirick, her father, a day's travel west of the pass.

"Iolen wanted to use the Cascade to make himself king; he never said so, not even to his own people, but it's clear enough. He bribed his way to the mages who helped Maridon, tricked them into revealing all they knew about the Cascade, and tried to get you to give him your new version of the schema. That was where his plan broke down. He thought you were working for me and that all he had to do was pretend that he was working for me too."

Coelus nodded. "I did not give it to him for the same reason I would not give it to you."

"Yes. A week ago I was willing to accept that. A week hence, Iolen will be in Forstmark and everything he knows about the Cascade will be on its way to whatever mage the Forstings think can best reconstruct your work. That means that I need the Cascade now. The royal mages have implemented your protective schema, so His Majesty is for the moment safe, but there is no way we can hold Northpass or the Keep if the Forstings have all the magic on their side."

"And if I still refuse?"

"Do you? I think I have made it clear what is at stake."

Coelus held his voice steady. "I will be happy to work on designing further defenses against the Cascade, perhaps even a way of making it impossible. No more."

The Prince shook his head. "That no longer suffices; we do

not have time to try to work out something new. If you will not give me what I require to defend the kingdom willingly, I will take it by force."

He hesitated, but only for a moment. "You know how to make the Cascade work and I am willing to gamble your lady knows it as well; you have made it clear enough that she had been working with you. There are ways of forcing knowledge from a mind, even a mage's mind. Dangerous ways, sometimes fatal, but they exist, and they usually work. If you refuse to tell us what you know, I will use them on her; I regret the necessity, but it exists.

He turned to Ellen. "I did warn you, in this room the last time we spoke."

"You did."

"And you warned me; I took my precautions accordingly. An hour ago you held all our lives in your hand; I know what an angry fire mage can do. Wilham is the strongest water mage I know and you are now linked to him, your talent cancelled by his."

"The business with the wine cup?"

The Prince nodded. "We arranged matters so you both drank from the same cup, one after the other, water and burnt wine mixed. Part of the spell."

Coelus finally spoke. "And if neither of us knows how to make the Cascade safe, will you destroy us both trying to tear the information from us?"

"If neither of you knows the solution you have only to tell me so; one of my men at the door is a truth teller."

Coelus opened his mouth, closed it again, said nothing.

"You have until morning to make your decision. Until then Wilham will keep your lady company. No harm will come to her tonight."

* * *

Ellen waited until the mage in the other bed was asleep, judged at least by his breathing. Eyes closed, she let her mind explore the room. Iron bracelets were riveted about her wrists, the chain between them wrapped once around the oak plank that joined the bed posts. Enough slack to lie comfortably but no more. The key to the iron lock to the bracelet around her right wrist was not in the room; she had seen it leave with the Prince. The cup…

Outside the room two guards, two more by the inn door, a mage with them. The Prince was being careful.

She moved her perception to the other bed; Wilham was indeed soundly asleep, his head beside the pillow. Everything in the inn was quiet save for a faint murmur of voices from the guards by the door. One step at a time. Shadows, at least, there was no shortage of. She wove them carefully about the head of the sleeping mage, that nothing she did would wake him.

Next the chain. Too strong to break, and she could get no hold on the mechanism, shielded as it was by the iron case of the lock. The bed then; the frame was held together by glue and the tension from the rope mesh that supported the mattress. She felt her way into one of the sockets, into the linked fabric of glue and wood, unwove it.

When she had finished with the glue joints she eased herself out of the bed, shifting her weight from the mattress and the rope mesh beneath it to one of the side boards of the frame. She wrapped both hands around one of the head posts of the bed, set her feet against the other, pushed the two apart with all her strength. For a moment nothing happened. Again. The far post moved. Another inch and she was just able to ease the end of the plank she was fastened to out of its socket.

Once free of the bed, she slid the plank back into its socket, pulled the bed posts back together and rewove the glue; the Prince might as well have a puzzle to occupy his time. Wilham still slept. She crossed the room silently, slid her hand under his pillow and drew out the wine cup, wrapped in a silk cloth. Clay not metal, but with at least five men awake in the inn, noise would be a problem.

She felt a touch of cool air and looked up; the shutter was open a crack. She slipped to the window, swung it wide, unwrapped the cup, and threw it as hard as she could. It shattered on the stone flags of the inn courtyard. One of the guards at the front door of the inn said something; a moment later she heard the door opening and voices in the courtyard.

The guards at the door heard footsteps coming up the stairs, and abruptly came to attention as their commander came into sight.

"Any problem in the room?"

"No sir. What's happening?"

"Someone in the courtyard; I sent Hermann to check it out. But just to be sure..."

He opened the door quietly, looked in. Both beds were occupied, mage and lady prisoner sound asleep. He eased the door closed again.

Once the guard captain had gone, Ellen went back to work. When she was done her bed sheets were gone and in their place was a long rope of tightly braided linen. She tied one end to a foot of Wilham's bed; he should be easily heavy enough. The other end of the rope went out the window; Ellen followed it. The rope tightened with her weight, then loosened, shook itself, and came free from the foot of the bed. A few moments later Ellen was standing in the courtyard hidden in the shadow of the inn wall, the rope coiled at her feet. She pulled shadow as a cloak around her, paused to be sure nobody had seen her escape, then set off for the jeweler's shop.

Once safely inside she went to the large casting furnace at the back of the workroom—the small furnace had gone with its owner and contents. The lid came off easily; under it was a layer of fire bricks, under that a collection of flat wooden chests. The second of them contained jeweler's files; she set to work with them on the iron bracelets chaining her wrists.

* * *

Coelus looked around the small stable, one of the inn's outbuildings hastily converted into a cell for his benefit. The mage sitting in the other chair gestured at the empty bed. "I don't know what His Highness wants of you and don't want to know, but most things are easier with a night's sleep."

Coelus shook his head, said nothing. If there was something he could do to escape, he could not see it. Unless Durilil came back, which seemed unlikely, or his daughter found a way out of the trap they were in. The Prince had made one mistake that Coelus could see—he had once made the same mistake himself—but he doubted that it would be enough.

Rorik, the mage guarding him, was surely both stronger and more skilled in the application of magic than he—at least applied to situations like this. Inventing spells was a useful skill, but he was used to taking weeks to do it, not hours or minutes. No doubt there was some spell ideal for the circumstances. No doubt he would come up with it a week too late.

Absent force or guile to use against the Prince, what about persuasion? Ellen did not, after all, know how to construct the Cascade. The Prince's truthtellers would vouch for it if she said so. But then there would be more questions. Whether she knew what had gone wrong, first with Maridon and then with Fieras. That knowledge, forced from her, could cost her father's secret as well as his.

It occurred to Coelus that he had one advantage in any conflict with the Prince's people; they could restrain him but could not risk any serious injury. No doubt His Highness had made that clear.

Looking down, Coelus noted a tiny dust devil swirling a foot from his chair, recognized it for his own absent minded work. Fire was good for killing people; how could air be used? He gradually eased the miniature whirlwind along without looking at it until it was spinning a few feet behind his guard's back. The floor of the stable was dirt, dried dirt was dust. Dust…

It took most of five minutes to sweep enough dust into the whirlwind, now a good deal less miniature. Coelus stood up.

"I suppose you are right; I'm for bed." He took two steps towards the bed and the door behind it, spoke a Word, bolted for the door. He heard a crash behind him as Rorik pitched over his bed and down.

The door was closed but unbarred; Coelus pushed it open, stepped into the darkened courtyard, and collided with a large, solid figure. Effortlessly, the guard picked the mage up, carried him back into the stable and held him firmly until Rorik, face dripping, returned with his eyes cleared of dust.

Coelus spent the next hour in bed pretending to sleep, feeling through memory for voices and words while Rorik, his chair pulled back into a corner, watched him. It took two hours more to assemble the pattern of voices, spells, and acts, occasionally mumbling sleepily to himself. The first few times, Rorik came over to the bed to listen, returning to his chair only as Coelus fell silent.

Outside the door the air began to move. The faint moonlight would have shown a watcher, had there been one, a spiral of dust and straw, its top knee-high to the silent guard whose eyes were fixed on the door. The baby cyclone drifted across the yard, picking up air and force from gusts of wind blowing past the corners of the outbuildings, straw from the ground, more as it passed over a half-full manger, growing. It was a column of whirling straw nearly twelve feet high when its foot touched the guard's lantern, caught fire.

Rorik heard footsteps outside, a clamor of voices, then one he knew, the Prince's, pitched as in speech but loud as a shout. "Fire. A Fire mage."

By the sound of it, one of the horses must have taken fright. Men were yelling. The Prince's voice was heard again, lower, from just outside the door: "You had best come with me."

Rorik glanced at the figure on the bed, spoke three Words, made a twisting gesture, and went to the door. The Prince was out of sight, but the cause of the commotion was clear enough, a towering figure of flame twice a man's height moving about the inn courtyard. He stood frozen for a moment. The sound of the Prince's voice from the far side of the figure sent him off around the courtyard in search of it.

Coelus tried to throw off the blanket; nothing happened. His arm was limp against his chest, his muscles like water. He took a deep breath; his torso at least was still his, and his voice. A wriggle and twist got him to the edge of the bed, to the floor in a tangle of blankets. With luck, with the mage who cast the spell gone, the shock would be enough. He made it to hands and knees but no farther, and in a moment collapsed back onto the ground.

Water. The words of Rorik's spell; Coelus reached back through his memory. Water and weakness. The fourth counterspell he tried worked; this time he made it to his feet. The other mage's cloak and hood, both of dark wool, were on the back of his chair; in a moment Coelus had them on and was out of his cell into the chaos of the courtyard, whipping more wind into the burning column of straw.

The back door of the inn opened, a tall figure against the fire-lit room. This time it was the Prince's real voice, lifted in a yell; Coelus filed it in his memory for future use.

"The fire mage is out. Ward as best you can."

Behind the Prince a second figure. Coelus discerned Wilham's voice, words in the true speech, moving hands.

The burning whirlwind went out—where it had been was a column of steam that a puff of wind blew away from the inn door. Shadowed by its spreading fog, Coelus darted for the nearest passage between two outbuildings. In a moment he was in the street beyond.

"Get rid of the cloak; they may be able to track it."

Coelus spun around, saw nothing, reached out, gathered Ellen into his arms.

Chapter 21

An hour north of town, the two mages stopped to rest their stolen horses in the shelter of a grove of trees just off the royal road. When they had dismounted, Coelus gave Ellen a long hug. "I was afraid I was going to lose you."

Barely visible in the thin moonlight, she shook her head. "Never. Who would you talk to?"

"That too. But I am afraid we may be making a mistake."

She looked up at him curiously. "In running from the Prince?"

"No. In running to your parents.

"I have been listening for pursuit and thinking about what the Prince will do. Chasing us would be risky; he can't afford to kill us and he has no way of knowing how willing you are to kill him or his people. Nor does he know what our limits are, especially after tonight. If I were the Prince I would have people following us, far enough away so that we wouldn't spot them; he may have someone whose perception is even better than yours. Once he knows where we have taken refuge he can recapture us at his leisure with as many of his people as he thinks he needs."

Ellen looked unconvinced. "Can he afford to take that long?"

"After what happened tonight, I think he will take as long as he thinks necessary. While he is looking for us he can have another team recreating the first Cascade, the way Iolen did, by trying to work out what went wrong. They do not have to know exactly what the problem was. I didn't. My best guess was that Maridon had tapped the sun, but I think the solution I came up with would have worked. Whoever is doing it only has to realize that there is some enormous source of fire out there to be tapped, then figure out how not to take too much of it."

"What should we be doing, then?" Ellen spoke softly, but he could hear the note of worry in her voice.

"Your woven protection, the one that makes you invisible to perception. That's part of the answer."

"And if His Highness's mage spots two horses galloping side by side along the highway with nobody riding them?"

"Is there any reason you can't weave it around the horses too?"

There was a long silence before she spoke. "Have I ever mentioned that sometimes I am very stupid?"

He shook his head. "I don't think so. One more thing we have in common."

After another hour of riding Ellen led them off the Royal Road on a track that ran east, through a patchwork of field and forest. Before dawn she found a haystack in a field with no farmhouse in sight and a convenient stream where they could water the horses. The horses tethered to a nearby oak, the two mages burrowed into the haystack. Coelus forced his eyes open to put a final question. "If someone happens to come by and sees two unguarded horses do we get to walk the rest of the way?"

"Nobody is likely to see the horses unless he stumbles over them. I can't put a shadow cloak on them, or on you for that matter, but I wove protections into their manes that should make them hard to notice. Go to sleep."

He half woke at noon, reached out, felt the reassuring solidity of Ellen beside him, fell back into a pleasant dream. It was mid afternoon when he reached out again, felt nothing, and came abruptly awake. He struggled clear of the hay, looked around. The horses were gone. A moment's panic before he heard splashing from the direction of the creek.

When Ellen came back, leading both horses, her hair was dripping, her tunic damp; she stood in the sun steaming while she combed out her hair. Coelus watched for a moment before turning to the horses' gear, mostly hung up over branches the night before. The first saddle bag he checked turned out to contain courier's rations, dried fruit, meat and twice baked bread.

"I suppose the horses were waiting in case His Highness needed to send a message somewhere in a hurry."

Ellen nodded. "That was my guess when I spotted them and the groom. If nobody noticed where he was lying and woke him they may not have found out until morning. I have looked over horses and gear and I cannot find any spells on them other than mine."

At nightfall the two stopped again, this time in a forest with neither farm nor haystack in sight. The horses were unsaddled and tethered a little way off the road, rubbed down with cloths from the saddlebags. When they were done, Ellen reached into her saddlebag and pulled out a heavy roll of fabric. "Last time I came this way I put up in farm houses, but I don't want to risk word getting back to His Highness. So while you were sleeping like a log this afternoon, I was working."

She shook it out, a yellow cloth thick as a quilt; he examined it curiously. "Straw?"

She nodded. "It won't be missed, but I'll do something for the farmer in payment next time I come by."

They made their bed under a tall pine from a pile of needles it had dropped that spring, with half the width of the cloth under them, the other half over. It was deep night when Coelus woke with Ellen sleeping quietly in his arms, her head against his chest. He lay watching the stars, listening to the soft sound of her breathing, before he fell back to sleep himself.

The next morning, several miles farther along, Ellen was roused from her thoughts by Coelus' voice: "You are going the wrong way."

She brought the horse to a stop at the left hand side of the fork. He had taken the right and was now sitting atop his horse impatiently waiting for her to join him.

"How do you know which is the right way? You have never been here before," she said.

His expression shifted from impatient to puzzled. "I don't know; this just feels right."

She nodded, thought a moment. "Close your eyes and think through your favorite song, words and music; just let your horse follow mine."

"I don't have a favorite song; I can't sing. Will reciting the beginning of the First Treatise do?"

"Admirably."

In a few minutes she told him to open his eyes; he looked around curiously. "What was that about?"

"Why you need me to find Mother; she has the house warded against mages. It does not affect anyone else, but there are two or three forks where a mage will go the wrong way. I am so used to ignoring them that I forgot you weren't."

It was late morning when Ellen finally turned her horse off

the track; the path she followed led past an ancient oak and into a farmyard. The farmer waved. Ellen slid off her horse, walked it over to him; Coelus, after a moment's hesitation, did the same.

"Back for the summer art thou, Miss Ellen?"

"Indeed, and a friend come with me to visit. Dan, this be my friend Coelus; Coelus, old Dan, who taught me to ride back when I needed a long ladder to reach the horse's back."

The farmer looked Coelus over carefully, finally nodded to him, turned back to Ellen.

"Expect thy ma'll be pleased then."

Ellen nodded.

"Expect she will. Canst board our horses? 'Twill be for longer than t'winter past."

"In the back pasture, with thy old pa's pack mule. I'll rub them down for thee; thy ma will be hot to see thee I make no doubt."

"Father is back?" Ellen was unsaddling her horse as she spoke.

"Four days back, thou'lt not call me a liar if 'twas five. Doubt not he'll be glad t' see thee as well."

When both mounts had been stripped of saddle, saddle cloth, bridle and saddle bags she let the farmer lead them off, hoisted her saddle bags onto her shoulders, set off back to the road, Coelus following with his saddle bags.

Another half hour brought them into the main and only street of a small village. Ellen led Coelus to one of the larger houses, surrounded by a less than orderly planting. Much of it was blue flax mostly blown, but some of the other colors were still bright. She stopped at the door, hesitating a moment. From inside came a cheerful voice.

"Come in love, and your friend too."

They went in. The speaker was a small woman sitting by a loom, a length of cloth half woven on it. Her hair was grey, face wrinkled. She rose, stepping around her loom, dodged a chair and a small table and caught up her daughter in a hug. Kissing both cheeks, she let go of her to turn to her companion.

"And this is the young man you have told me about? You are most welcome, learned sir, and more welcome if I can persuade you to explain a few things I could not get clear from my daughter's account."

Coelus eyed her uncertainly. "I will be happy to do what I can. What sorts of things?"

"Basis stars, mostly. Why we think there are only a fixed number and what you base your guess on about what that number is. Also concerning the elementals, or more precisely the pure forms, whether the elementals and the naturals and the rest can all exist at once, or if making one set declare themselves reduces the others to mere potentials. If the Salamander and the sylph are real, does that mean that the web and the warmth are not? Also ..."

Ellen interrupted.

"If you do not mind, Mother, we have more urgent matters to talk with you and Father about first. I will be happy to turn Coelus over to your tender mercies thereafter."

Melia turned back to her daughter.

"You mean the Prince? As your father will be delighted to report, His Highness is energetically searching the College and the village for you. So you should be safe enough here. His opinion of your abilities has been growing rapidly the past two days, although I expect he gives some of the credit to the learned magister here."

"But we left the village two days ago."

"I know that and you know that, but fortunately the Prince does not." The voice from the other side of the door was Ellen's father; a moment later he came through it. His hair was grey, his voice vigorous.

Ellen gave him a look of mingled affection and irritation.

"I am sure you have been very clever, father. Do you mind telling us just how?"

"Not at all, love. But I would rather do it sitting if you don't mind."

He sat down on a chest at one side of the doorway; Melia returned to her chair. Ellen pulled a second chair out of a corner for Coelus, sat down on a stool, and gave her father an inquiring look.

"Two days ago, the morning after you left His Highness's hospitality, a messenger arrived for me from an old friend of ours in the capital. He hardly gets out nowadays but he is still well connected. He had heard that Lord Iolen had taken off north for the Forsting border with His Majesty's men in hot pursuit. His Highness, oddly enough, had gone east instead, with a substantial contingent. He thought I would be interested, so sent someone he trusts a three day ride with the news.

"There was only one thing I could think of worth his Highness's attention in the east." Durilil nodded towards Coelus. "It took me a couple of hours of peering through various fires to see what had happened. Kieron has enough mages with him to run the Cascade and enough information about your first attempt to try to copy it. If he doesn't yet have a competent theorist to work on improving the schema, I expect he can find one." He looked up at Coelus; Coelus said nothing, only nodded. Durilil continued:

"The four of us should be able to work our way through your present puzzle; Olver's messenger brought some suggestions that might help. But we are not going to do it overnight, so I thought it prudent to slow things down a little."

"How?" That was Ellen. Her father smiled.

"At noon on the day after Kieron's little feast, every scrap of paper he and his people had with them caught fire and burned to ash. When they went to the College to arrange to run the Cascade inside the protective sphere, they couldn't get in; Magister gatekeeper could not or would not open the sphere for them. That night they all had a cold dinner because nobody in the inn could get a fire to light."

"Wasn't that risky, father? Once they found out it was being done by someone from miles away?"

Ellen stopped speaking, her face lost its puzzled expression. "Oh. I think I see."

"More important, His Highness saw. He saw a fire mage of unknown abilities vanish from a guarded room after he had taken care to neutralize her power and chain her to the bed. And a second mage, one original enough to have contrived a spell that had been absorbing most of the Prince's attention, vanished at the same time under circumstances strongly suggesting the use of powerful fire magic. At some point I want an account of how both of you did it. But not just now.

"If two mages with unknown powers had vanished an hour's

ride out of the village and things suddenly started to go awry in the village itself in a mysterious, incendiary fashion, it was obvious who must be responsible. If they could do magic in the village they had to be in the village or at least close. So there was no point in searching for them elsewhere.

"That's why the Prince's people have been tearing the village and the adjacent countryside apart looking for you. They would be tearing the College apart, too, if they could get in. The Prince, I suspect, has been racking his brains trying to figure out in what ingenious place and by the use of what exotic magic you could be hiding. The busier he is at that, the less time he has to spend on other things we don't want done."

Durilil sat back, looking distinctly self-satisfied.

Chapter 22

"I have at least a little good news, Highness."

Kieron, looking rather the worse for wear after two nights of little sleep, glanced up from his breakfast table at Alayn, a chunk of bread in one hand. "That being?"

"The College is no longer sealed. One of their servants came out this morning; Johan went in and asked after Magister Coelus. He hasn't been in the College for days. Should we search it?"

The Prince shook his head. "The only reason to think Coelus was there was that we couldn't enter; if it is now open, he isn't there. And my last attempt to get his cooperation was not so successful that I'm eager to try again. We are doing more harm here than good. The more we search for Coelus and his lady fire mage, the more likely others are to notice and draw conclusions."

"Does it matter, Highness? Your secret is on its way to Forstmark with Lord Iolen. The odds are a hundred to one against stopping him."

"The situation is bad, but perhaps not as bad as it seems. Running away to Forstmark is better than being beheaded for treason, which is the direction my unfortunate nephew seemed headed. But allying with the Forstings carries its own problems.

"Suppose he tells the Forsting Einvald all he knows about Magister Coelus's spell. First the Einvald has to decide to believe him. Then he has to decide to reward Iolen instead of cutting his throat to make sure he does not try to resell the information to someone else. And then the Einvald has to decide what to do with the spell."

"Isn't it obvious?" Alayn said, sounding puzzled. "The spell would give them a huge advantage in any magical conflict. They have been getting up the nerve to attack us for the past two years. Wouldn't this settle the matter?"

The Prince shook his head. "The spell gives huge power to one mage. The Einvald of Forstmark isn't a mage, any more than my brother is. He seized power four or five years ago; half the reason for all the war talk is to deter a fresh challenger any time soon. Where can he find a mage he can trust not to seize power either for himself or to install a puppet? It is not as if the Mage's Guild was under the Einvald's control or even solidly in his faction. If I were him and Lord Iolen showed up at my door, I would learn what I could from him, tell no-one, then have Iolen discreetly disposed of. Perhaps Iolen is counting for his protection on being of some use to them as a pretender to our throne, but ..."

"Surely Your Highness has considered that Iolen anticipates all this? If you were Iolen ..."

"If I were Iolen, I would consider presenting myself to the Einvald as a royal pretender to the throne of Esland while saying nothing about mage secrets. If the Forstings invade and install him as their puppet, he can surely find an opportunity to use the spell himself. If they continue to threaten without going to war, he might establish himself well enough to explore the spell on their side of the border. As a pretender, he is more useful to the Einvald alive than dead."

"Unfortunately we cannot get this wise advice to your Highness's nephew."

"That is one of the reasons why I would like to have the spell myself. Perhaps there is some compromise or some guarantee Magister Coelus would be willing to accept in exchange for its secret. But he is not here, and he is a stubborn man."

"If Your Highness wishes to communicate with Magister Coelus, I can think of at least two ways of trying."

The Prince looked at his guard commander curiously. "I did not realize that you too had become adept in new spells."

"Those I leave to Your Highness and the other mages; I was thinking of more mundane solutions. The simplest is to leave a message for him in the College; once we leave, he will probably return to his post and his duties."

"And your other solution?"

"The Lady Mari. Give her a message to pass on to her friend, who can pass it on to her companion. The students will in due time return to the college, and Magister Coelus' incendiary lady is also a student."

* * *

Ellen surveyed her old room, hers again with the beginning of fall term. The bed was made; someone had put fresh ink in the desk's inkwell. Several codices were missing, most notably her private copy of Olver's treatise; presumably Iolen's people had taken them in their search for clues to the workings of the Cascade.

There was a knock on the door. She looked up.

"Come in."

Mari entered in traveling garb carrying a cloth wrapped package that she set down on the desk.

"His Highness wouldn't tell me anything, but he did give me this and a message for you."

She handed Ellen a tightly rolled scroll. Ellen glanced at the seal, put it in a drawer of her desk, and looked back at her friend.

"And how was your summer?"

"Not as exciting as yours. I hope whatever you did to him has not permanently frightened Kieron off lady mages."

"Has it? You should be the first to know."

"Not that I can see. He and Father had to deal with problems up north and we traveled together, so we saw a good deal of each other. Two days after we got back Jon showed up with your message and Kieron took off for the College. He paid us a visit when he came back. He was in an odd mood, as if he wasn't sure if he should be disappointed or glad."

Ellen considered the virtues of silence, its cost, decided against. "His Highness tried to force me and Magister Coelus to do something we thought ought not to be done. He threatened me to persuade Coelus. We departed without his leave."

Mari looked concerned. "I see. That explains both his disappointment and his relief."

Ellen nodded. "Yes. I do not think Kieron is a bad man, but he is too used to having his way."

"A fault, but perhaps not incurable. And how is Magister Coelus?"

"I took him home to Mother. Between teaching her theory and learning about weaving magic from her, I fear he got very little rest. He now plans to persuade his colleagues that since women students have talents neither the magisters nor the tutors are competent to train, they need to recruit women tutors."

"Witches as tutors? That will take some persuasion."

Ellen nodded. "Diplomacy is not among Coelus' talents. Since his arguments are correct, the rest must of course accept them."

Mari pointed at the package she had brought. "Aren't you going to open it?"

Ellen looked the package over carefully before unwrapping the cloth. It contained two bound codices, a thin stack of paper covered with neat writing, and a note which she read, smiling.

"Iolen made off with some things of mine. His Highness is returning them."

After Mari had left, Ellen took the scroll out of her desk, broke the seal, unrolled the paper, and watched with only mild surprise as the writing, once read, faded away. A few minutes later she was in Magister Coelus's office. "Mari is back, and she brought me a message from His Highness."

"One for me as well. What did yours say?"

"A qualified apology, a promise of good behavior in the future, and a brief description of his plans. He thinks Iolen hasn't told his hosts about the Cascade and will hold it in reserve against future opportunities. His Highness won't use it now, does intend to be able to if necessary. Do you think he can manage it successfully?"

Coelus nodded. "Yes. He's got Hewry working for him now, one of my students from a few years back. Hew is competent enough, if a bit slow, and I expect he can produce a version of the schema that will work tolerably well. His Highness would still have to find someone he trusts enough to control the spell."

Ellen shook her head.

"If His Highness does the Cascade, I expect he will be the focus. He can trust himself."

"And His Majesty?"

"His Majesty trusts Kieron absolutely. According to Mari, during the succession troubles King Thoma was willing to support Kieron instead of Josep. The King wanted anyone but his eldest son and Kieron was more popular with the lords. Kieron ignored his father's hints as long as he could, then left court. When the King finally moved against Petrus, Kieron hid his brother until their father finished dying, then helped him deal with Josep and his supporters.

"Kieron is the one mage His Majesty can trust. If the situation is bad enough to require the Cascade, it will be with Kieron at focus."

They were silent for a few minutes, thinking; at last Coelus spoke. "I doubt that anyone will do the Cascade in the immediate future. But eventually someone, Kieron or Iolen, will. That means we have to find a way of blocking it first.

"It comes down to two problems: how to protect someone against being pulled into the Cascade well enough so that more magery will be needed to pull him in than can be pulled out of him, making the Cascade converge. I think we know how to do that. Then, how to spread that to enough people to keep the Cascade from working."

Ellen cut in: "Would it be enough to protect only the mages? Once other people are in the pool they contribute, but in the initial stage do they yield as much as it costs to pull them in?"

Coelus shook his head. "No. Good point. In my original design, surplus from the mages pulled other people in. Most would not get pulled in until after all the mages were in the pool. So we only have to protect the mages. But I still do not see how we are going to do it."

"Can we design the protective spell so that it spreads? Put a bubble around one mage and gradually draw enough power from him to put another bubble around a second mage—the same principle as the Cascade?"

Coelus considered the idea briefly.

"The Cascade pours its power into the pool; the mage at focus uses that power to pull in more people. The bubbles we designed are pretty simple; what you are proposing is much more elaborate, a static spell that could cascade itself. I do not see how to do it, and if I did I would worry about what else could be done with it."

Ellen got up. "It's late; we won't solve the problem tonight."

"No. But we have to solve it soon. The first half we can do, but we want to do it better. Somehow we need not only to make the Cascade converge but let the bubbles get thicker over time, using some of the power the Cascade is pulling out of protected mages, so that eventually the mages that were pulled into the Cascade drop out again. Otherwise, even if the Cascade converges ..."

Ellen finished his thought. "Even if it converges, the mages in the pool gradually recover their magic. If they have enough time they can do another round, and another, and gradually spread the pool. I do not know what the limit is to how long one person can hold the focus or whether once the pool is well established the first focus could pass it on to someone else. You are right. We need to design a better bubble. But not tonight."

* * *

The next day Ellen and Mari took lunch into the orchard, joined by Alys, who put her first question to Mari while sitting down. "What is the Prince like? Set a date for the wedding yet?"

Mari looked amused. "What wedding, Alys? Are you marrying someone?"

Alys, undeterred, shook her head. "Not me, you. Everyone says that Prince Kieron is going to marry you."

"Then everyone is better informed on the subject than I am."

"But you spent the whole summer with him, didn't you?"

"I spent the summer with my father. For the early part of it His Highness guested with us at Northpass Keep, where he and my father were inspecting its defenses."

Alys grinned. "I'm told that His Highness is very handsome. No doubt defenses were the sole topic discussed." Over her shoulder Mari saw Jon and Edwin come into the orchard, headed in their direction. As they sat down, Alys tried again, this time with Ellen.

"You have to tell me all about it, the Prince and Lord Iolen and everything. Did Magister Coelus really get a spell wrong and go crazy? I saw he was back; are you sure it is safe to have him for your tutor?"

Ellen said nothing. Mari looked up at the curve of the containment dome, glowing with dispersed sunlight.

"Nice weather we are having, isn't it?"

Edwin sat down on the other side of Mari and Ellen from Alys. "I heard from one of the grooms on the coach that both the Prince and Lord Iolen were in the village this summer and there was a lot of commotion. There seem to be six or seven different stories about what was happening. I hoped somebody in the College could tell me which one was true. Were any of you here then?"

"You say Lord Iolen was here? In the College?"

The speaker was a stranger, a large young man, well dressed.

Alys looked up at him, patted the grass at her side. "Come join us. Ellen and Mari usually know everything; I'm trying to get them to tell and could use some help. Do you know Lord Iolen?"

"You are welcome to join us," said Ellen. "We're all friends from last year; are you new here?"

"Not new. I was here year before last but took last year off. Now I'm back, most of my friends have graduated, and it feels like one of those dreams where you are walking through the courtyard into your own hall and all the faces have changed. My name is Anders."

The group introduced themselves. "You might want to fetch some food from the refectory if you're hungry. As you can see, we have moved our lunch outside."

Anders sat down between Alys and Ellen. "Thank you. I had lunch early, but would be happy to join your conversation. Was Lord Iolen here?"

Ellen nodded. "He spent several days in the village this summer. Do you know him?"

"Not exactly know, but I've met him; Father holds from Earl Eirick, and Iolen is married to the Earl's eldest daughter. I know about him, that he ought to be on the throne if he had his rights."

That got Jon's attention. "Why do you think Lord Iolen's claim is better than His Majesty's?"

"Because the old king, Thoma, named Josep, Iolen's father, as his heir. Petrus ended up King only because he and the youngest prince murdered Josep and usurped his throne."

Jon looked puzzled. "But surely Petrus was the older. It's true that King Theodrick chose his heir, but none of his sons were alive, had to choose among the grandsons. Eldest son inherits, or so Gerrit says in his *History of the Kings.* Was just reading it yesterday in the library."

Anders shook his head. "I don't know what the books say, but in the North we have long memories. Ever since Esland broke free from the League and Theodrick reestablished the monarchy, custom has always been election by the great lords from among the royal household. It's true that the eldest son usually gets elected, but King Thoma summoned the Lords and they confirmed his choice of Josep."

Mari looked up. "How many Great Lords make up the

Council?" By her tone, she might have been asking about the weather.

"Forty, I think."

"Yes. And how many were present at the meeting at which King Thoma named Josep as his heir?"

"I don't know, but it doesn't matter; they approved it."

"It doesn't matter? If Thoma invited three of the Great Lords to consult with him and two approved his choice, would that be election according to the ancient customs?"

"Of course not, but it wasn't just three."

"No. Six of the northern lords came to Council at the King's command; five supported his choice. Three came from the court itself, two of whom had had their offices from Thoma's hand. Eight votes out of forty. Learned as you are in custom, does that suffice?" Mari's voice was still calm.

"If it's true that only nine lords came to Council, that's the fault of all the other lords who stayed away. "

Jon interrupted.

"Gerrit's book discusses that, actually. Old custom was election by a majority of the Great Lords, not of whatever lords came to council. Without that, King could control the succession by when and where he called council."

Anders turned back towards Mari. "How do you know how many came, or how they voted? Did you read that in a history book too, or were you there counting?"

Mari shrugged. "The count is my father's. He was one of those not present, being at the other end of the kingdom when His Majesty sent out a summons for a council three days later."

It occurred to Ellen that Anders looked a bit like a bull doing his best to ignore the flies that were biting him.

"Perhaps there wasn't a majority, but it doesn't really matter, because everyone knew that Petrus wasn't really King Thoma's son; that's why the King didn't want him as heir."

Mari's voice was still calm, but with an edge to it:

"Do you know why they say the hyena is the most prudent of beasts?"

"No. Why?" Anders replied.

"Because it waits to attack its prey until it is safely dead. The Queen Dowager Elinor was a formidable lady; it is surely prudent to wait to slander her honor until she is four years in her grave."

For a moment everyone was silent, Mari's face expressionless, Anders' flushing with anger. Jon's voice broke it. "Did you know the library is older than the college?"

For a moment nobody responded, then Ellen picked up on the line. "No. Was it the oldest part of the old monastery?"

Jon shook his head. "I don't mean the building, I mean the collection. When Durilil and Feremund started here, wasn't really a college. Just two mages, their apprentices and a library."

The distraction having succeeded — at least, neither Mari nor Anders had tried to interrupt — Jon continued with growing enthusiasm. "Old days, mages didn't share their spells except with their apprentices. One of the reasons to be an apprentice, so the mage would pass his spells down to you. It was the library here, our library, that changed that.

"Durilil and Feremund wrote all the spells they knew down, made an open offer to every other mage in the kingdom. Any who could tell them a spell they didn't already know got to pick any spell from their collection and learn it. Mage could share a spell didn't think worth much, get the most useful he didn't already know from the collection. Library could use the same spell in trade over and over again; wasn't losing spells, was gaining them."

Edwin cut in. "But wouldn't that mean that the library got mostly minor spells, for banishing horseflies and the like?"

Jon shook his head. "Spell that banished horseflies not minor on a farm. And mage who wanted ten spells, only had eight he didn't mind sharing, might end up offering a couple of his better ones. Idea wasn't to get powerful spells anyway, was to get lots of different spells in hope of figuring out more about magic, how spells were put together."

Ellen nodded. "Then Olver showed up and what he had been looking for was sitting in the library waiting for him. Olver didn't need powerful spells. What he needed were multiple spells doing the same thing in different ways using different talents. If you could banish horseflies with a spell of fire and air and get exactly the same result with a spell built only from heat, that meant that in some fashion heat was fire plus air. How the spell was constructed let you figure out just how the air and fire were put together. Olver started with more than forty multiples — two or more spells that did the same thing in different ways. When he was finished he had the science of magic as we now know it—the different basis stars, the central paradox that any one star spans all of magery, and the rest. That was the first big breakthrough in three hundred years, since the Dorayans worked out the basic principles by trial and error.

"If he had a spell that used warmth he could make one using air and fire, so mages were no longer limited to using only spells that fit their particular talents. Jon is right; the library came first. The theory of magic was built on the library; the College was built on the theory of magic. The talented came here because it was the only place in the world where they could learn not only what worked but why."

Edwin looked over at Anders, listening intently. "Welcome to Ellen's noontime seminar. But one thing is still missing; we do, after all, have our traditions. Mari?"

Mari reached into her wallet, removed a small wheel of cheese covered in wax, cut a slice and held it out to Jon. He took it. She cut more pieces for each of the others, finally a last piece that she offered to Anders.

He looked at her uncertainly.

"Take it. I should not have spoken so harshly; you were only repeating what you have been told. I don't suppose you ever met Elinor, so how could you know how impossible that old slander was to anyone who knew her?"

Anders hesitated a moment, then reached out, took the slice.

* * *

"Will Lady Mari be coming to visit again?"

Prince Kieron looked up from his book, struck by the tone more than the words; it was not an idle question.

"Not soon. She has resumed her studies at the College. It is a long day by horseback, even the way Mari rides, and two days by coach. I doubt we will see her until midwinter break."

"But she will be back?"

"I expect so. She knows she is welcome here. Do you like her?"

Kir nodded. "Yes. She is the only one of the ladies who doesn't bring me sweets."

"You like Mari because she doesn't bring you sweets?"

"They want me to persuade you to marry them. Mari is the only one who treats me like a person, not a pet. I've been teaching her chess and she has been telling me about magic. She is very nice."

Kieron waited a moment, was about to return to his book, when Kir spoke again. "Are you going to marry her?"

Kieron's first thought was his usual noncommittal answer. But there was no one, with the possible exception of his brother the King, with a better right to the truth. "Do you want me to?"

Kir nodded. "Then she would be here all the time. And she's much nicer than … I think Mother would have liked her."

Kieron reached out, pulled his son into his lap — at ten Kir still fit comfortably — hugged him, the boy's head against his father's shoulder. "I intend to ask Mari to marry me when she is home for midwinter. I think she will say yes, but that is her decision and her father's, not mine."

Chapter 23

"I have found a solution to the second half of our problem. Or, more precisely, you have," Coelus announced. His face was aglow. Ellen closed the door of his office and took a chair.

"The first half of the problem," he continued, "is how to shield someone against the Cascade. We have solved it, and I have an idea for an improvement, a way of diverting the magery tapped for the Cascade to strengthen the barrier around the individual mage. When it gets strong enough to cut off the flow, he drops out of the pool. Once I write it out in full I will show it to you and you can poke holes in it.

"The other half is how to get enough power to protect everyone. It occurred to me last night that you gave me the answer to that almost a year ago."

Ellen looked puzzled. "That was before we started working on the problem."

"You were solving a different problem at the time. One of those I set you."

He stopped, waited; enlightenment took only a few seconds.

"The elementals."

Coelus nodded. "The elementals. You pointed out some of the things one could do if only one had use of one or more elementals. Now we do."

"Only one."

"One is enough. We need a pool that spans all of magery, which means all four elements. We can get that with four mages plus a fifth at focus—just like the Cascade. We can also get it ..."

"With four mages and an elemental; of course. Unlimited power, even if only in one element. If we design the spell to ... I don't see why it wouldn't work, but I will have to consult with Father; he knows more about the practical end of that problem than we do. And he probably has to be the focus. Who do we get for the other mages?"

Coelus thought a moment. "We need earth and water. The problem is finding ones we can trust who will be willing to help. You might think about whether any of the second or third year students are possibles; you probably know them better than I do. And we will have to be careful; if the Prince hears about it..."

"How will he know what we are doing?"

"He won't. But if he knows we are trying to put together an elemental star of mages, he will conclude that we plan to do the Cascade and use it somehow to stop him."

* * *

"If it comes to a vote, you will lose."

Coelus responded to Hal—the two were alone in the senior common room—in a puzzled tone. "How can I? It's obviously the right thing to do."

"Obvious to you."

"Obvious to anyone. It has always been our policy to provide tutors for all the kinds of magery, up to the bounds of what is permitted. That's why Reymer comes for spring semester, because none of us is a competent truth teller. Healing is magery. Important magery. We have students who want to learn it, so we need a tutor who can teach it. All of the really competent healers are women, so..."

Hal considered, not for the first time, the problem of making the facts of life and their application to academic politics clear to his friend. "You assume that all that anybody cares about is what is true, what arguments are right or wrong. Truth is not the only thing that matters to people."

Coelus shook his head. "Not the only thing. But truth is a means to all other ends. Staying alive might be more important to someone than the truth about how magic works, but how can you know how to stay alive without knowing the truth as to whether the food put before you is poisoned or the horse you plan to ride likely to throw you?"

"What if admitting that truth prevented you from achieving some other end you desired—getting a royal pension on retirement, persuading more parents to send their children here, or being respected by colleagues you value? Olver's view that witchery is merely another application of the laws that govern all magery has only started to spread beyond this College in recent years. Most of the senior mages in the Kingdom and practically all of the people who we hope will send their talented children here grew up with the view that witchery was only a useful craft, magery the noblest of sciences. It makes no more sense to them for us to teach witchery than for a master painter to give lessons to his apprentices in painting barns."

"But the evidence is perfectly clear. Olver made the case nearly forty years ago, and Henneck proved it experimentally twenty years later, and I …"

Hal interrupted him. "And most of the people I am talking about, not to mention a fair number of our colleagues, have never read Olver and would not understand him if they did. Or Henneck. Or you. And besides, once people learn something most of them never unlearn it. If you did manage to persuade our colleagues that, having decided to admit women as students, we now have to hire one as a tutor, they would conclude that the first decision was a mistake. I don't think that's the result you want."

For a moment Coelus was too shocked to answer. "They couldn't. Ellen proves that decision was right; she's the best student we've had since I came here. Easily the best theorist and one of the best applied mages as well. If you don't believe me, ask His Highness."

"I believe you; I am not the one you have to convince. I would be perfectly happy to have a healer here as a tutor, although I am not sure that with only six girls in the second year class there will be enough students to keep her busy."

The puzzled expression had returned to the younger mage's face.

"What does the number of girls have to do with it? You were not assuming that only women would want to learn healing, were you?"

"I was, actually. Was I wrong?"

"Of course," Coelus said. "Part of the point of what Olver taught us is that the same spells can be performed with more than one set of talents; you just have to work out the correspondences and go from there. The average man may not be as well suited to healing as the average woman, but some male mages have talent mixes that would work, and many more could do at least minor healing using reagents to fill in for the missing talents. I did the rough calculations last month, after spending some time with a very accomplished healer; my estimate is that almost a quarter of our students could learn a useful amount of healing—more than what war mages learn now. Of all the kinds of mages, healers are what we need most; think of how many people die each year because the nearest healer is a day's travel away, often more."

"I suspect that hiring a woman to train our male students, whether in healing or anything else, will be even less popular with our more conservative colleagues than hiring a woman to tutor female students. So we still have a problem. To which I think I have a solution."

"Other than forcing our colleagues to agree that two and two make four and that being healed is better than dying?"

"Forcing people to agree to things does not usually work very well.

"On the other hand," Hal continued, "since being healed is better than dying, especially if you are the one who is dying, most of our colleagues would be delighted for the College to have a healer of its own instead of relying on Janis from the village or one of the handful of healing spells we happen to know. Three years ago, as you may remember, Bertram came close to dying before we managed to bring a sufficiently accomplished healer from the Capital to get his heart working properly again. Instead of hiring a healer as a tutor, we should get a healer to move to the village on retainer from the College…

"Once there is a competent healer in the village, there is no good reason why she shouldn't tutor anyone who wants to learn healing. She wouldn't be called a tutor, at least not until more of our colleagues get used to the idea. What she was doing would not count officially as a tutorial, but what matters is what students learn, not what we call it. Your friend Ellen has been teaching some of the other students for the past year; Lady Mariel, at least, refers to their lunches as Ellen's tutorial. It isn't on the College records, but that does not mean nobody is learning anything from it. If she wanted to do the same thing after she graduates…"

Coelus shook his head. "Ellen wouldn't want to set up as a healer; it isn't really what she does. But I know a very accomplished one with the makings of a first rate theorist as well; I only wish the students in my class were as interested in learning what I have to teach as she was. I don't know if I can persuade her to come here, but if I could…"

Hal considered how to put the obvious question tactfully. "It is none of my business, but you don't think Ellen would be uncomfortable if you brought another female mage here? You and she are obviously pretty close."

Coelus shook his head. "I do not think that would be a problem in this case."

* * *

"... and so, with gratitude for Your Grace's kind invitation, I must regretfully decline."

Dur added his signature, put the letter aside to dry. The regret was real enough, even if not, as Mari's mother would assume, for a lost commission. Almost fifty years since he had visited the Northfire and come away with its heart; it would be interesting to see its present condition. And no doubt there would be doings of note in Northpass Keep. As always, it was a temptation to meddle.

Most of a week each way in a coach as Master Dur, a week more in the keep itself, would be difficult and perhaps dangerous. If he was correct about what the Duchess wanted him for, the Prince would be there as well, a further risk. Better not.

But for the Northfire itself, he did not have to send his body; his mind would do. His link with the Salamander was stronger now than then; it should be safe enough. Dur considered the matter for a few minutes more before standing up from the desk and going down to his workshop.

It was nearly an hour later that he finally eased himself free and let the cold world wash back over him. The signs were clear. Something was happening under Fire Mountain that was no work of his. Something he had best deal with.

He would have to write Her Grace another letter.

* * *

A knock on the door; Ellen looked up from the paper on her desk, wondered what Mari could want; in another half hour they would both be at dinner. "Come in."

Mari opened the door, came in, politely averted her eyes from Ellen's unmade bed. Ellen laughed and said, "You have had servants to wait on you all your life; I have never had a servant. So why is it that you manage to keep your bed, and your rooms, so much neater than I do?"

Mari, used to her friend's random curiosity, considered the matter briefly before answering. "You grew up learning to do magic; I grew up learning how to run a household. As my mother pointed out to me long ago, you cannot get servants to do something properly unless you know how to do it yourself. That includes making beds, cooking dinner, sewing, and quite a lot of other things.

"What I wonder," glancing around Ellen's room, "is how you can have both such a messy room and such a tidy mind. But that isn't what I came to ask. Come visit us at Northkeep for Midwinter break. I can offer you my company, as much snow and mountain as you want, and a bath every day — the hot spring is inside the walls."

"A hot spring? Are there volcanoes? I have never seen one."

"One volcano, Fire Mountain; the pass goes by one side of it. But it's dead since long before I was born. An old man in the Keep told me that when he was a child he saw it erupt, but that must have been at least fifty years ago, probably more, assuming he wasn't just repeating a story he had heard. Still, you are welcome to investigate the volcano, as best you can without burning yourself up or freezing to death in the snow.

"And I expect my mother and father would enjoy meeting you. You might find meeting my father useful as well as interesting."

Ellen gave her a puzzled look. "Useful how?"

"Useful if you have to deal with the Prince, or Lord Iolen, or other powerful men. Kingdom politics is a complicated web; the more people you know the less power any one of them has over you. Speaking of which, I should warn you that the Prince will almost certainly be there too; I don't know what terms you and he are on at the moment. And Father asked me to invite Magister Coelus on his behalf, to help him and the Prince figure out what the Forsting mages have been up to all this time."

"It's tempting; let me think about it. Is Northpass Keep where you grew up?"

Mari shook her head. "I grew up in our lands, in the East. The Keep isn't ours; it belongs to His Majesty. Father just takes care of it for him."

"Why your father, and not ..."

"One of the northern lords, such as Earl Eirick? You know the history of the succession troubles, that Anders was talking about the first time we met him?"

"Only the parts you have told me about; I do not think Northpass Keep came into that."

"During the troubles, Father kept as far from court as he could. Anders was right about that part, although I couldn't say so. Father got messages from both sides and ignored all of them. As it happened, the Castellan of Northpass was one of our people in the royal service. Father could see what was going to happen, so while the Princes and His Majesty feuded, he did everything he could to get Northpass Keep ready, spent money repairing the defenses, hired troops, recruited mages. When the Forstings decided we were close enough to a civil war for them to intervene they brought an army over the pass; the Keep refused to surrender so they laid siege to it. After a month they gave up and went home.

"His Majesty, who has more sense than his father did, decided it would be prudent to put that key to the kingdom in the hands of a lord more concerned with protecting Esland than trying to decide who was king. So Father tells His Majesty who he should appoint as Castellan and His Majesty appoints him; His Majesty pays the official garrison and supplies it, and Father provides whatever else he thinks the Keep needs.

"Anders is a fair sample of the Marcher lords. Prince Josep's wife, Iolen's mother, was from the north, and most of her kin supported Josep's claim. Nobody ever found out if the Forstings were coming in on their invitation, but His Majesty garrisons the Keep with his own people, not local levies."

An hour later, at dinner, the question of Northpass and the Forstings came up again, this time raised by Alys. "Isn't it terribly dangerous for you and your family to spend Break there? Everyone says there's going to be another war; if the Forstings invade you could end up trapped. And if they take the Keep..."

Mari failed to react with appropriate horror.

"If they take the Keep, all sorts of terrible things could happen. But to take the Keep in midwinter they first have to learn to fly, which doesn't seem likely. That's why our skirmishes are always in spring or summer; this time of year the pass is ten feet deep in snow and ice. It might be possible to get a few men on snowshoes over Northpass, but not an army. We'll be at least as safe in Northpass Keep as you will be in the capital, probably safer. After all, we have a garrison of loyal soldiers to protect us; you're at the mercy of any passing footpad."

And with that, Mari turned back to her plate.

Chapter 24

"Where do you hide a salamander?"

Durilil, his head resting in his lover's lap, looked up at the face inverted above him, marveled again at his good fortune.

"Why would I want to hide a salamander?"

Melia shook her head.

"Not you. One of the few things we know about the Elementals is that nobody has found one. And if Olver is right... "

"Any decent fire mage should be able to see the thing from ten miles away. Yes."

He thought a moment.

"If I were hiding a salamander, I would hide it in the biggest fire I could find."

He reached up, caught her hand, brought it down to his lips.

Now he was back where the search had led, directly underneath him the trailing skirts of the Northfire, its heart barely ten miles away. From where he lay he could smell sulfur in the air. It was probably why Duke Morgen's residence was on the other side of the keep from the hot spring, bath house, and spare guestroom above it.

Why he was installed there was clear enough; Her Grace, intending him as a surprise for her daughter, wanted him out of sight until the proper time. One of the chests he had brought contained cut gemstones, sample pieces, drawings, paper and pens, everything needed to design the jewels for a royal wedding. Over the next few days, if all went according to Duchess Gianna's plans, the Prince would propose to Mari, Mari would accept, the two would inform her father, and Gianna and Mari would set about planning the details of the wedding. With a jeweler conveniently at hand.

Of course, it might also have occurred to Duchess Gianna that a man of Master Dur's age would be glad of a warm room in winter, despite a bit of sulfur in the air. If so, she was correct. Any room occupied by Master Dur and his luggage was going to be warm, with or without a hot spring underneath it. There was much to be said for a room that people expected to be warm.

Which brought him back to his reason for being there, which had nothing to do with jewelry. Having come this far, he felt an odd temptation to finish the matter once and for all, close the circle. It would be easy enough to put the Salamander back where he had found it, to make the choice the Mage King had made at a still more advanced age. He wondered how the imperturbable Duchess would react to finding an impossibly aged corpse in her guest room bed.

He put the idea firmly aside; he had not come here to die. Not, at least, if he could avoid it. What he planned would require returning the Salamander to the fire's heart, at least for a little while, but if all went well... He could not possibly retrieve it from a distance of ten miles, so he had to go too, if not quite all the way to the fire. It had been a long time, but he thought he could still find the way. If, of course, it was still there.

It was dark outside. The servants, having brought his dinner and cleared away what he left of it, were unlikely to come again. Still, it was best to be safe; Durilil spent several minutes making sure that anyone who came to his door would pass it by. The lid of one of the two traveling chests was warm to his touch. Inside was a leather bag; he put the carrying strap over his shoulder, felt the warmth of the box inside it against his side. That done he wrapped himself in his cloak — he was already dressed in his warmest clothes — and left the room.

* * *

All Johan could see, looking out the postern gate, was snow, lit by the lantern hanging above him. With twenty or thirty miles of snow between Northkeep and the nearest Forstings, it was not entirely clear to Johan why the gate needed guarding. But he knew his duty. At least he could guard the lantern.

Suddenly, the lantern went out. Surely he had filled it before dark; perhaps a gust of wind had somehow gotten through the horn panes. He untied the lantern rope, let it run up through the pulley as the lantern lowered. He unhooked it. The guardroom fire was an entirely illicit charcoal brazier his superior officer, having stood watch himself in past winters, scrupulously failed to notice. It would do to reignite the lantern.

The brazier too was out, its charcoal ash. Laurens must have forgotten to fill it on his watch earlier that evening. Odd. It had been going well enough just a while ago. Johan had warmed his hands over it. There was more charcoal in the corner, a bundle of kindling, flint and steel and tinder in his pouch. In a few minutes the charcoal was again beginning to glow, the lantern relit, Johan again at his post.

Looking back out of the night, Durilil could see the lantern and make out the figure of the guard; the guard, his eyes blinded by the lantern's light, saw nothing but snow.

An hour's walk brought him around the wall and a mile or so towards the pass. The road was bordered by evergreens; Durilil took shelter under one of them to rest. Master Dur was in good shape for his age, but miles of walking, uphill through snow, was not a task for an old man. The box in its leather bag was almost too hot to touch; he let his hand rest on it, fire pouring up through his body.

Some hours later, where the road bent left to find its way through an old lava flow, he stopped, stood for some minutes wrapped in his cloak, eyes closed. Still there, but blocked. He turned off the road, scrambled along the edge of the lava, uphill through the snow. Arrived at his destination he let his mind sink into the stone, felt for fire, found it. Unlimited fire, and nobody within miles to see. For once...

He pointed with his right hand, the other resting on the rune that was the lid of the box; water ran steaming away. Where there had been a bank of unmarked snow was now bare rock, the cave mouth showing clear. The first few feet were half choked with dirt and broken rock where part of the roof had fallen in. His mind filled with fire, he pointed again.

No. Carefully, strand by strand, the mage pulled his mind free from what he carried. Turning broken rock molten might clear the cave, but while the Salamander could take no harm, his own body was flesh and blood. Hands might be slower, but a great deal safer.

It took him an hour to open a sufficient space to crawl through. Once past the rock fall, the tunnel, a vent formed long ago by hot gases through molten lava, was high enough for him to stand. Half an hour more brought him to the chamber at the tunnel's end. He folded up his cloak, lay down at full length upon it, the Salamander's box resting on his chest. The floor was warm, but not as hot as he remembered. Eyes closed, he felt through rock.

The fire at the mountain's heart had cooled a little in fifty years, the crust that roofed it thicker than he remembered. It took a moment to realize that what he was looking for, the work of the Forsting mages, would be found not at the top but the side, where the road through the pass ran by the flank of the mountain. The mages themselves he could barely make out through the greater flame, but their workings were clear enough. The pattern bright in his mind, Durilil reached up, undid the catch, slid open the lid of the box.

Chapter 25

From where they stood on the parapet, the flattened cone of Fire Mountain was outlined against the evening sky. The wind off the mountains was cold; Mari let the Prince draw her into the shelter of his heavy cloak. When he spoke it was with less than his usual assurance.

"Will you marry me?"

Mari stiffened against his arm. "Perhaps. You and Father have agreed on your terms; I have yet to set mine."

"What are they?"

"Nan was a good and gentle lady. But I do not think that in all the years you were together she ever said no to anything you asked."

"And you?"

"And I am not Nan. If we wed I will deal with you honestly, serve King and Kingdom as best I am able. But merge my will in yours, no. If I believe you are mistaken I will say so, and I will act as I think right, with your leave or without it."

"You drive a hard bargain, lady mine. I could name three or four maidens of rank who would have me with no such conditions."

"If you would rather wed one of them..."

"I think not. I know both sides of my bargain with your father; if I accept your terms, what do you offer in exchange?"

"Besides my person? You have not declared your love; are you inquiring as to mine?"

"If I say that I love you more than sun and moon and stars, will that suffice?"

"Too much and not enough. No."

"So far as the charms of your person, you are certainly the most desirable lady I know, but I do not think that is the question you are asking."

Mari said nothing, waited.

"You are the only lady I would be willing to have to wife on the terms you offer. I accept them. Does that suffice?"

"And does your son ...?"

"Agree? Yes. I asked him before I made my final decision."

"That was well done. Then to answer your question, if I had my choice out of all men alive there is none I would rather wed."

The two fell silent, Mari held in the Prince's embrace. After a long minute she pulled free. "That's impossible."

"That you should permit me to kiss you?"

She shook her head. "Listen."

He listened. A moment later he moved to the rampart's edge; looked down. The ground below was dark. "It sounds like running water."

Mari nodded. "It sounds like the stream out of the pass when the snow melts in spring, but even louder." Before she had finished speaking the Prince was at the stairs leading down from off the rampart; she followed him.

By the time they reached the Great Hall it was clear that they were not the only ones to have noticed. Duke Morgen was already there; a moment later Bertil, the Castellan, joined him. Morgen gave him an enquiring look.

Bertil was the first to speak. "The stream is running, and running fast. The water isn't hot, but it is warmer than any water outside the hot springs has any cause to be this time of year."

Morgen thought for only a minute before he started giving orders: "I need four messengers, two to His Majesty, two to the Earls. Now. I also want Magister Coelus brought here as quickly as possible."

He saw the Prince, motioned him over. "The streambed down from the pass is running full; I think I know what the Forsting mages have been doing for the past year. With luck Coelus can give us at least a guess at how they are doing it."

"You think they are using magic to melt the pass clear? There aren't enough fire mages alive."

Mari broke into the conversation. "Can't fire mages channel fire as well as making it?"

The Prince nodded, his expression shifted. "You are saying that ..."

"The hot springs. There is a reason it's called Fire Mountain. I expect there is enough fire under it to melt clear a hundred passes."

"And the mages don't have to make it, just channel it. It must still have been a massive undertaking."

Duke Morgen turned back to them. "They have had most of a year to do it in. Do we have any idea how soon we can expect to see a Forsting army coming through the pass?"

The Prince shook his head. "Ask Coelus. Here he comes now."

By the time Morgen and the Prince had finished explaining the situation to Coelus, the Castellan had returned with four of his men. Morgen turned back to them.

"It looks as though the Forstings have found a way of clearing the pass in winter and are about to descend on us in force; I must get word to His Majesty. They are obviously planning to cross the pass and take this castle before any help can arrive. One way of making sure they succeed is to ambush any messengers we send; they may have gotten a few men across already, and there may be people in place here to help them.

"I want two of you to leave tonight, separately, each carrying letters to His Majesty. Assume anyone you meet might be an enemy. Get as far as you can from here by dawn, get to the capital as fast as you can. I am giving you courier chits to get you remounts at the stations, but don't use them until you are well out of the Marches; at that point I think it will be safe to assume that the people at the stations can be trusted. The other two are going to the Earls to warn them."

The Prince broke in. "Are you asking them for troops for the garrison?"

Morgen shook his head. "Not yet. For one thing, I want to see if the mages we lent Frederik a week ago come back." He turned back to the four men. "You know yourselves better than I do; you and Lord Bertil can decide who does what. How soon can you be packed, mounted and ready to go?"

"Half an hour, Your Grace."

"Meet me then by the front gate; I'll have the letters."

He turned back to Coelus. "Do you agree with His Highness about what is happening?"

Coelus nodded. "I expect they used a lot of static spells, set up over the past year. Probably started at the north end of the pass. If the melt water is coming south, the melting must be this side of the crest of the pass by now. Exactly how they are doing it and how long it will take I don't know, but we may be able to learn more."

"So if you are right, we will be blocked from the pass until the last moment, when they melt through the snow at this end, by which time they will probably have troops already filling the pass. Can they use the same heat against us—roast us in the keep?"

Coelus shook his head. "A disturbing thought, but I doubt it. Even if the magma layer under the mountain extends this far—as for all I know it does—they do not have the spells set up to use it. The snow they are melting where they have their spells is just above the fire they are melting it with; we're miles away. It might be worth figuring out how they are doing it so we can set up spells here and try to roast them next time, but I doubt it will help just now."

The Prince touched Morgen's arm, as he turned spoke in a low voice. "The Marcher lords?"

Morgen shook his head. "That we will have to see. I can assure Your Highness that I will be careful."

Morgen spent the next half hour dictating letters, having them copied, signing and sealing, while the Castellan made his own preparations to ready the castle for what might come. Once the messengers were out the gate, Morgen and the Prince returned to the Great Hall. Coelus and Mari were still there, but the Prince noticed that Ellen, who had come in with Coelus, was gone. He turned to Mari: "Has your friend sensibly gone to bed?"

"I don't think so; she spoke with Magister Coelus, then went off with a determined expression."

Coelus heard, turned away from Morgen to the Prince. "Ellen has gone to see what she can about what the Forstings are up to."

"Alone?"

"It seemed prudent. I realize there might be enemies watching the castle, but Ellen is good at not being seen. I don't suppose His Grace has any invisible guards to keep her company."

"I concede your lady's skill with magery. Also that, despite appearances, she is probably the most dangerous person in this castle; I would not care to be the man who tried to take her prisoner. Is she also a practiced mountain climber?"

Coelus shook his head. "Not that I know of; I do not think she plans to go that far. Her perception is much better than mine and probably better than yours, and she is, among other things, a fire mage. Her plan was to get to where the mountain starts and see as much as she can from there."

* * *

Ellen joined the others at the morning meal, looking tired but undamaged. Coelus looked up from his plate. "Were we right?"

She nodded: "They are tapping fire from the magma under Fire Mountain, using a series of static spells to channel it, I think, under the control of fire mages. A lot of fire mages. There's a channel that lets out its fire near the peak of the pass, another a ways this side of it, several the other side but too far to make out much detail. I couldn't tell if they were set up to open more channels farther south; they may just plan to use warm water coming down through the pass to melt the rest of it clear."

"Nothing you could see that ..."

"We could do to stop them? If I were at the top of the pass and nobody was paying attention I might be able to do something to interfere with their channeling, but not at this distance. It would take far more power than any single mage has."

The Prince looked up as if he were about to say something, didn't.

It was well past noon when a guard came down from the keep roof seeking the Castellan. Lord Bertil listened to him, then sent for Duke Morgen and the Prince.

"There's a fair sized force approaching from west of here; my guess is it's Earl Eirick. One of the men thought he saw something the other direction but wasn't sure."

The Prince looked puzzled. "That's fast work; your messengers only went out last night."

Bertil and Morgen exchanged glances; Morgen spoke: "Impossibly fast—it's most of a day's ride from Eirick's keep here, and nearly as far from Frederik in the other direction. Neither retains an army feasting in their halls all winter; they would need to call men up from the lords in allegiance to them. If that's who it is, it isn't our messengers that brought them."

An hour later, the western force was close enough to show both size—substantial—and banners, a red axe on a white field, the banner of Earl Eirick. A second force was approaching from the east but not yet as close. Morgen, standing with the other two on the eastern ramparts, turned to the Castellan. "The garrison is ready, the walls manned?"

Lord Bertil nodded. "Yes, Your Grace. I hope needlessly."

Morgen nodded agreement, turned to the Prince. "They will send someone to tell me who they are and what they are doing here; I will arrange to speak with him just inside the gate. They may not know of Your Highness's presence; from the second story of the gatehouse you will be able to hear without being seen." The Prince nodded agreement.

Earl Eirick's force stopped a little out of bowshot from the walls; from there a single horseman rode to the front gate, where he was met by the Castellan and led in on foot.

"My Lord Eirick has word of a Forsting threat from over the pass. Considering how small your garrison is this time of year, he thought it prudent to offer your lordship reinforcements. Since he did not know what would be required, he brought all the force he could. If the threat is not urgent, he proposes to station as much of his levy as you require in the keep, return home with the rest, and be prepared to come back if necessary."

Bertil thought a moment before responding. "I am grateful to His Lordship for his assistance, but I do not think we can provide accommodations within the wall for his forces. He himself, of course, I will be happy to guest, since I would like to combine his information with ours."

The messenger looked around the almost empty courtyard with a puzzled expression. "I see room enough for a considerable force. We can, of course, camp for a little while outside the walls, but if the invasion is imminent that could be risky."

Bertil smiled. "There is room enough, but we are holding it for royal forces expected to arrive imminently to reinforce the garrison. If His Lordship wishes, he could make camp between us and the pass; as you will see, there is no shortage of fresh water there just now. With sentinels in the pass, there should be no difficulty falling back on the keep if there is need."

The messenger, still looking less than satisfied, bowed to the Castellan. "I will bring your message and invitation to my Lord."

The Prince waited until the messenger had gone to join the other two.

It was less than half an hour before a guard came down from over the gate to tell them that a party was approaching from Eirick's force. As it drew near, they could see that it was led by a young man in Eirick's livery, accompanied by four others. They stopped in front of the open gate, where Lord Bertil was waiting.

Two of the four unfurled banners; the other two raised trumpets, sounded them. As the echoes died away their leader stepped forward, spoke in a loud voice: "On behalf of my Lord Earl Eirick and his lord Prince Iolen, rightful claimant to the throne of Esland, I demand that this castle be yielded up, to be held for His Highness by those loyal to him!"

Bertil stepped forward, replied in a voice even louder: "And on behalf of my lord His Majesty Petrus, rightful king of this land, I name Earl Eirick traitor, faithless, foresworn of his oaths to his king. This castle I hold from the King's hand, and it I will defend with all my strength against my kingdom's foes and the traitors who ally with them!"

There was a brief pause, then the trumpets cried out again. As silence returned, the Earl's herald spoke: "Then, in the names of Earl Eirick, Earl Frederik, and their liege lord Prince Iolen I summon Northpass Keep to siege."

He hesitated a moment, as if waiting a reply. Bertil spoke softly to the guard beside him, stepped back. The gate swung shut.

Ellen, watching from the ramparts, turned to Mari. "You recognized him?"

Mari nodded. "Anders makes a good herald. I hope it doesn't end up costing him his head."

Less than an hour later, Coelus and Ellen met with the Prince at his invitation in a room in the keep. He offered them seats, himself remained standing.

"I need your help. I make no threats; the last thing we need at the moment is conflict among ourselves. I ask only that you hear me out before you make your decision.

He hesitated, continued: "As matters stand now, it is very nearly certain that this keep will fall. The winter garrison is small and Frederik's treachery has left us with only a handful of mages. The forces of the Earls we could probably withstand, but in another day or two there will be a Forsting army besieging us, with siege engines and ten or twenty times our number of mages. A Forsting army allied with the marcher earls will advance into the kingdom, probably driving for the capital. We may hope that one of our messengers got through; if so His Majesty will at least be warned. Whether he will be able to defeat the invaders I do not know; we will not.

"I see one way, and only one, of saving the Keep, stopping the invasion, ending the rising of the northern lords. As Lady Ellen said, interfering with the magery that is melting clear the pass requires more power than any one mage possesses. We know, you most certainly know, a way of getting such power.

Coelus shook his head; the Prince continued. "I understand your arguments against letting the Cascade become known, and on the whole I agree with them; it might be better if the spell had never been invented. I can see how you might truly believe making the spell known to be too high a price even to save the kingdom from the horrors of an invasion. But that is not the choice you face.

"I know how to do the Cascade, although not without risk. Lord Iolen knows how, or knows enough to learn it. Both of you know. Your secret is out, and it cannot be put back in the box.

"I want you to help me implement the Cascade, use it to destroy the workings of the Forsting mages and as many of the mages themselves as we can. If you refuse, the Keep falls. Any of the three of us that survive its fall will be captives.

"Magister Coelus once spoke to me of the limits of magery to extract information without destroying the mage one used it against. It had not occurred to him that the combination of torture with truth telling, a simple magery familiar to our enemies as to us, provides a means of extracting information from a prisoner with no injury to his mind, only his body. You may believe, with some justice, that the means I have been willing to use to obtain information from you were less scrupulous than they ought to have been, but I can assure you that our enemies are far less restrained. If we are taken prisoner, they will learn, by one means or another, all we know. And that most certainly includes the Cascade.

Ellen looked up, face set, started to speak; the Prince gestured her to silence.

"We might try not to be taken alive, though all plans are hazardous in the chaos of battle. But this still would preserve your secret for only a short while. His Majesty knows much; the Learned Hewry, now safe in the capital, knows, at least believes he knows, how to accomplish it. Magister Coelus described to the Learned Gervase the precautions he intended to take when next he implemented the spell, information Gervase passed on to Hewry, who made use of it and all else he could learn. If the kingdom is threatened I have no doubt that my brother will use every weapon he can, that included.

"And there is Lord Iolen. If the invasion succeeds, he will be king and will no doubt take the opportunity to complete his knowledge of the spell. If it succeeds only in breaking free the Northern Marches under Iolen's rule, he still will have all the resources needed for that project and reason to use them. I see no future that leaves your secret secure.

"Among the remnant of the Keep's mages there are, by great good fortune, one each of earth and water. With them, the two of you for fire and air, and myself at focus, we have what we require to implement the schema. With the knowledge you possess we can do it safely, at least more safely than I could have without that knowledge. I could promise that if you help me in this I will not use the spell again, but if I did you would not, should not, believe me. No promise will bind if the need is great enough. I can say truthfully that I think the secret is less likely to get out into the world if you aid me than if you do not, but on that you will have to trust to your own judgment.

"I ask no answer now; you will wish to consider the matter. I go to take council with His Grace and the Castellan as to the defense of the Keep; when you have made your decision, tell me."

The Prince bowed to Ellen and Coelus, turned, and left the room.

* * *

Kieron glanced over the top sheet of paper, covered with neatly written instructions for his part in the schema, at Magister Coelus.

"This is it?"

The mage nodded.

"Instructions for all five of us. I believe I know what

happened last time and have taken precautions; I cannot guarantee that nothing will go wrong, but I am fairly sure that particular thing will not go wrong. Before we start I should tell you what I believe will happen and we should discuss what you will be doing with the pooled power."

Prince Kieron nodded agreement, waited.

"The first stage is creating the pool; this room should be big enough. I brought chalk to mark our positions. The three of you should go over the instructions several times in advance and keep them before you as the schema starts. Once the pool is formed, the second stage is in Your Highness's hands; it starts below the red line halfway down the sheet.

"As the Cascade spreads, it uses the power from each new mage pulled into the pool to pull in the next. While it is spreading there will be little power available to you to use. Since this time we are not working within a protective sphere, there is no external limit, or none I know of, to how far it can spread. I have accordingly designed a limit into the schema itself. When the Cascade has reached a radius of about thirty to forty miles, if our calculations are correct, it should stop spreading.

"The pool will then contain the power drawn from the last cohort of mages pulled in, which ought to be considerable. Instead of being spent pulling in more mages, it will be available for your use, as focus. You will have to be careful; power is peril, and you will be using more power than any of us has ever had to draw on before.

"In addition to what is in the pool, there should be a gradual inflow from all the mages that have been pulled into the pool, as their own pools of magery slowly refill. With luck you will not need that. The longer you hold the focus, the greater the danger to you. My advice would be to do whatever you think needful to end our current peril as quickly as possible and then release. Releasing should be easy, but I have additional instructions at the bottom of the sheet just in case."

Prince Kieron waited to be sure Coelus had finished, turned to Ellen. "Do you have any advice to add, lady?"

She shook her head. "It's all on the sheets, and what Coelus just said."

"Then, while the two of you lay out the pattern, I will

consider what I can do with the power you are providing me. Am I right in understanding that I will have not only power but a mix of talents under my control, a mix spanning all of magery?"

Coelus nodded. "Yes. You start with a complete basis star here, and of course the magery pulled in will be of all sorts. But you will still be limited by your own knowledge; if you intend to do things that are more than your accustomed uses of magery, you had best plan out the spells with the same care you would use for any new spell."

"That had occurred to me. There are only three things I intend to do with the power, and I think I know how to do them all. The only difficult one is canceling the Forstings' static spells. I will have to work out the details of that when I see their precise nature. Either of you could do it better, I expect, but as I am neither air nor fire I cannot replace either of you in the star."

Outside the room Mari was waiting. There was no one else in the corridor. The Prince took her hand, drew her away from the door, spoke softly. "Coelus and your friend Ellen have agreed to help me with a spell that should, if all goes well, end what the Forstings are doing; we will be starting shortly."

He stopped a moment, looking down at her.

"Coelus has done the spell once before; it killed the mage controlling it. He believes he knows what went wrong and that he has altered the spell so that it will not happen again. I am willing to stake my life that he is right, there being no better gambles available. If I lose, there is nothing I will regret so much ..."

He stopped speaking, unable to continue. Mari put both arms around him, hugged him tightly.

"You will do what must be done. If Coelus and Ellen think it is safe, it is probably safe. If not ... "

"If not, you will take care of Kir for me?"

She nodded, said nothing, held him tighter.

* * *

Kieron reviewed the sheet of paper a last time, closed his eyes, and watched the web grow; in a moment it was a star traced in the colors of the four elements, himself at the center. He raised his hand, spoke the final Word, and felt it roll through him, then lifted his hand. Three bright lines, each in mixed colors. By their direction they were pulling the mages in the north tower into the

Cascade. More lines from other directions in the castle. Two were brilliant red, brighter than the others — not from the castle then. The earls must have brought fire mages in their company. Magery poured through him into the pool, out again into the world, a thick cluster of lines pointing at the pass, the Forsting mages.

He felt a surge of relief as the web ceased its growth; it felt to him that he was already full of more magic than he could possibly contain. No new lines, but something was still happening. His hand was pouring out what seemed, to his perception, a cloud of soap bubbles. For a moment he remembered Kir, the bellows-powered bubble machine someone had given him, and the resulting mess. What he saw accorded with nothing in the descriptions he had heard of earlier experiments. But they had ended sooner than this, and the schema had been changed. When it was done he would ask Coelus. For now there were more urgent matters to deal with.

First and easiest, the forces of the two earls. Any mages guarding them were now pulled into the Cascade, their power his. His own perception was brighter, more detailed than ever before. He let it move out to the western camp. There a wagon full of grain, here a massive stock of hay. With his new power, dealing with them was a moment's work. Another wagon was stacked with beer kegs; Eirick treated his men well. But not for long. He pulled back, expanded his view. Over the camp, plumes of smoke were rising. With a last twist of fire he set the Earl's tent ablaze. Next the other camp.

If there were only the rebels to deal with, he would be done; without supplies for men and beasts they could not long maintain the siege. But now he must confront the real threat.

He tried to throw his perception north to the top of the pass, failed. For a moment, he was lost in a wilderness of snow and trees. He pulled back. Better, if slower, the way he knew, the road he had many times ridden. Up the road into the pass, mind moving faster than any rider. At the top of the pass, the head of the army. Within it a dozen mages, each linked to him by a line of light, their own power dimmed. He would deal with them, but first their work. His mind's vision scanned the mountain slope, searching for magery.

Something was wrong; holding the vision in his mind was

getting harder and harder, the picture shredding away at the edges into mist. The magery that filled him, still far more than his own, was less than it had been. He had spent too much of the pool. He needed to wait while it refilled sufficiently to let him finish his set task. Kieron let go the vision of pass and mountain. He knew that, when he wished, he could have it back. He opened his eyes.

He was still standing in the same room, its stone floor marked up with chalk, the center of a star of mages. He drew in deep breaths of the cold air. Closed his eyes.

The lines linking him to the mages in the north tower were gone, with them the two brighter lines of fire. Even as he watched, one of the other lines blinked out.

* * *

"It didn't work."

Mari looked up from the chessboard at the tone of the Prince's voice; Kir kept his eyes focused on the pieces. "The spell?"

"The spell. I don't know what went wrong—everything seemed to be going fine, and nobody casting it got burned up this time. I think it may buy us a little time—I don't expect any enemy mages in the pass will be doing much for the next few hours. And I managed to destroy quite a lot of the Earls' supplies. But it was supposed to do a lot more than that, at least stop the magery thawing the pass. And with luck kill the mages controlling it. Perhaps if I had moved faster... but the spell ran out sooner than I expected."

"What happens now?"

"What happens now is that Eirick and his allies lay siege to the castle and the Forstings bring a real army over the pass to help them. Even if one of your father's messengers gets through—and with the North rising against us that is far from certain—it is going to take longer for the royal forces to get through the rebels, assuming they can, than we can expect to hold out. Especially with almost no mages.

"Your friend Ellen has extraordinary abilities, as I discovered to my cost some time back. I am going to ask her if she can get you and Kir out and away to someplace safe—east to your father's lands if she can manage it. If the keep falls, I expect the marcher lords and their allies will move on the capital."

"And you?"

"Will do my best to make myself a bad prophet. With magister Coelus to help, and good fortune, we might have a chance."

"Father, look. The sky's burning."

Kieron spun around. Two steps took him to the window; he undid the catch, swung the two sides in. The shutters were open already. The sky was red with reflected fire. The whole top of Fire Mountain was ablaze, a thin trickle of lava pouring down the side.

Into the pass.

* * *

Durilil lay in bed, eyes closed, mind wrapped in fire, watching. The burning mountain was too far for unaided perception, even his, but to the Salamander all fires were one; merged in it, he could look out of the mountain at what he had done. There was a limit to how much a human mage could channel, but none for the Salamander during the hours it had poured its fire directly into the mountain's heart. The crust of rock that had roofed the Northfire was gone, the accumulation of decades melted away in days.

The south end of the pass was filled with steam where lava pouring out of a crack in the mountain's side boiled off the snow and ice that still choked that end of the pass. The north end, already swept clean by magery, was clear. Someone on the Forsting side had kept his head; lines of troops were streaming north out of the pass in an orderly torrent, leaving behind piles of abandoned supplies. Where the slow advance of lava had reached the rear of the debris, a siege engine was burning.

Between the burning engine and the rear of the retreating army, a man was sitting his horse, looking uphill towards the lava. Curious, the mage let the vision expand. Ten miles and more from where Durilil lay in the keep, and even he had his limits, but perhaps...

Iolen took a last look at the road home; no magery, whether from the Forsting guild or the College, would open it again until the mountain subsided. It would go hard on the loyal earls, but there was nothing he could do beyond persuading the Einvald to offer refuge to those who escaped the failed rising. Frederik, still vigorous, might make it even in winter over the high pass that his castle guarded, but he had little hope for Eirick. As to his own position, whatever had gone wrong had been the failure of Forsting magery, not of his part in the plan.

That would do him little good if he chose to remain where he was until the lava reached him. He reluctantly turned his horse about and started after the tail of the army which should have put him on the throne his father had lost. As the road emerged from the crease between Fire Mountain and its eastern neighbor the left side dropped away. Iolen held his horse hard to the road's right.

Just in front of him, a stand of dried grass burst into flame; he wondered how the volcano had reached so far. The horse shied left; he snatched at the reins too late.

Chapter 26

Duchess Gianna took a final look over the scene, nodded to the servants to open the doors. The dining room in the residence was smaller than the Keep's great hall—also more comfortable and, with fires blazing on both hearths, warmer. A much more suitable site for her purposes. Later in the evening Castellan Bertil would carry the news to the Keep; between them they had made suitable arrangements for celebration by the garrison.

Gianna watched Mari and Prince Kieron come in, not quite hand in hand. Certainly a daughter to be proud of. The one skill that mattered in the long run was that of choosing friends wisely and winning their love. If she was not very much mistaken, the triumph about to be announced was as much Mari's work as hers.

Looking down the table, she noticed that Mari had put Kir next to her, beyond him her friend Ellen. A delightful if odd young lady, but a puzzle; Ellen spoke freely of her mother but had never mentioned her father. The obvious explanation felt in this case unconvincing. Gianna liked puzzles.

Morgen came in with Bertil; Gianna waved them to their seats, took her own, the Prince on her right hand. Circumstances had delayed her plans a little, but between the incompetence of the enemy mages and the diplomacy of her husband the difficulties had and would be dealt with. And a little peril, jointly shared and overcome, was not a bad start for a life together.

The guests all seated, she caught her husband's eye; the Duke rose, the table fell silent. "Before we begin our dinner, I have two announcements to make. The first is that, in Lord Bertil's judgment, the Keep is now safe. The Forsting invasion was ended when Fire Mountain erupted into the pass. The rising is not yet over, but the Earls have agreed to send one of their people to hear what we have to say and I have good hopes that we can offer them terms they will accept."

He paused a moment; the silence held. "My second announcement is that His Royal Highness Prince Kieron has made an offer of marriage to my daughter the Lady Mariel, which offer she has accepted. They plan to wed in early summer, when Mari will have completed her studies. The wedding will be held in the capital; everyone present is of course invited to attend."

The dinner over, congratulations given and received, Gianna drew her daughter aside. "Now that the preliminaries are done with, we can leave what is left of the revolt to your father and your betrothed while we take care of the serious business of planning a wedding that will have the whole capital talking. I have a small surprise for you."

Mari gave her a curious glance, followed her to the door to one of the side rooms.

"A wedding, a royal wedding, requires jewelry. Spectacular jewelry. Accordingly, I have provided us with ..."

She opened the door. "A jeweler. Your favorite jeweler and, as of the pieces he made after you introduced him to me, mine as well."

Master Dur looked up from the table. Gianna noted, to her surprise, that he was looking not at Mari but through the door. Turning, she saw Ellen looking in from the near side of the dining room with an astonished expression on her face. Of course; she too would know the jeweler and be as surprised as Mari that he was here, not a hundred miles away in Southdale. Gianna nodded politely at her daughter's friend, closed the door, and turned back to the table with its stack of sketches, two burning candles, and a small bowl filled with glints of brilliant color.

Ellen watched the door close and turned back to the table where Coelus was deep in discussion with one of the mages from the garrison. When it ended she caught his eye, nodded towards the door into the hall; he followed her. Without speaking, she led him to the hall's end, through an open door into an empty room. "Master Dur is here."

"Master Dur. You mean ..."

She held up a hand; he fell silent. They were not the only people in the Keep who could see, or hear, through walls. "Master Dur, the old jeweler from Southdale. I think Her Grace brought him as a surprise for Mari; I expect they are in there now planning out jewels for the wedding."

"I see." He paused a moment, considering how best to put the question. "The eruption was great good fortune; do you have any more ideas as to how it happened? It must have been due in some way to the channeling spells; it is too great a coincidence otherwise that it should occur just when it did. But I cannot figure out how. One would have thought …"

"That the spells would draw fire out of the mountain, making an eruption less likely, not more. I do not see any mechanism in magery by which the spells could cause the eruption, but I agree that there must be some connection."

Their eyes met; he nodded, spoke. "Perhaps, when Mari and Her Grace are done for the moment with their consultations, you can find Master Dur. If he left the village after we did, he may have news from home."

"And I would like to see what he is planning for Mari, if it is not all a deep secret. He was in the room next to where we dined; perhaps we can catch him on his way out."

* * *

Anders looked about the room. Mari was seated at one end of the table. Next to her sat a tall stranger, well dressed, and next to him Duke Morgen. Morgen motioned him to a chair. "I asked to have you taken to the tower roof so that you could view the eruption for yourself. As you can see, it is still in progress. I think I can say with some confidence that no Forsting army will be using Northpass in the next few weeks, probably not for considerably longer than that. Do you agree?"

Anders hesitated, nodded reluctant assent.

"There are, of course, other passes. But they are still choked with snow, and the mages I have consulted doubt that the spells that used the mountain's fire to melt Northpass could clear places so distant, even if the Forsting mages had not lost control over their own creation and brought out more fire than they had any use for. And even in summer Northpass is the only pass in the range low enough and wide enough to let through an army and its supplies.

"It will not be easy for Earl Eirick and his allies to take this keep without Forsting support. Lacking Forsting mages and Forsting engines you will have to either storm the walls at the cost of many lives, with no certainty of success, or siege it—and we are better supplied for siege than you are. Frederik's treachery has deprived us of many of the mages stationed here for the keep's defense. But, by good fortune, my lady daughter's friend Elinor and her teacher Magister Coelus are guesting with us. They are both, as you may be aware, accomplished mages.

"I sent messengers as soon as we discovered the pass was being cleared. If one got through, you will be facing a royal army within weeks—sooner, if His Majesty has received word of your rising from another source, and such secrets are hard to keep. The men of the Northern Marches, the liegemen of Eirick and Frederik and the rest, are brave and accomplished soldiers. But with the whole rest of the kingdom against them they cannot long prevail. You know that and they know that—it is, after all, the reason you chose to call in the Forstings in support of your rising.

"If you continue to fight, by the time it ends the holds of Eirick, his allies and his liegemen, your father among them, will be destroyed, and many will die."

Anders looked up with a fierce expression. "Not all of them ours."

"Not all of them yours—which will make things still less pleasant when the fighting is over. There will be new feuds between lords that supported Eirick and lords that support the King. And the more of our people are killed the more reason His Majesty, who did very little against the lords who supported Prince Josep against him, will have to wonder how prudent mercy to the defeated would be this time.

"When this is over, the Marches will still be part of the kingdom. Every soldier killed, Marcher or loyal, weakens us when next the Forstings move against us. Not all who will be killed will be yours—but all, on both sides, will be ours."

"Your Grace's point is?" Anders' voice was steady.

"My point is that I want to end this now, on terms, before any more people die."

There was a long silence before Anders spoke again. "I will carry any message you give me back to my liege lord. But whatever terms you offer, he will ask me what authority you have to offer them. What assurance do we have if we agree to your terms that His Majesty will honor your side of the agreement? Your Grace is high in His Majesty's council, as all men know. But what authority have you to make promises that will bind His Majesty?"

"None. That is why I have asked His Highness Prince Kieron,

who also was guesting here, to join us."

The tall stranger who had been sitting by Mari stood, pushing back his chair, the noise loud in the silent room. "After consulting with His Grace, I am prepared to offer the following terms on behalf of my brother. Earls Eirick and Frederik, as leaders of the rebellion, are to be permitted to go into exile, succeeded in each case by one of their sons acceptable to His Majesty. Any damage done to property held by those loyal to His Majesty to be repaired at the cost of those responsible. Any deaths of those in service to His Majesty or those loyal to him to be compensated according to the customary schedules of the northern marches. Those terms met, all remaining rebels willing to swear allegiance to His Majesty directly or through their own lords are to have a free pardon."

"Your Highness's terms are generous. There remains one question the lords I serve will certainly put to me, and so I must put to you: What reason have we to believe that what was spoken here will be remembered after we have laid down our arms? I cannot speak of my own knowledge to the rights and wrongs of the past. But Your Highness played a role in the conflicts at the Old King's death that was not highly regarded in this part of the kingdom."

The Prince thought a moment before replying: "I will, of course, put the terms agreed to in writing, signed and sealed. Beyond that, and so far as your own knowledge is concerned, you are I think acquainted with the Lady Mariel, daughter to His Grace. You may if you wish take private council with her as to what my word is worth. It is a matter on which she may be prepared to offer an opinion. Three days ago she accepted my offer of marriage and is now my betrothed."

* * *

"Can we trust him? It is my neck, and the necks of my kin, at stake."

Mari thought a moment before answering. "I think so. I would not have agreed to marry Kieron if I did not think he was, on the whole, an honest man. He is, as Ellen puts it, too used to having his own way. But among us—I, Ellen, and your fellow rebels—we may have convinced him over the past year that having his own way is not something he can always rely on. I do

203

not think he has it in him to first promise you all pardons, then massacre you after you lay down your arms.

"Further, I think I can myself provide at least a partial guarantee. Kieron has spent the past six months and more courting me, with reasons both political and personal. We do not plan to marry until this summer, when I will be done with my studies. If between now and then I discover that he has committed such treachery and made me the instrument of it, he will have to find himself a different bride, and I have no doubt he knows it. For sufficient reason he would pay that price. Kieron feels deeply his obligation to his brother and the kingdom. But he would not pay it willingly.

"More important still, I have discussed affairs of the kingdom at length with His Highness and my father. Both have long regarded the disaffection of the northern marches as a serious weakness to the kingdom. By getting rid of the leaders of the insurrection and replacing Eirick with his son Eskil while dealing generously with the rest, they can help mend that weakness. Killing the rebels or forfeiting their holdings after promising pardon would open new wounds that would take a long time to heal. I think you may rely upon His Highness's honesty. I am confident you may rely on his sense."

Mari paused for a moment before continuing. "One more thing. I know that you, and those you follow, rose for Lord Iolen, that you believed in the justice of his cause and claim. Ellen says Iolen is dead. When Fire Mountain erupted he was in the pass and his horse took him over the edge. She did not say how she knew, and I did not ask. But Ellen is, in my experience, truthful to a fault, and I have no doubt that it is true."

Epilogue

Coming to Northkeep, they had been four: Mari, Ellen, Coelus, and one of the Duke's retainers. Returning there were three. Or perhaps, considering the contents of the case on the seat next to Master Dur and the warmth of the carriage, again four. The road was a good one, the coach well sprung; the Duchess did her best to provide for the comfort of her guests. Ellen, half asleep with her head resting on her companion's shoulder, tried to feel her way into the case to its contents, but the blocking spells were tightly woven, too strong even for her. Her father, seated across from them, was speaking softly to Magister Coelus; she kept her eyes shut, listened to their voices over the rumble of the wheels.

"We can talk freely; neither the coachman nor the groom is talented.

"My half of the story is simple enough. I saw what the Forstings were doing, guessed why, and so accepted Duchess Gianna's invitation. The Salamander left the Northfire fifty years ago. Since then the fire has slowly cooled; I put it back for long enough to change that."

"The day after I finished doing so, someone invoked the Cascade. I could feel it drawing fire from both of us, on a less lethal scale than last time. When it stopped I discovered that I and the Salamander had each somehow acquired a protective shield strong enough to cut off the flow. It looked to me as though His Highness had invoked the Cascade and then, a few minutes later, the two of you had invoked your spell to block it. Where he and you found enough mages for two stars at once, or how you managed the necessary power without my assistance, I have not yet figured out. I wondered if perhaps you had limited the protection to just the mages in the Keep. But I would have thought that by the time it started, the Cascade would have spread farther than that."

"It had. Much farther. We did two spells, but it only took one star for both of them."

"You used the Prince's Cascade to power your spell, to shield every mage in the area?"

Coelus nodded. "Every mage for about fifty miles around, if I got it right. To spread it farther we'll have to do it again later, with your help and two more mages. The pool was supposed to have power enough from the final stage of the Cascade to both spread the shield and let the Prince undo the magery that was melting the pass clear. But he didn't quite make it. Once the bubbles got thick enough to start cutting mages out of the Cascade, there was no more power coming into the pool—and no way of getting more even if we had been willing to run the Cascade again. I spent several hours afraid that my cleverness had killed all of us, until Fire Mountain erupted. It did not occur to me that that might be your work until Ellen told me you were here."

Ellen opened her eyes. "You mean our cleverness, don't you, love? If we had ended up killed by the Forstings it would have been my fault as well as yours. I did not know Father was here either."

Durilil smiled. "Both of yours equally, I think. Dying for your principles is all very well in stories, but on the whole I prefer to live—it makes it easier to fix my mistakes. If you only spread the shield for fifty miles, someone would eventually have tried the Cascade somewhere where it would work. Some of the Prince's people know enough to do it, I expect, and not all of them were in the Keep. And there was Iolen too. You were very clever indeed, but you should have allowed more of a safety margin. It is not as if the Prince had ever had that sort of power to play with before."

Ellen let her eyes close again, her mind drifting. Mari's wedding, Mari resplendent in silk and jewels, Mari some day as queen. Perhaps Ellen should volunteer herself as royal mage. It was amusing to imagine how Kieron would respond. But no, Coelus would never leave the College willingly.

Weddings…

Made in United States
North Haven, CT
22 February 2023

33015535R00126